From The Ashes

Claire Sanders

I0673389

FROM THE ASHES

Contact Information: titleadmin@pelicanbookgroup.com

Scripture quotations, unless otherwise indicated are taken from the King James translation, public domain.

Cover Art by *Nicola Martinez*

White Rose Publishing, a division of Pelican Ventures, LLC
www.pelicanbookgroup.com PO Box 1738 *Aztec, NM * 87410

White Rose Publishing Circle and Rosebud logo is a trademark of Pelican Ventures, LLC

Publishing History
First White Rose Edition, 2014
Paperback Edition ISBN 978-1-61116-319-3
Electronic Edition ISBN 978-1-61116-318-6
Published in the United States of America

Dedication

For Anne Wheeler, a wonderful, loyal friend.

1

In the eastern curve of Texas, forests grow as thick as abandoned resolutions. Trees aspire to be mainmasts for schooners, and morning's quicksilver light seeps through the canopy with dewdrop speed. In this wildwood, red eared sliders sunbathe and butterworts wait patiently for insect meals. This is the land of the Caddo, where runaway slaves and Confederate refugees hid. The people who live there call it treasure.

But amid the thickets and cane brakes, an old hatred festers. There are some who exploit deep-rooted fears and threaten those who dare to stand firm.

It is an intolerance that true Christians fight with determined love.

෨෬

Piney Meadow, Texas
Present day

Jacob Fraser aimed the stream of high-pressure water towards the burning roof of All Saints Community Church. This was the fourth church fire he and the other volunteer firefighters had fought, and his heart sank lower with each blaze. Someone was intentionally destroying places of worship.

Familiar faces were in the huddled groups of onlookers. Arsonists liked to watch their handiwork.

Was one of his neighbors the culprit? Maybe it was George Hampton, his old Boy Scout leader, or Marvin Simpson, his Little League baseball coach. Maybe he didn't know the people of Piney Meadow as well as he thought.

Henry Washington, the pastor of the church, stood in front of a separate group of bystanders. His dark skin glowed in the firelight, but the brightness in his dark eyes was more than mere reflection. Was it anger, righteous indignation, or something more that ignited the fire inside the African-American pastor? Henry raised his Bible towards the flames and his congregation gathered around him.

Some embraced and others cried, but most stood in silence, their backs straight and their gazes fixed on their suffering church.

Above the roar of the fire, voices sang a familiar hymn.

Jacob's heart swelled with admiration. The fire might destroy their building, but not their faith.

A second truck from a neighboring community arrived, but there was no saving the All Saints Community Church. Jacob and the other firefighters could contain the blaze, but the church was beyond rescue.

At last, Chief Dutton gave the order to turn off the hoses.

While Jacob's team stowed the equipment, other volunteers raked through the charred ruins, putting out hotspots.

The county sheriff, Vince Miller, clapped Jacob on the shoulder. "Good job keeping the fire contained."

"We were lucky there's so little wind tonight."

"Is Chief Dutton around?"

"I saw him just a few minutes ago." Jacob scanned the area, and then pointed to a man talking into a radio. "There he is."

The chief raised one hand in acknowledgement and strolled towards Jacob and the sheriff.

Sheriff Miller shook hands with the other man. "What do you think, Emmett?"

"Same as the others. It burned too fast to be anything other than an accelerant." Chief Dutton removed his wire-rimmed glasses and wiped his sooty face with a bandana. "When are you going to call in the cavalry?"

"Already done it. The FBI is sending a special agent from the hate crime task force."

Chief Dutton let out a low grunt. "Hate crimes in Piney Meadow. Didn't think I'd ever see the day."

The scents of smoke and sweat clung to Jacob's skin as he removed his heavy firefighter's jacket.

Four churches in three months, all belonging to African-American congregations, and now the FBI was coming. What was happening to his hometown? Piney Meadow had always been a place where neighbors could live and work without the threat of violence.

He'd needed just such a haven after his stint with the Houston Police Department. Now crime menaced his refuge as sure as a nest of copperheads.

☙❧

Rain clouds darkened the summer sky when Jacob returned to the site the next afternoon.

Henry Washington raised his hand in greeting and called to Jacob in a deep, gravelly voice. "Mornin' Jacob. Appreciate you meeting me here."

Jacob shook hands with the older man. "Sorry we couldn't save your church, Henry. At least no one was hurt."

"Yes, we were blessed in that regard."

Jacob's chest tightened as he walked through the rubble. Water-swollen hymnals lay amid pieces of broken pews, and shards of stained glass crunched underfoot. Burning a church was like hitting a baby; they were both defenseless and innocent. "I saw the sheriff at the diner this morning. He said he'd finished with the crime scene and you could start cleaning up." He bent to pick up the remains of a book, and then realized it was a Bible.

Henry took the Bible from Jacob and cleaned it with his handkerchief. "We plan to rebuild, of course, but a lot depends on the estimate you give me for the lumber and other building materials."

Jacob swallowed the lump in his throat. "I don't suppose you had fire insurance?"

Henry shook his head. "Heavens, no. My congregation is so poor the collection plate is often filled with pennies. You know my wife and I both have jobs. Our building was simply a meeting place for those who wanted to worship the Lord."

"What are you going to do until you can rebuild?"

Henry pursed his lips in thought. "I've been wondering about Isaiah Beecham's place. That old church on his land is still standing. Think my congregation could meet there until we rebuild?"

Jacob rubbed the back of his neck while he thought. "I don't know about that, Henry. The land was deeded to Isaiah's granddaughter. You'll have to contact her."

Henry's eyebrows shot up. "Didn't know Mr.

Beecham had a granddaughter. Any idea how I would go about talking to her?"

"It might be easier than you think. I spoke with the lawyer handling the will because I want first chance at buying the Beecham acreage. He told me Isaiah's granddaughter is coming from Dallas this afternoon."

"Is Walter Davidson handling Mr. Beecham's estate?"

"That's right. Only lawyer Isaiah ever trusted."

"He's a good man, all right," Henry replied. "I'll give him a call. Think the granddaughter would be willing to lend the church to us?"

"Isaiah would've been glad to let you use it," Jacob said. "But the decision is up to his granddaughter."

"Have you met her?"

"I saw her at Isaiah's funeral, but didn't really get to talk to her."

"What about your family? If you buy the Beecham land, will my people still be able to use the church?"

"Shouldn't be a problem. But you know, that old building hasn't been used for more than twenty-five years. No telling what kind of repair it's going to need."

"Buying the materials might be a challenge, Jacob, but my congregation will supply the workers. As it says in Second Chronicles 'So the workmen labored, and the work was completed by them; they restored the house of God to its original condition and reinforced it.'"

Jacob grinned.

Henry was one of the few people who could pull out a Bible verse the way some people pulled out photos of their grandchildren.

"If you get permission to use Isaiah's old church,

my family will help however we can. Get somebody to look at the place, make a list of what you need, and then come down to the lumber yard." Jacob offered his hand to Henry.

"Bless you, Jacob. When I look at what's left of our church, all I can see is the remnants of hatred. But then you come along and blow that hatred away."

Thunder rumbled overhead as Jacob turned away from the older man. "Knock it off, Henry. You know how I feel about that kind of talk."

Henry chuckled deeply and clapped Jacob on the back. "All right, friend. I won't embarrass you any longer. I guess I'd better get into town and talk to the lawyer."

"I'll follow you there." Jacob climbed into his pickup truck and followed Henry onto the highway. Springing his offer on Isaiah's granddaughter might not be the best way to introduce himself, but not getting the Beecham land would mean he'd lost another important deal for his family's lumber business.

Hopefully, Isaiah's granddaughter would be sensible enough to follow good advice when she heard it. If she sold her land to Jacob, she could pocket the money and go back to her life in the city.

And Jacob could present four hundred acres of heavily timbered land to his family.

2

While a summer rain fell steadily against the louvered windows of Walter Davidson's law office, Judith Robertson tried to understand the document spread before her.

"I've marked the boundaries of your grandfather's property on this tax map," Walter Davidson explained. "As you can see, it borders the Sabine National Forest. I'll drive you out there if you'd like because you'll never find it on your own. Once you get off the main highway, most of the county roads are unmarked."

Judith frowned over the unusual document, embarrassed to admit she couldn't make heads or tails of it. The tax map looked like someone had served spaghetti on top of a crossword puzzle. "Your letter said there were buildings on the property."

"Three, as a matter of fact. There's a barn, a small cabin where Isaiah lived, and an old church."

"A church?"

"That's right. It was used by a nondenominational group for a while, but when they got enough money, they built a fancy place in town."

Judith crossed her legs under the table in an effort to stop her knees from shaking. There was nothing to be afraid of in the lawyer's office.

A soft knock at the doorway interrupted them. The lawyer's wife stepped halfway into the room. "Walter, Jacob Fraser and Henry Washington are here and asking to meet with you and Miss Robertson."

"That's fine, Dorothy. Just ask them to wait a few minutes."

The woman smiled politely at Judith and closed the door.

Curiosity pushed Judith's fear to the side. Those two men had obviously known about her appointment with the lawyer. "Why do they want to meet with me?"

The lawyer cleared his throat. "Jacob Fraser most likely wants to talk to you about buying all, or part, of your grandfather's land. His family runs the largest business in Piney Meadow—a lumber mill and a building supply. Henry Washington works as an accountant, but he also leads a small church group in town. I don't know why he's here. If you're not ready to see them now, I'll put them off."

Judith uncrossed her legs and straightened her spine. "I might as well see what's on their minds."

Mr. Davidson opened the door and called to the two men. "Come on in, Jacob. How are you, Henry? Gentlemen, I'd like you to meet Judith Robertson."

Judith stood and shook the older man's hand. He was a middle-aged, well-dressed man with kind eyes and a patient manner that put her at ease.

"Good afternoon, Miss Robertson. I'm Henry Washington, pastor of the All Saints Community Church."

"Nice to meet you," she said politely, and then turned her attention to the other man.

"Jacob Fraser," he said, shaking the hand she offered.

As his calloused hand gripped hers, Judith looked into his cobalt blue eyes.

Jacob Fraser was tall and broad-shouldered, dressed in a flannel shirt, faded jeans, and work boots covered with red dirt. His light brown hair was flecked with gold and his rolled-up shirtsleeves revealed well-muscled forearms. He wasn't the first good-looking man she'd met, but he was the first one who'd made her mouth dry up with a simple handshake.

"Sit down," the lawyer invited, "and tell us what's on your minds. I was just showing Miss Robertson where Isaiah's property is located."

"You'll never find it by following that map," Jacob said, settling his lean body into a chair across the table from her. "It's at least twelve miles from the highway."

"That's what I told her," Walter said with a chuckle. "Do you want to see the property, Judith?"

Judith gave a curt nod. "Definitely. Is it possible to see it this afternoon?"

"Yes." Walter answered. "But I've got another appointment at three and can't take you until later."

"I'd be glad to take you out there," Jacob volunteered. "But there's something I'd like to talk to you about, first."

"Me, too," Henry said.

Judith waited for her heartbeat to return to its regular rhythm. She was alone with three men, but that didn't necessarily signal danger. She reasserted her take-care-of-business façade.

Henry Washington smiled good-naturedly, calmly waiting for her reply.

Jacob Fraser, however, had a serious look about him, as if he had important business that couldn't wait.

Judith took a drink of water and concentrated on making her voice not quiver. "What's on your mind, Mr. Fraser?"

"Call me Jacob," he said with a friendly smile. "Mr. Beecham sold timber to my family over the years, and I was negotiating a sale before he passed away. I'd like to make you an offer."

"And you, Rev. Washington? Do you also have a business deal to discuss with me?"

"No, ma'am," he said, his eyes twinkling. "What I'd like to talk to you about is more in the line of a favor. I've been the pastor of the All Saints Community Church for the past ten years. We're a small congregation of local folks who meet twice a week to study God's word and to praise the Lord."

Judith tried to give her full attention to the preacher, but could not tune out the way Jacob scrutinized her. While Henry spoke in a soft, earnest voice, she could feel Jacob's gaze travel from her feet to her face. Determined not to blush under his inspection, she concentrated on the preacher.

"A few nights ago," Henry continued, "our church was burned to the ground. We have nowhere to meet."

The last piece of the puzzle fell into place.

"And you want to use the church on my grandfather's property."

"That's right. But there's more you should know. During the last few months, there have been three black churches burned in this county. My church made the fourth."

Judith's stomach clenched with disgust. Burning a church was a particularly heinous form of hatred. But, as her minister had often said, there was no such thing as a fortunate coincidence. She'd been given a church for a reason.

She had so much to think about. So much to pray about. "When do you need an answer, Mr. Fraser?"

"My name's Jacob," he said, "and although I'd like to close the deal quickly, I can understand if you need a little time."

"And you, Rev. Washington? When do you need an answer?"

"I don't have a deadline, Miss Robertson, but I am anxious to get my flock under a roof. Mr. Isaiah's church is going to need some repair before we can meet there, and, if it's all right with you, I'd like to bring members of my congregation out to your grandfather's place to inspect it."

Judith felt the men's expectant gazes. Her first reaction was to out-and-out give the church to Rev. Washington, but she'd learned the cost of making rash decisions. "I'd like to see the property before I decide, but I will tell you this much. There won't be any decisions made in haste. You gentlemen might as well know that up front."

Jacob and Henry traded long, meaningful looks, and then Henry smiled at Judith. "That's fine, Miss Judith. I understand completely. I'd best be on my way. It's been a pleasure to meet you."

She shook Henry's hand and he stepped out of the room. If he was disappointed, it didn't show in the straight set of his shoulders or the air of quiet dignity that radiated from him.

"If you'd still like to go out to your grandfather's place," Jacob said, "I've got time."

Judith's throat tightened with a familiar anxiety. She'd just been informed that her grandfather's property was secluded. She wasn't about to go there with a strange man. She focused on the lawyer. "Was there anything else you needed to tell me, Mr. Davidson?"

"No, that's it. Now that you've signed the papers, I'll take care of the rest. The land is yours, free and clear. But keep my number handy. If there's anything my wife or I can do for you, just give us a call."

Judith gathered her purse and shook Walter's hand. "Thank you, Mr. Davidson. I'll be in touch."

A minute later, Judith stepped into the misting rain and looked at Jacob. He seemed like a nice person, but one could never be sure. Accepting a ride from a man she'd just met was definitely on the list of stupid moves made by naïve women. Even if that man was handsome in an overgrown, clean-cut sort of way.

She tried to clear the lump in her throat. "I appreciate your offer, Mr. Fraser, but I'd rather find my grandfather's place on my own. I'll be in touch when I decide what to do with the land."

Jacob smiled down at her and slid his hands into his back pockets. "It's no problem for me to take you out there now."

"No, that's OK. I'll ask Mr. Davidson to write down the directions or I'll use my GPS system to find it."

"There's no way a GPS has your grandfather's property in its memory. The last two miles are dirt roads. Is that your roadster?" He gestured with his head.

"Why do you ask?"

"The low clearance on that car is going to make it difficult to drive on our dirt roads. Plus, it's been raining for the last two days. The road will be mostly mud."

Judith examined Jacob. If only she could see into a person's soul and know if he was trustworthy. It was the only superpower she'd ever wanted. "Hold on just a minute." She stepped back inside the lawyer's office. "Mrs. Davidson?"

The lawyer's wife looked up from her desk. "Yes, Miss Robertson? Did you need something?"

Judith's heart pounded as she peered through the window to make sure Jacob couldn't overhear, and then returned her attention to the lawyer's wife. "I know this is awkward, Mrs. Davidson, but I don't know who else to ask."

The older woman smiled encouragingly. "What can I do for you?"

"Jacob Fraser has volunteered to take me to my grandfather's place. Is it safe for me to do that? Can I trust him?"

Mrs. Davidson nodded. "I'd trust any member of my family with Jacob. Not only is he a former police officer, I've known his family for most of my life. They don't come any better than Jacob Fraser."

"OK," Judith said, blowing out a breath. "Thanks." Surely she could take the lawyer's wife's word. For the past year Judith had been praying for the courage to trust. Perhaps this was another opportunity to face her fears. At least she could take her own car. That way, if something did happen, she'd have a way to escape.

She stepped outside to find Jacob patiently leaning against a muddy pickup truck. "OK," she said with a confidence she didn't feel. "I'll follow you in my car."

"It'd be best if you rode with me. Like I said, the dirt roads are muddy and if that *is* your sports car, it'll never make it. I'll bring you back here when we're finished."

Judith considered her next action. She couldn't go through the rest of her life second guessing every decision. Mrs. Davidson had vouched for Jacob Fraser, and that would have to be good enough. "OK," Judith said, inwardly wincing at the tremor in her voice.

❧

Jacob steered his truck onto the highway and glanced at Judith. He liked what he'd seen in the lawyer's office. Tall and slender, with dark curls escaping from her ponytail, Judith had a type of careless beauty, as if she simply accepted her looks without worrying about the latest fashion. "I hear you're from Dallas," he said.

Judith tucked a stray curl behind her ear. "That's right. What about you?"

"Born and raised in Piney Meadow."

Her fingers shook as she dug through her purse and fished out a small notebook and a pen. "I'm going to write down the directions so I can find the place on my own."

"Good idea. Not only are most of the back roads unmarked, it's so dark at night you couldn't read the signs if they were." He drove a mile in silence, glancing over at Judith from time to time. She looked like a city girl in her black slacks and blue blouse, and those were probably real diamonds dangling from her ears. "I'm sorry I didn't get a chance to talk to you at your grandfather's funeral."

"You were there?"

"My parents and I attended."

"I couldn't believe how many friends Granddad had."

"He was a good man, and he'd lived here his whole life."

"I would've liked to have stayed longer and met

more people, but my father had to get back to Dallas for work. Mr. Davidson told my dad that he'd handle Granddad's estate and get in touch with us." Judith crossed her legs, and then re-crossed them. She was as nervous as a fly in a spider's web.

Jacob tried more small talk to put her at ease. "I'm surprised you came by yourself today. Do you have family?"

"Just my father."

"No husband?"

"No, I'm not married." She grasped the notebook in one hand and fingered the pen with the other. "And, by the way, Mr. Fraser, I charge by the question. So far, you owe me forty dollars."

Jacob smiled at the subtle way she'd told him to mind his own business. "Forty dollars, huh? Well, I can afford it. And my name's Jacob."

She returned his smile, but it wasn't a genuine one. More like the polite smile a woman gave him when he held a door open. Why was Judith so anxious?

"It certainly is pretty country around here," she said. "I guess you're used to it."

"Never get used to it. Sometimes, when I'm out in the forest by myself, the beauty of God's creation still catches my breath." Jacob made the first turn off the highway.

Judith scribbled a note on the paper. Then she licked her lips.

He reached down to the floor of the pickup and retrieved a small ice chest. "I've got some water in here." He set the chest on the seat between them and handed her a cold bottle. Maybe she'd relax if she had a drink.

Judith drank deeply from the bottle. "Thanks."

If he knew why she was so nervous, he might be able to put her at ease. "I've been to Dallas a few times. What part of the city do you live in?"

"Do you have family here?" That was the second time she'd changed the subject.

"I've got so much family around this area it's hard to stretch without hitting someone."

"That must be unpleasant."

Jacob grinned at her joke.

Even though she was tense, Judith had a sense of humor to go with her good looks.

He turned off the two-lane road and onto a gravel one.

Judith wrote another note.

"Do you work?" he asked.

"I'm an illustrator."

"An artist?"

"In a way," she answered with a small shrug. "My latest project is illustrating children's books."

"You should meet my niece, Chloe. She loves to read. My sister has to take her to the library twice a week just to keep her satisfied."

"How old is she?"

"Seven. At least I think she's seven. It's hard to keep up with all my nephews, nieces, and cousins. But Chloe just finished second grade. At least I'm sure of that."

"How many brothers and sisters do you have?"

"Two of each. I'm the baby of the family."

"Awfully big baby."

Jacob grinned again. Judith Robertson definitely had a sense of humor. He'd had his fill of women who wore their troubles like chevrons on their sleeves and seemed to think he had the power to rescue them. And she was definitely more relaxed when she wasn't talking about herself.

He turned off the gravel road onto a dirt one. "Now here's where you might run into trouble if you come out here by yourself. We're lucky the rain has stopped, but as you can see, it's left some big puddles. And the mud can be thick and slippery."

Not that she would be coming out here very often, Jacob thought. After a tour of her grandfather's land to satisfy her curiosity, surely she'd be ready to listen to an offer. After following the muddy road for several minutes, Jacob turned into a shady drive and stopped in front of a small wooden cabin. "This is it."

Before Jacob could open her door, Judith slid out of the truck and stood in front of the unpainted cabin. Jacob studied her reaction as she took in the simple structure. What would Miss Judith Robertson of Dallas think of her grandfather's three-room cabin? "Have you ever been here before?"

"No. The last time I came to visit, my grandfather was still living in a house in town. I didn't know he owned all this land." She stepped onto the small porch and nudged one of the two rocking chairs, setting it into motion. A sad smile whispered around the edge of her mouth. Then she seemed to catch herself. When she turned to face Jacob, her demeanor was all-business. "Mr. Davidson didn't give me the keys."

"Probably not locked." Jacob opened the screen door and turned the knob of the inner door. When it swung open with ease, he smiled down at her.

Judith took two steps back. "Don't tell me people around here don't lock their doors."

"People in town probably do, but out here...well,

the nearest neighbor is a quarter mile away."

Judith stepped through the doorway. She trailed a hand over the worn leather couch, walked into the small kitchen, and then turned the handle on the faucet. "The water's still on."

"That's not city water," Jacob explained. "There's a well out back."

"I didn't think about that," Judith said, cupping her hand and filling it with water. She certainly was out of place. Never lived in a house with a well, drove a car designed for city streets, and had probably never seen a forest except from an airplane window.

Judith walked into the bedroom, leaving Jacob in the small kitchen. "Did my grandfather die in this cabin?" she called.

Jacob took four steps from the kitchen and leaned against the frame of the bedroom door. "Yes, but not in bed. I came out to visit and found him in one of the rocking chairs on the porch."

Her gaze swung to him. "You found my grandfather?"

"That's right."

Judith looked at him expectantly.

Jacob realized she wanted details. "Mr. Isaiah had a morning routine. He got up, made himself a cup of coffee, and then went to the porch to study his Bible. I dropped by around ten o'clock. At first, I thought he'd fallen asleep. But…he wasn't sleeping."

"Mr. Davidson told me my grandfather sold his house in town. Do you have any idea why he moved out here?"

"Sorry, but I can't answer that. I met him for the first time two months ago."

"Were you trying to talk him into selling his land

to you?"

The question felt like an accusation. Jacob rubbed a hand across the back of his neck and considered his answer. "My father asked me to find out if Mr. Isaiah might be interested in selling some land. But don't get the idea that was the only reason I visited."

Judith's posture hadn't relaxed one bit. She looked as though she was questioning a witness in a courtroom. "What other reason was there?"

"I admit I probably wouldn't have gotten to know him if I hadn't been interested in the land, but I enjoyed talking to him. He knew a lot about the history of this area, and he taught me quite a bit about the forest that I never learned in college."

Jacob waited for Judith to challenge his statement, but instead she walked past him and made her way to the fireplace. She picked up one of the framed photographs on the mantel. Jacob craned his neck to look at the picture. "Cute baby."

"It's a photo of my mother and me. I was about a year old when this was taken."

"Your mother had dark hair and dark eyes like you."

"Yeah, but her hair was straight. Nobody knows where my curls came from."

An urge to touch one of those curls, to twine it around his finger and feel its softness against his skin, came over him. He stuck his hands in his pockets.

Judith returned the photo to its place on the mantel. "May I see the rest of the buildings, now?"

"Sure. There's a barn in the back."

Judith followed him off the porch and around the cabin where an unpainted barn on the verge of collapse sat under a canopy of pine boughs. "Did my grandfather keep animals?"

"No. He mostly used this as a garage. His truck is still in there." Jacob pushed open the wide barn doors to reveal an old blue pickup. "I guess it's yours now."

Judith walked ahead of him and peered through the driver's side window. Her nerves seemed to have calmed since their arrival at the cabin, but she was far from being relaxed and friendly.

"The keys are in the ignition," Judith said. "Think it still runs?"

"Mr. Isaiah drove it all the time, but it's been sitting in this barn for several months. Give it a try."

The truck door groaned as she opened it, but the motor roared to life when she turned the key. "That answers the question," she yelled over the noise, and then turned it off.

"If you're interested in selling the truck, you'd best take it to my mechanic. He'd know of anyone who'd be interested in buying it."

"OK, thanks. Where's the church Rev. Washington asked me about?"

"It's about a hundred yards up that path. Want to see it now?"

"Might as well."

"We can either take my truck or cut through the woods. The dirt road curves around to the church, and then joins up with the paved road that leads to the highway."

"I'd rather take the path, if it's OK with you."

"Fine with me."

Jacob led the way on the narrow, winding path through the dense forest. Judith's curiosity was natural, he supposed, but there was no way he could show her all four hundred acres in one afternoon. He glanced back to check on her and noticed that she'd stopped, her head thrown back to look at the sky.

"Something wrong?"

"Perspective," she called back to him.

Jacob knew the word, but suspected she meant something else. "Perspective?" he repeated.

"We have trees in Dallas, but nothing like this. How can so many tall trees grow so close together? And from this viewpoint, the tops look like one giant canopy. Drawing this one scene would take weeks. So many intricate details. And painting it...look," she said, pointing upwards, "One step forward and I can see blue sky peeking through the cloud cover. Do you think there's wildlife nearby?"

"Oh, the animals are here, all right. No doubt looking at you with as much interest as you're looking at the forest."

She dropped her head and caught up to him. "Just be glad I don't have my sketchbook. Otherwise, I'd sit right here and start to draw."

"Be a shame to get those fancy clothes dirty."

"Never stopped me before."

He'd grown up with the forest and worked in it every day, but she had a different way of looking at things. "Ready to see the church, now?"

"Lead the way."

A hundred feet farther, Jacob stepped into the circular clearing where the old church stood.

Judith moved towards the structure, her head cocked to one side as she studied the building. "It's..."

"Old? Abandoned?" Jacob volunteered.

"Quaint," Judith said.

Jacob frowned at the plain wooden building. The flakes of white paint that clung to gray boards hinted of a time when the church had been lovingly tended, but now it suffered from decades of neglect. If she wanted to call that quaint, he wouldn't argue.

As if reading his mind, Judith continued. "It reminds me of a mother waiting patiently on a playground bench while her children are off having fun. Her children may have left, but she knows they'll come back."

Jacob looked at the church again. Some of the foundation blocks had sunk into the soft earth, causing the building to list slightly to one side. He squinted, trying to picture the image Judith had seen.

"And there's a bell!" Judith pointed with delight.

At last, she'd said something he could agree with. The small steeple did indeed hold a cast iron bell. "Mr. Isaiah told me that when the wind is strong enough, that bell will ring."

"I wonder what it sounds like." Judith walked up the rickety wooden steps to the front door and turned the knob. "I think this door really is locked."

"More likely just stuck. Here, let me try." Jacob put his shoulder against the door and pushed. When it gave way, he stumbled through the entryway.

Sunlight streamed through uncovered windows, highlighting a dust-covered pulpit, a small choir loft and pews stationed on either side of a central aisle. A plain wooden cross hung in the center of the back wall.

Judith walked softly, running her fingers along the edges of the worn pews. "Peaceful here," she said in hushed tones. "Like it's sleeping."

Jacob found a light switch near a side door and flicked it. "No electricity. Probably just a matter of getting the wires inspected and the power turned on."

At the altar, Judith turned. "It's a beautiful little

church. Obviously made with loving hands. Is it really big enough to hold Rev. Washington's entire congregation?"

Jacob walked slowly towards her. "I think so. You need to understand, Henry's group isn't part of some recognized church. They're just a group of people who get together once or twice a week to worship."

Judith walked the perimeter of the altar area, her eyes cast down to the worn wooden floor. She was definitely less nervous now that she was out of the truck and investigating her grandfather's property. He'd give more than a nickel to know what Judith was thinking as she paced in front of the pulpit.

She came to an abrupt halt and lifted her gaze to his. "I've seen enough. Will you take me back to my car now?"

Just like that?

"Sure you don't have any more questions?"

She didn't answer, just stepped out of the quiet church leaving Jacob no choice but to follow.

During the trip back to town she was too quiet.

Jacob's attempts to engage her in conversation were met with grunts or head motions, but few words. When he parked in front of the lawyer's office, Judith finally spoke.

"Mr. Fraser, is there any reason I shouldn't let Rev. Washington use that old church?"

He rested his hands on top of the steering wheel. "My name's Jacob, and there are some things you might want to consider. First, talk to Mr. Davidson about any legal issues loaning the church might cause. You may want to get some kind of insurance. The second reason makes me ashamed of some of the people of Piney Meadow."

Judith's expression went to stone as she waited for him to continue.

"There are some people around here who will be angry if you let Henry's group meet in your church," Jacob explained.

"The same people who burned Rev. Washington's other building?"

Jacob nodded. "They're just as likely to burn Isaiah's place."

A long moment of silence stretched between them.

"I need to protect my grandfather's church," Judith finally said, "but turning away Rev. Washington's group feels wrong."

"What are you going to do?"

Judith didn't answer. She slid out of the truck, walked to her car, and placed her purse inside it.

Jacob got out of his truck and leaned against the hood.

Judith's keys dangled from one finger. "Like I said earlier, both you and Rev. Washington will have to wait until I make up my mind. I will tell you this much. Tonight, I'm driving back to Dallas. Then, sometime next week, I'll be moving into my grandfather's cabin."

"You're going to live there?" Jacob couldn't keep the surprise out of his voice. "By yourself?"

"That's the plan. Thanks for showing me around today."

"Hold on, Judith. I don't think it's a good idea."

Her lips trembled and her voice sounded strained. "Why not?"

"It's just...you've never lived in the country before, have you? It might be a difficult adjustment for you."

Judith bit her bottom lip. "Is that the only reason?"

"Guess so. Why do you want to live out there anyway?"

Judith slid into the driver's seat without answering his question. "I'll let you know if I decide to sell all or part of the acreage, Mr. Fraser. Don't worry; I'll let you make the first offer."

"My name's Jacob," he called as she backed out of the parking lot. He watched her drive down the highway, worry nagging the edges of his mind.

❧❧

Judith blew out a shaky breath, the last of her nerves fading like wisps of fog in sunlight. She'd been all right once she'd gotten out of Jacob's truck, where she could run, if necessary. But Jacob had done nothing to put her on edge. She'd created all her fears by herself. As usual.

When she and her father had visited Granddad at Christmas, he hadn't mentioned his property, or his plans to leave it to her. He hadn't told her about his plans to sell the home where her mother had grown up, and from what she'd seen in the cabin, he'd brought very little with him from the house. Maybe he'd been preparing for his transition, ridding himself of earthly possessions and getting his affairs in order.

She should have visited more often. But that was the regret of every mourner. She never traveled outside of her neighborhood unless her father went with her, so trips to Piney Meadow had been few and far between.

Her father had invited Granddad to visit Dallas, but he'd always scoffed at that idea. "I belong in the city about as much as a mule belongs in church," he'd said. Still, the call from his minister had surprised her. Even though her grandfather was in his eighties, she'd never thought his time was near.

She relaxed into the driver's seat as she turned onto the interstate leading to Dallas. She had a three hour drive ahead of her, plenty of time to wonder about her impulsive decision to stay in her grandfather's cabin. She lived in a condominium with neighbors on every side. Her condo featured state-of-the-art security and the guard was only minutes away. And yet something had prodded her to move into that isolated cabin.

"It's You, isn't it, Lord?" Judith smiled as she prayed. One of the benefits of living alone and working out of her home was that no one thought it odd that she kept up a running conversation with God. "I know I've been resisting Your will. I've felt the restlessness in my soul, like a captive bird yearning for blue sky, and I know that's You prodding me to make some changes. But do You really want me to live in the middle of nowhere, Texas?"

Yes, Judith realized, that was exactly why she'd made such an uncharacteristically rash decision.

The Lord wanted her in Piney Meadow.

It was no coincidence that she'd inherited a church just when a congregation needed one.

3

"You've caught me by surprise."

Judith looked at her father's lined face. His smile conveyed approval, but she needed to make certain. "Good surprise or bad surprise?"

"Good," he said, settling into the upholstered chair next to Judith's drawing table. "Just a few months ago, I spoke to you about your reluctance to leave this condo. Now you tell me you're moving to your grandfather's cabin. What's gotten into you?"

Judith gathered her clean paintbrushes and placed them in a cardboard box. "Some of my reasons are practical, the others are spiritual."

"Tell me the practical ones first."

"On the practical side, I could use a change of scenery. I have several illustrations to finish for the children's book about fairies, and zero good ideas. For the first time in my life, a blank page feels like torture."

"When's your deadline?"

Judith blew out a breath. "September. That gives me a little over two months to finish and there's no reason I can't work in Granddad's cabin."

Her father ran a hand through his gray hair. "You said the other reasons are spiritual. What's that about?"

Judith smiled at her father. He'd always accepted her, the good and the bad, and that had made it easy for her to tell him everything. "You were right about challenging me to get out of my condo."

He leaned forward and placed a hand on her arm. "Judith, what happened when you were a child was a terrible thing. No one should ever have to go through something like that. But you can't let it paralyze you."

"I know, Dad. And if I don't do something, I'll grow old in this little condo with no family of my own. That's not what I want."

"It's not what I want for you. You're a beautiful young woman with lots of love to give. I hope you won't let fear cheat you out of a happy future."

"I've been praying for the courage to embrace whatever future God has planned for me. But you know that saying, 'be careful what you wish for'?"

Her father nodded.

"I prayed for courage and the Lord put me in situations where I got to try out my newfound bravery."

He grinned and his dark eyes sparkled with interest. "Oh, yeah? Like what?"

"Losing you has always been my number one, Goliath-sized fear. So I prayed about it. 'Lord,' I said, 'I really want to stop being anxious and terrified whenever Dad goes out of town on business.' So, guess what happened?"

"Are you talking about the time I went to Boston?"

"Yep. You got caught in the worst blizzard in twenty years. No phone service for two days. Two days! I had nothing to sustain me but faith."

"Turned out all right, didn't it?"

"It did. When you called me on the third day I was relieved, but I also felt vindicated. Every time I was afraid during those two days, I would pray and listen for the Lord's voice. And every time, I heard 'all is well'. I admit it was a challenge, but I got through it. And I haven't been afraid for you since."

"Even when I flew to Mexico City last month?"

"I admit there were a few hours of anxiety when the news broadcast the story about a plane crash in Mexico, but I prayed, got the same 'all is well' message, and went on with my day. It was much easier the second time."

The corners of her dad's eyes crinkled as he smiled broadly. "I'm proud of you."

Judith's heart bloomed with warmth. "Yeah? Thanks, Dad."

"So, now that my little David has conquered that Goliath, what's next?"

Judith unzipped a large portfolio case and positioned her illustrations in the pockets. "Trust, of course. I still have a hard time with that one. I just can't get over how wrong I was."

A deep line formed between her father's gray eyebrows. "What happened to your mother wasn't your fault, Judith. I'll say it over and over until you believe it."

"It may not have been my fault, Dad, but you can't deny I let that man in our house. I learned the hard way it's wrong to trust everyone. But it must also be wrong to trust no one. How am I supposed to know who's trustworthy?"

"The trick is to trust just a little." Her dad held his finger and thumb an inch apart. "Then a little more." He widened the space between his fingers. "Until they've earned your trust."

"Right. Sounds good in theory. I'm just not sure I can put that into practice."

Judith's father propped his elbow on the arm of

the chair and rested his head on his fist. "Who do you trust now?"

"You, of course."

"That's all?"

"Hmmm…I think so."

"Is there anybody in Piney Meadow you trust?"

Much to Judith's surprise, she thought of Jacob. He'd been considerate during the hours they'd spent together. "The lawyer, I suppose. He doesn't have any reason to hurt me or to mislead me."

"Anybody else?"

"It's kind of too early to tell. You said to start small and work my way up. I've only met a few people in Piney Meadow."

"Fair enough. When will you be leaving?"

"Tomorrow, or the day after. Will you visit me there?"

"If you'd like. But I'll be praying for you. Not only for your safety and well-being, which I pray for every day, but also for your success. Discovering God's will for your life isn't always easy."

But worth the effort, Judith thought. Otherwise, she'd disappoint her father, herself, and her Lord.

కుం

A few days later, Jacob walked into the Timber Land Diner and slid into his regular booth. He didn't bother with the menu. The Wednesday night special was chicken fried steak, exactly what he wanted.

Jo Nell sidled up to his table with a glass of iced tea and greeted him. "How you doing, Jacob? By yourself tonight?"

Jacob looked into the familiar face of the middle-aged waitress, her red hair teased into a tall poof atop her head. "Yeah. I'll have the special."

"Knew that without asking." Jo Nell grinned and turned back towards the kitchen.

Jacob stretched his legs under the table and relaxed into his chair. He'd spent another long day negotiating with landowners about leases or purchases, and he hadn't gotten one step closer to making a deal. Of course, none of the other prospects offered anything like Isaiah Beecham's four hundred acres. Most of that land hadn't been touched since Isaiah had been a child, and the hardwood alone would make up for the deals Jacob had lost.

He took a long drink of iced tea and let his gaze wander around the diner. Then he saw something that caused him to choke on his drink. Judith Robertson sat in a nearby booth.

"Good evening, Mr. Fraser," she said.

Mr. Fraser again? Well, two could play that game. "Good evening to you, Miss Robertson. What brings you to town?"

"I moved into my grandfather's cabin this afternoon. Then I came into town for groceries and dinner."

Jo Nell brought Judith's food and slid the luscious chicken fried steak in front of her. "You need anything else, honey?"

"No, I'm fine. Thank you," Judith answered.

Jacob's mouth watered as he watched Judith cut into the tender meat. "Are you doing all right out there by yourself?"

"So far, so good. How have you been?"

"Me? Fine." He watched the morsel of food slide between her lips. What lovely lips they were. Full, soft, and enjoying the food he craved.

Judith raised her eyebrows and gazed at Jacob. "You're looking at my food the way a thirsty man looks at water."

He chuckled at the realization of how transparent he'd been. "Sorry. My stomach's been yelling at me for the last two hours, and now it thinks you're eating my food."

"Your stomach has a mind of its own?"

"It feels that way."

To his relief, Jo Nell brought his food and slid it in front of him. "You two know each other?" she asked, cocking her head towards Judith.

"This is Judith Robertson," Jacob answered. "She's Isaiah Beecham's granddaughter."

"Granddaughter?" Jo Nell repeated, looking at Judith with an inquisitive eye. "Didn't know he had one."

"Nice to meet you," Judith said. "You brought Mr. Fraser's food at just the right time. He was about to steal mine."

"Mr. Fraser?" Jo Nell repeated. "I guess I'll have to start addressing you with more respect."

Jacob grinned. "You used to be my Sunday school teacher, Jo Nell. Be kind of silly for you to call me anything except Jacob."

Jo Nell whisked away his plate of food.

"Hey!" he protested.

"You and this young lady know each other, and you're both eating alone, so you might as well sit together." She placed the food on Judith's table and walked away.

"Not exactly discreet, is she?" Judith asked.

Jacob remained in his seat. "Is it OK if I join you?"

"Sure. Besides, I don't want your stomach yelling at me."

He smiled in relief, gathered his utensils and glass, and changed seats. "Did you get settled into your grandfather's cabin all right?"

"Yeah, but I'm going to need the phone number for your mechanic. I thought I'd take my grandfather's truck in."

Jacob bowed his head to say a blessing, and then dove into his food. "Going to sell it?"

"Haven't made up my mind yet. But I met with Walter Davidson today. He's going to help me with transferring the truck title and getting an appraisal on the property."

There was only one reason a person asked for an appraisal. "You've decided to sell?"

"Back off, Mr. Fraser. I've made no such decision. I told you I'd let you make the first offer, and, if I decide to sell, you'll be the first person I call. You can draw up some proposals and I'll talk it over with my father. He knows a lot more about business than I do."

Jo Nell returned with a pitcher of tea and refilled their glasses. "Y'all want anything else? We've got lemon meringue pie tonight."

"Not for me," Judith said.

The waitress set a slice of pie in front of Jacob. "Didn't have to ask you. You always have dessert."

"May I have my bill?" Judith asked.

Jo Nell tore a small piece of paper off a pad and set it beside Judith's plate. "Pay up front when you're ready."

Jacob fumbled in his pocket for his wallet. "I'll get that."

"No, it's OK," Judith said. "Thanks, anyway." She

slid out of the booth, and then retrieved her purse. "See you later, Mr. Fraser."

"Yeah," Jacob muttered as he watched her walk away. Then he realized she'd zinged him with the name thing again and chuckled to himself. He was going to enjoy negotiating with Isaiah Beecham's pretty granddaughter.

∂∽∾

Judith awoke the next morning to sunlight flooding the windows of her grandfather's bedroom. She stretched the length of the bed, considered falling back to sleep, but then remembered what had woken her.

Birds.

She really was a city girl if birdsong at dawn would wake her from a sound sleep. She stretched and said her usual morning prayer, thanking the Lord for another day, and asking Him to guide her. Then she pulled on her jeans and shirt and shuffled barefoot into the kitchen for a glass of juice. Taking it outside to the porch, she sank into one of the rocking chairs and recalled how difficult her first night in the cabin had been.

Without the ambient city light, she'd experienced firsthand just how black the night could be. She'd felt alone and vulnerable as she traveled the unlit roads, the headlights of her car a poor substitute for powerful city streetlights. Darkness loomed like a sinister shroud on either side of the highway.

She'd known the surrounding forest was alive with nocturnal animals and she'd struggled to keep her imagination at bay. "You're safe in the car," she'd told herself over and over. "No raccoon is going to carjack you."

When she'd finally found the cabin, relief washed over her. She'd run from her car to the cabin, trying to keep images from childhood ghost stories out of her brain, and closed the door firmly behind her. She'd automatically reached for the lock, remembered there wasn't one, and pushed the couch in front of the door.

Walking around the cabin in her pajamas hadn't been a picnic, either. Why hadn't she noticed the windows were uncovered? Not a curtain in sight. She'd considered tacking up towels, and then realized there was no one around to see her, anyway. Unless an armadillo took up spying, curtains wouldn't matter.

After leaving the bathroom light on, she'd finally snuggled into the bed. But her eyes popped open when the silence disappeared and the noise of the surrounding forest flooded the room. An urban girl couldn't begin to identify the sounds, but whatever they were, they would keep her awake.

She'd stared at the bedroom ceiling, listening and praying, until, at long last, sleep defeated fear.

But she'd made it. She drained the last of the juice. She'd conquered the dark, the silence and the noise. Now she had a full day ahead of her. She grabbed her sketchbook and shoes and stepped outside. If she lived in a forest, she may as well make use of it.

Pine needles rustled underfoot as Judith went into the dense woods. Although there was no discernible path, she was able to pass through the undergrowth with little difficulty. A few steps at a time were all she needed, for each stopping point revealed new wonders; a circle of toadstools, vines that wrapped themselves around towering trees, and decomposing logs that flaunted colorful fungus.

Heedless of the dirt, she crouched close to the forest floor, her pencil racing over the pages of her sketchbook until they overflowed with detailed drawings of the small marvels she found.

She pushed farther into the woods, not noticing the branches that slapped against her face, until she reached a clearing. Settling against a fallen log, she quieted her mind and let her senses absorb her surroundings.

There, the call of a crow and the buzzing of insects. Nearby, the sound of a small animal burrowing amid the dry leaves. Overhead, the wind's song as it danced amid the treetops.

She took a deep breath of the pine-scented air and resumed her sketching. The light that filtered through the canopy seemed to sanctify the small clearing, as though she'd stumbled into nature's cathedral.

Had her mother been here when she'd been a girl? Had she played among the trees, picked wildflowers, or dreamed here?

She prayed here.

The thought formed in her mind, not as a spoken answer, but as response to Judith's question. "Thank you, Lord," she whispered.

A sense of well-being washed over her and she lifted her face to the sun. Once again, the Proverb had been proven right. Judith's heart had led her this way, but the Lord had directed her steps.

❧

It was late morning when Jacob parked his truck behind Judith's sports car. He stepped onto the porch of her grandfather's cabin and knocked loudly on the screen door.

No one answered.

"Judith?" he called loudly.

Still no answer.

She couldn't have gone too far. He settled into a rocking chair. But a few minutes later, a troubling thought crossed his mind. What if Judith was in the cabin, but hurt? He wasn't one to trespass, but a quick look through the cabin wouldn't hurt anything. If she was hurt, it would be a good thing he checked, and if she wasn't in the cabin, no one would know.

Surely, she hadn't gone exploring in the woods by herself. A city girl like Judith would get lost in the maze of pines. After all, the forest didn't exactly have street signs or a marker with an arrow pointing towards civilization. She was most likely in the cabin. After another minute of debate, he sprang from the rocker and stepped inside.

One look at the artwork taped to the walls stopped him in his tracks. "Holy cow." On every wall were photographs of fairies. No...that couldn't be right. No one could take a photograph of a fairy. He stepped closer to inspect the picture. It was a painting. A painting so realistic, it looked like a photograph.

"Good morning, Mr. Fraser."

Jacob jumped and turned to see her stern face.

"You didn't touch any of those, did you?"

"What? Oh...no. I...uh..."

Judith arched an eyebrow and crossed her arms in front of her, waiting for him to explain.

"Sorry," Jacob said as he straightened and faced her. "I came out to give you the mechanic's name and number. You left the diner before I could give them to you."

"And you decided to make yourself at home? Is that common practice in Piney Meadow?"

"It's not uncommon when you're visiting a friend's house, but I thought you might be hurt. So, I, uh…" Jacob studied Judith's serious face. Was she really angry to find him in her cabin?

Just when he thought he'd have to apologize, her stern frown melted into a mischievous grin. "Well…I suppose I can overlook trespassing this time."

He relaxed with a smile of his own.

"So, what do you think of the paintings?" Judith asked.

Jacob turned back to the wall. "These are amazing. They look just like photographs. Who did these?"

"Who do you think?"

"I don't know."

"That's what I do for a living. Remember?"

"You told me you drew pictures for children's books."

"Uh-huh. These are for a book about fairies."

She stepped beside him and he caught the faint scent of gardenias. Not an overpowering perfume, but a feminine scent that matched the attractive woman who stood next to him.

"I've got the paintings laid out in the order of the pages," Judith explained. "The whole book is about how fairies are real and live among humans in secret."

"I love this one," Jacob said, tearing his gaze away from her and pointing towards fairies playing in a department store.

"How many fairies can you find in that picture?"

Jacob narrowed his eyes and studied the artwork. "One on the mannequin, two on the light fixture, one behind the perfume bottle…"

"That's good," Judith complimented him. "There are two more. Want a hint?"

"Give me a minute."

From the corner of his eye, Jacob could see Judith watching him as he inspected her painting. "In the shoes. And they look like they're having a great time."

"I only have three more paintings to go. But the publisher has OKed the thumbnails and sketches, so now all I have to do is finish."

Jacob gestured to the drawing board beside the largest window. "You're going to work out here?"

"That's the plan. The first part of the book was about urban fairies, the middle part about suburban fairies, and the last part is about—"

"Rural fairies?" Jacob finished for her.

"Exactly. I thought I'd take advantage of living in a forest to get some ideas. I went out sketching this morning."

"You went by yourself?"

"Sure."

"Good thing you didn't get lost."

"I may be from the city, but I did remember to bring my brain with me."

In other words, don't underestimate Judith Robertson. Jacob gestured towards the sketchbook tucked under her arm. "May I take a look?"

"Sure, help yourself." She handed it to him. "Can I offer you something to drink?" she said over her shoulder.

"Got any coffee?"

"Sorry, don't drink coffee. How about a soft drink?"

"Fine." Jacob leafed through the sketchbook,

stunned by the intricate drawings. He chuckled at the fairies using acorn caps to slide down snow-covered hills and the cross-section of a pine that served as a high rise apartment building. "These are amazing, Judith. You did this with just a pencil?"

"Yep. Glad you like them." She handed the drink to him and their gazes connected.

An awkward moment of silence stretched between them as an unspoken current of attraction sparked.

Did Judith feel it, too, Jacob wondered, or was he making a fool of himself by staring into her dark eyes?

"So, do you have that phone number for me?" Judith asked.

Apparently the attraction was all one-sided. "Oh, yeah," Jacob answered, fishing his cell phone from his pocket. He pushed some buttons and handed it to Judith.

She jotted down the number and returned his phone. "Thanks. I'll give the mechanic a call and take the truck in. Do you think he'll give me a ride back here?"

"Probably. But my mother wants to invite you to Sunday dinner. If you'd like, I can meet you at the mechanic's and after dinner, bring you back here."

Judith took in a quick, sharp breath. Her gaze darted from Jacob to the front door and back again. "Why does your mother want to meet me?"

"She knew your mother when they were both girls. She says she hasn't seen you since you grew up."

Judith's eyebrows drew together and she rubbed her palms on the legs of her jeans. "Will it just be your mother, you, and me?"

"No, my whole family meets at my parents' house after church."

"The whole family? Didn't you say you had two brothers and two sisters?"

"That's right. They'll be there with their wives, husbands, and kids."

Judith's eyes widened and she stepped away from Jacob.

He closed the sketchbook and handed it back to her. "Are you all right, Judith?"

She let out a shaky breath. "I'm fine."

Jacob returned his gaze to the art work on the wall. For a few minutes, Judith had been relaxed, even playful. But at the mention of a family dinner, she'd reverted to the same nervous woman he'd met last week. "This picture is really clever." Jacob nodded to the first illustration. "I love the idea of teams of fairies playing aerial baseball. But these fairies over here are causing a lot of trouble."

Judith stepped next to him to look at the scene he indicated.

"Messing with the traffic lights is going to lead to chaos." Jacob grinned at her.

"It's my explanation of why the Dallas traffic is so awful."

"Must be the fairies."

"Must be."

Judith gazed up at him and smiled. "Thanks for inviting me to your family's Sunday dinner. What time should I meet you at the mechanic's?" She'd beaten back whatever had made her anxious.

That was twice now Jacob had seen her afraid, but proceeding nonetheless. Judith had courage. "Church usually lets out around noon. How about I meet you at twelve-thirty?"

Judith nodded her agreement. "OK. I'll see you

then."

Jacob headed towards the door, and then stopped and turned back to her. "Just one more thing. When you're at my parents' house on Sunday, you're going to have to call me Jacob."

"Why's that, Mr. Fraser?"

"Because the house will be full of Frasers. If you call me Mr. Fraser, no one will know if you're talking to me, my brothers, or my father."

She pursed her lips in thought. "I'll think about that."

"You do that, Miss Robertson," he said. "I'll see you on Sunday."

❧❦

Jacob's truck drove away in a plume of red dust.

She'd be meeting his family in a few days.

Another opportunity the Lord had put in her path. Large social groups could be especially challenging— so many people wanting so many things, and all of them talking about next to nothing.

She'd always avoided large parties, but she was determined to change her solitary ways. Dinner with the Frasers was as good a place to start as any.

It should be interesting to talk to Jacob's mother. Other than the stories her grandfather had told her, Judith knew little about her mother's early life. But did Jacob's mother know the details of Mom's death?

Judith squeezed her eyes shut. Every second of that awful day was permanently etched in her memory. Judith wrapped her arms around herself and bowed her head. "Let not your heart be troubled, neither let it be afraid," she murmured. That verse from the Book of John had comforted her many times. She whispered the verse again and waited for the pain in her chest to subside.

Like drops of water melting off an icicle, grief and guilt slowly loosened their hold on Judith.

Then the Lord blessed her with a memory.

Christmas. The house smelled of the fresh evergreen tree they'd yet to decorate, and patches of snow covered the yard. Her mother, young and carefree, helped Judith make Christmas cookies. How her mother had laughed when Judith insisted they use the cookie cutters from Halloween. "Stars and snowflakes," her mother had said between giggles. "The wise men didn't bring scarecrows and pumpkins."

Someday Judith wanted to make cookies with her own children. But that dream would never come true if she settled for a life of fear. A rush of air escaped her lungs. She could have lunch with the Frasers. She could even learn to like it.

4

Judith awoke the next morning to the sound of a prowler. Someone, or something, was pacing the length of the narrow front porch. Her pulse thundered in her ears and she struggled to listen as the footsteps first crept, then sped across the front of the cabin, followed by what she swore was a child's giggle.

Judith eased herself out of bed and tiptoed on shaky legs to the kitchen. Half hiding behind the cabinets, she watched the uncovered front window, trying to determine who, or what, had decided to visit her.

Less than a minute later, a dark head passed along the bottom of the window frame.

Her fear vanished as she realized there was a child on her front porch. As Judith neared the front door, she saw a small, dark-skinned girl, crouched on all fours. Judith cracked open the door and met the girl's round-eyed, startled gaze. "I see I have a visitor."

The girl sprang to her feet, the startled look dissolving into a wide smile of perfectly formed teeth. "Mornin'," she said, beaming up like sunlight on morning dew. "Do you always sleep so late?"

"Sorry to have kept you waiting," Judith answered, barely able to keep from laughing. "What's that under your shirt?"

The girl tightened her grasp on the wriggling lump near her stomach. "Nothin'. Are you Mr. Isaiah's granddaughter?"

"That's me. My name's Judith."

"Judith?" The girl rolled the name around her mouth like a candy she'd never tasted. "Is that a Bible name? Don't get me wrong, it's a pretty name and all, but it sounds so serious. Like someone who's at least a hundred years old."

"What's your name?"

"Keneisha," the young visitor announced with pride. "Keneisha Lewis."

"Nice to meet you."

The girl's eyes grew wider and she bent at the waist. "Ouch! Quit moving around, will you?"

"That nothing under your shirt wants to get out. I think you'd better tell me what it is."

"It's just a little kitten," Keneisha explained as she freed the animal and lifted it up to Judith's face. "I brung it for you."

The orange-and-white kitten hung helplessly from Keneisha's hands, its back legs pushing against the empty air as it struggled against the girl's tight grasp.

Concern for the animal swept through Judith as she gingerly accepted Keneisha's gift. "I've never had a pet before. Are you sure it's OK with your mother?"

"Sure it is. She don't care. She said to tell you she'll be by later with some things from the garden."

Judith snuggled the kitten into the crook of her arm and ran a finger along the top of its tiny head. "Do you live close by, Keneisha?"

"Yep." The girl pointed towards the back of the cabin. "You go through those woods there, and then follow the dirt road to our house. Can't miss it. Can I come in?" Shyness was foreign to Keneisha.

"I guess so," Judith answered. "You'll have to

teach me how to take care of this kitten. Does it have a name?"

"Not yet," the girl answered as she followed Judith into the cabin. "I decided to let you name it. But Pumpkin would be an awful good name because it's orange like a jack-o-lantern."

Judith spooned a bit of tuna into a shallow bowl and set it and the kitten on the kitchen floor.

The kitten took in its surroundings, tested its feet on the worn vinyl, and promptly scampered out of the room and under the couch.

Keneisha giggled at the cat's antics. "That crazy little cat don't want the food."

Judith frowned at the spot where the cat had disappeared. "Do you think it's OK under there?"

"Sure. It'll come out after it stops being scared. You got any ice cream?"

"For the cat?"

"No," Keneisha said between giggles. "For me."

"Oh. No, sorry. No ice cream. How about a drink?"

"Got any soda? I love a good, cold soda."

Judith retrieved the drink for her new friend and passed it to her. "You sure your mother won't be worried about you? Does she know you're over here?"

"Nah, she don't worry. She knows I can take care of myself." Keneisha opened the can and took a long drink.

"How old are you, Keneisha?"

"Nine. How old are you?"

"Seventy-five." Judith struggled to keep a straight face.

"Wow. That's even older than my momma. You must be about to die or something."

"Never know," Judith said. "Now finish that drink while I get dressed. Then I want you to show me where you live. Plus, you have to tell me how to take care of Pumpkin."

"You gonna name that cat Pumpkin? Hot dog! I told you that would be a good name."

A few minutes later, Judith followed Keneisha along a rough path through the forest until she stepped onto a dusty, red dirt road.

"That's our house there," the girl said, pointing to a small metal-roofed frame house at the end of the road. "I'll tell my momma you've come to pay us a visit."

The girl skipped ahead of Judith, her black braids bouncing happily as she called to her mother. As she ran to the garden patch beside the house, a woman rose from her knees and turned to face the road. Shading her eyes with one hand, she waved the other in a wide arc above her head. "Come on, Miss Judith! You saved me a trip."

Judith waved back and made her way towards the house. To one side, several old cars were parked for eternity, half-covered with tall grass and climbing plants. She stepped onto the wide porch where three cats stretched lazily on the arms and back of a couch. One, a skinny orange and gray male, rubbed itself against her leg. "I bet you're Pumpkin's father, aren't you?"

Keneisha's return shooed the cat away. "My momma's coming. She said I should offer you something to drink. You want something?"

"Maybe later," Judith answered.

"Keneisha! Get over here and help me with this basket," a woman's voice called from behind the house.

The girl pushed herself off the couch, hopped off the porch and disappeared around the side of the house.

A minute later, a large woman wearing a flowered blouse and shorts stepped onto the porch. "Miss Judith, so glad you came. I was just picking some okra for you."

Judith offered her hand to Keneisha's mother but the woman ignored it and pulled Judith into a sweaty embrace. "Oh, I know Mr. Isaiah's happy you're here."

"You knew my grandfather?" Judith asked as soon as she was free from the hug.

"Sure did. He was my neighbor. Come on in and sit a while. I made a pudding cake this morning. Keneisha, give Miss Judith that little basket, and then go get the big one and bring it in the kitchen."

"Yes, ma'am," Keneisha answered, handing a small basket to Judith. "Can I have some cake, too?"

Keneisha's mother frowned at the girl. "You go do what I told you, and then we'll talk about cake."

Keneisha's laughter rang through the summer air as she hopped off the porch to carry out her mother's instructions.

"Is Keneisha your only child, Mrs. Lewis?"

"Heavens, no. I've got two grown sons who live and work in San Augustine. Keneisha there, well you might say she was a little surprise my husband left me just before he went to be with the Lord." She opened the screen door and motioned for Judith to enter.

"She certainly surprised me this morning," Judith said as she stepped through the doorway.

Keneisha's mother let her head fall back as she gave a loud bark of laughter. "I told her to wait to go visiting, but she's been pestering me every day. 'Can I go visit our new neighbor? Can I give her one of our kittens?'" The woman's smile faded as she cocked an eyebrow towards Judith. "You don't mind, do you?"

"Of course not," Judith hurried to say. "But I don't have the slightest idea how to take care of a cat."

"Nothing to it," Mrs. Lewis answered, leading Judith into a large, tidy kitchen. "Put out some food and water and they take care of themselves. A cat will keep the field mice and other critters away from your cabin. Some people like dogs, but all they do is bark and sleep. Me, I'd rather have a cat any day."

Judith eased into a straight-backed chair and examined the contents of the basket Keneisha had given her. "I appreciate the vegetables, Mrs. Lewis."

"My name's Beverly. Since we're neighbors, you call me Beverly."

"Fine. But my name's Judith. No need for the Miss."

"Oh, that's just something we do around here to show respect. You're from the city, aren't you?"

"I guess it shows," Judith answered with a smile. "Dallas born and raised."

"Uh-huh. Well, it shouldn't take too long to get the city off you. You know how to fix okra?"

Judith studied the fuzzy green pods in the basket. "Not really. But I've heard of fried okra. Do I fry the whole thing?"

Beverly barked another laugh and clapped her hands. "Heavens, no. I tell you what, after we've finished our cake, I'll show you how to cut it and fry it up. Then you can have some for your dinner."

Beverly removed the lid of a metal cake pan and sliced a piece of yellow cake. "Brother Henry told me you were gonna let us use Mr. Isaiah's old church."

"You must mean Rev. Washington. I met him last week."

Beverly slid the slice of cake onto a saucer and handed it to Judith. "That's right. It's wonderful how you're gonna let us use that old church. You'll see. We'll get it all fixed up and it'll be as good as new."

"I don't want you to get your hopes up. I told Rev. Washington he could come by and inspect the church. I didn't say he could use it."

"Oh, I have faith that everything will work out OK. What else can I get you, Judith? Something to drink? Another slice of cake?"

"First a kitten, and then food. Are you trying to bribe me, Beverly?"

"Oh, I'm just trying to sweeten you up a bit so you'll let the Lord work through you. Mr. Isaiah's church has been waiting for a long, long time. Waiting for somebody to come and lift the rafters in song. God sent you at just the right time, Judith. Yes, ma'am, at just the right time."

"Momma!" Keneisha's lively voice called from outside.

"What's that girl up to now?" Beverly asked as she headed for the door. "Raising that child is like trying to nail pudding to a tree."

Judith waited at the kitchen table, absently using her fork to mash cake crumbs. Even though she hadn't agreed to anything, it was obvious Beverly was making plans for Granddad's church. But Jacob's warning had been clear. If she loaned the church, she'd put it in danger, and she wanted to protect that dear, little church.

෧෧ඤ

Sheriff Miller was pouring a cup of coffee when Jacob stepped into his office. "Morning, Jacob," the older man said. His tan uniform sported sharp creases and his salt-and-pepper hair was cut short.

Jacob shook hands with the lawman. "I got your message."

"Have a seat and help yourself to the coffee."

"No, thanks." Jacob sat down. "What can I do for you?"

The sheriff glanced through the glass walls of his office. "See those two men sitting by the door? They're from the FBI's task force on hate crimes. I'd like you to take them to the scenes of the church fires."

"Not much left to see."

"I know. They got here yesterday and they've been looking over the case files, but they want to see the places for themselves. I don't have the manpower to spare so, as usual, I'm asking you. Have you thought any more about my invitation to sign on as a deputy?"

"I've thought about it, but let's keep things the way they are for now."

"A man like you should be more than a volunteer deputy. You've got more training than some of my full-time guys."

Maybe he'd return to law enforcement. Once he could remember his mistake without his gut clenching. "Is there anything new on the fires?" Jacob asked.

"Nothing I can talk about. Arson isn't a federal offense, but the FBI can prosecute arson of ethnic churches as civil rights violations. One thing I've learned is to never turn down offers of help, so I'm glad for any assistance those agents can give. Come on.

I'll introduce you."

The two agents wore white shirts and ties, their suit coats hung over the backs of their chairs. They stood as Sheriff Miller and Jacob approached.

"Jacob Fraser, this is Charles Lawson and Mark Grey. Jacob is one of our volunteer firefighters. He was on the scene at all four fires. I've asked him to give you a tour of the sites."

Lawson was a bear of a man, all chest and arms, in his mid-thirties. Mark Grey was taller and older, with silver flecks in his dark hair.

As Jacob shook their hands, it became clear that Mark was in charge of the two-man team.

"Thanks for taking the time to play tour guide," Mark said with a friendly smile.

"No problem," Jacob replied. "The scene of the most recent fire is the closest. OK if we start there?"

"Sure. Lawson is going to meet with an investigator from the state fire marshal's office, but I'd like to check the sites myself. Just give me a minute to grab my gear." Mark retrieved a case that resembled a tackle box and followed Jacob outside. "How long have you been a volunteer firefighter?"

"Two years," Jacob answered as he pulled his truck away from the sheriff's office. "We don't have the population to warrant a full time force, so everyone's a volunteer. Chief Dutton retired from the Dallas Fire Department several years ago, and he's the one in charge."

"Yes, I met him. Sheriff Miller told me you used to be with the Houston P.D."

"That's right."

"Big city wasn't for you?"

"Something like that." There was more to the

story, of course, but Jacob wasn't about to tell everything to someone he'd just met. "I noticed you brought an evidence kit. What do you hope to find?"

"The investigator from the state fire marshal's office asked me to collect a soil sample from the burn sites. Accelerants sometimes seep through the floor and accumulate in the soil."

"How will that help?"

"If the same type of accelerant was used in all the fires, there's a high probability we're looking for the same arsonists. Were you ever trained in arson investigation?"

"No."

"It's not my specialty either, but I've learned a lot since I started working on the Hate Crime Task Force."

"I still can't believe a place as small as Piney Meadow is the scene of hate crimes."

"Maybe it's not. But the burning of four African-American churches in three months certainly points to that possibility."

A few minutes later, Jacob stopped at what remained of the All Saints Community Church.

Mark looked over the site. "This place wasn't very big, was it?"

"I'd estimate it at about two thousand square feet."

Mark opened the evidence kit and removed a small plastic jar and a pry bar.

Jacob leaned against his pickup and watched the agent.

Mark slowly circled the perimeter of the building, and then walked into the debris. He squatted and used the pry bar to lift what was left of the floor. He returned to Jacob's truck a few minutes later, the plastic jar full of soil. "Do you know what this congregation is planning to do?"

"They're hoping to use an abandoned church building. They just need to get the landowner's permission, and then do some repair work."

Mark's face took on a serious look. "I hope the landowner knows what he's risking."

"Another fire?"

"Could be. Is the church building near a populated area?"

"Not hardly. The woman who owns the land is staying in a cabin about a hundred yards away from the church. Other than her, there's nobody around."

Mark shook his head. "That's not good. People who commit hate crimes don't always stick to just property damage. If she decides to lend her church building, she shouldn't stay there alone." Mark walked back to the evidence kit.

Jacob's gaze returned to the ruined church. The agent's words sat in his stomach like sour milk. Judith shouldn't have to deal with hate crimes. No one should. But if the arsonists had burned Rev. Washington's church once, they were likely to do it again, and this time Judith might be in the way.

She hadn't resolved the question about lending the church building yet, but he expected her to agree to Henry's request. How could anyone with a conscience turn him down?

Jacob recalled her nervous manner. If she was the anxious type, the kind of woman who lived on the border between reason and foolishness, dealing with this problem might convince her that Piney Meadow was the last place she wanted to be.

His throat tightened at the thought of Judith

leaving. Although he couldn't explain why, he suspected it had nothing to do with timber.

After driving Mark Grey back to the sheriff's office, Jacob headed for a lunch meeting with his father and brother. As he parked in front of Fraser and Sons Building Supply and Hardware, he let his head drop against the back window. Lunch with his father and brother was usually enjoyable, but today's meeting was undoubtedly about the recent drought of timber deals he'd been able to close. With a sigh of resignation, he got out of the truck and climbed the stairs to his father's office.

His brother and father were seated at the conference table eating sandwiches.

"There you are," David said around a mouthful of food. "We waited for you."

"Yeah, I can see that." Jacob sat and opened the bag with his sandwich. "Sorry I'm late. I was playing chauffeur for the FBI."

His father's eyebrows lifted. "The FBI?"

Jacob bowed his head over his food, said a silent blessing, and then explained the circumstances of his involvement as he ate.

John Fraser listened to his son, his expressive face clearly showing concern. "So we've got the sheriff, the state fire marshal's office, and the FBI working together on these arsons?"

"That's the sum of it," Jacob answered.

"Makes you wonder what the world is coming to."

David shifted in his chair. "Not to change the subject, but have you met Isaiah Beecham's granddaughter?"

"Yep. In fact, she's coming to dinner on Sunday."

"What's she like?"

Jacob shook his head slowly. "I can't quite figure her out. She's a city girl, but she's determined to live in Isaiah's cabin. Sometimes she's skittish, other times she's calm."

"Does she work?"

"She's an artist, so I guess she makes her own hours. And she smells like the gardenias Mom grows."

David's gaze connected with his father's and both men chuckled.

"What's so funny?" Jacob asked.

"She smells like gardenias?" David asked. "That's the first time you ever described someone by the way they smell."

"I bet she's pretty, too," his father said.

Jacob looked from his father to his brother, understanding the reason behind their laughter. "All right, you got me."

"You're interested in her," his brother said.

"Too early to tell," Jacob answered.

"I hope this attraction won't interfere with business," his father said. "The Beecham acreage would go a long way in securing our production for the next six months."

"Judith said that if she decided to sell, she'd let us make the first offer."

"That's good," David said. "Where do we stand with Dwight Thompson?"

Jacob swallowed the sour taste Dwight's name always gave him. "Now that guy's a piece of work. He's sitting on a nice stand of longleaf pine and there I am, offering him cash, and he's stalling."

"What's he want?" his father asked.

"More money, I suppose. But I've already offered him top dollar."

"The Thompsons can be difficult people," David said. "Dwight's father wasn't much better."

"I don't know why, but dealing with the Thompsons has always been tough," his father said. "Your mother says they're jealous of our success and want to get one over on us. I don't know how to respond to that."

"Just keep offering them a fair price until Dwight either accepts or rejects the offer," David suggested. "There's nothing else we can do."

His dad laid a hand on Jacob's forearm. "I know you're doing everything you can, son. Just keep at it. This drought of prospects can't last forever. "

Jacob ate in silence as his brother and father talked about other business matters. Since returning to the family business, Jacob had been charged with securing timber deals with area landowners. He'd enjoyed meeting the salt-of-the-earth people who cherished the land as much as he did, and he'd closed many lucrative deals. Until now. The last two months had been fraught with one failure after another.

He couldn't disappoint his family after they'd welcomed him back. His parents hadn't understood his desire to move to the biggest city in the state, nor his decision to become a police officer, but they'd supported him, nonetheless.

He'd survived the academy, had excelled during his rookie year, and was moving up the ladder when all of his plans for a career in law enforcement crashed on one cloud-covered night.

If he couldn't be a cop and he couldn't help his family, what could he do? He'd failed as a police officer, and now he was failing in the timber business. He didn't owe his family, but he did want to justify their trust. Doing his part to sustain the business was the least he could do.

❧❦

After lunch, Jacob walked up the dusty path that led to Dwight Thompson's double wide trailer.

Someone had made an attempt to beautify the cement walkway that led to the front door. Spindly zinnias struggled to survive in the sandy soil.

Jacob's knock brought Dwight's wife to the door. The bedraggled woman barely resembled the girl Jacob had gone to school with. She extended one skinny arm to open the cracked storm door. "Hey there, Jacob. Nice to see you."

"Hi, Della. Missed you at church last week."

"Oh," she said, a hand flying to cover a faded bruise on her cheek. "I haven't been feeling so well."

"Sorry to hear that. Been to the doctor?"

"Oh, it's nothing. I'll be fine. You looking for Dwight?"

"Yeah. He around?"

"Out back with his brothers."

Tightness closed around Jacob's heart. He didn't care too much for Dwight, but Dwight's marriage was none of his business. "You know, Della, if you ever need anything…"

Della frowned.

Jacob hastened to explain. "What I mean is, if you ever need help—"

"Oh," she said. "No, it's OK. I've got my momma and daddy if…"

Jacob smiled and nodded, fully understanding Della's unspoken message. "OK, I'll go find Dwight," he said, taking a step back. "You take care."

Della closed the door and stepped back, her bony arms crossed in front of her chest.

Lord, please help Della. A prayer was the only way he could help the woman at that moment.

Dwight Thompson and his two brothers were gathered around an ancient pickup truck. As Jacob approached, Dwight lifted his head from under the rusted hood. "Hey, Jacob. We were just talking about you."

"I hope it was good," Jacob replied, exchanging handshakes with the three men.

"We were talking about your offer on that stand of longleaf pine. The Jacksons out of Lufkin offered twenty-five percent more than you."

Jacob processed the information quickly. The fact that Jackson Lumber was on the verge of going out of business made Dwight's statement suspicious, but calling him a liar was not the way to secure the deal. A sharp pain burrowed its way into Jacob's neck as he eyed the Thompsons.

Dwight sported a sly grin, but his brothers glared at Jacob as though he'd come to sell them a load of ripe manure.

"Well," Jacob began slowly, "if you think the Jacksons can make you a better deal, I'd understand if you went for it. But you also have to consider the integrity of your land. The Jacksons clear-cut. They'll take everything—the pine, the immature oak and everything else. It'll take decades for the land to recover. But my family will only take the mature pines and leave the other trees for the future."

The brother closest to Dwight mumbled something that Jacob couldn't make out and Dwight nodded. "Can you match the Jacksons' offer?"

"No. The offer I've made is the fair market value."

Dwight exchanged silent glances with his brothers. "We're going to think about it. Check back next week."

For yet another stalling tactic?

"Fine," Jacob said as he stepped away from the group. "I hope the truck is fixable."

"Oh, we'll get it running," Dwight boasted. "They haven't invented a car the Thompsons can't fix. By the way, have you heard anything about the FBI coming to Piney Meadow?"

"Why do you ask?"

"Just wondering. There's a lot of talk around town about some special task force the FBI has created to find out who has been burning churches. It's hard to believe the FBI could be bothered with a place as small as Piney Meadow."

"I know what you mean, but four church fires in three months...maybe the FBI can use its resources to find out who's behind them."

Dwight glanced at his brothers, and then back at Jacob. "I'm going to talk to the Jacksons again about their offer. I'll get back to you."

"Fair enough." Jacob ambled towards his truck, intent on hiding the discomfort that dealing with Dwight always brought him. His family might need Dwight's land, but Jacob refused to play the game.

Both this deal and the Beecham property were falling like rain through a lattice roof.

5

Jacob left the church service during the final hymn. If he stayed until the end, he'd get held up in the ritual of greetings that was as much a part of the Sunday service as the sermon. He'd been thinking all week about Judith, and he didn't want her to have to wait at the mechanic's.

As it turned out, he was the one waiting. He glanced at his watch several times, wondering what had held her up. Twelve-thirty came and went, but still no sign of Judith. If he'd asked for her cell phone number, he could have called to make sure she was still coming, but he'd abandoned that idea, thinking it too forward. After all, they'd only met three times. An involuntary smile crossed his lips as he remembered the moments they'd spent together.

She had a way about her. Part teasing, part serious. Part confident, part shy. It sure would be good to see her again.

If only she'd get there.

Just when he was considering driving out to Isaiah's cabin, a familiar blue pickup truck rounded the corner.

Judith was straining at the steering wheel until the truck stopped with a lurch. She cut off the motor, blew out a breath, and leaned back in the seat.

Jacob walked across the parking lot. Opening the driver's side door, he studied her with curiosity. "Did the truck give you problems?"

"Nothing a little more experience couldn't fix." At Jacob's frown she explained. "Manual transmission and no power steering. It took me a while to figure it out."

"You don't know how to drive a stick shift?"

"Knowing and doing are two different things when it comes to this truck," Judith answered as she grabbed her purse and got out.

"But you made it all right?"

Judith didn't answer. She examined her hands, flexing her fingers in open and closed fists.

"What's wrong?" he asked.

"My hands hurt. I must have been gripping the steering wheel too tight."

Jacob took one of her hands in both of his and massaged it. "Sorry. I didn't even think about Isaiah's truck being hard to drive. I could've come out to your place and driven it for you."

"It doesn't matter now. Besides, I made it OK. I just need more practice." Judith pulled her hand from his and another silence stretched between them as unspoken thoughts charged the air.

Jacob thrust his hands in the pockets of his dress slacks, wishing he could hold her hand a bit longer. "Hungry?"

"Sure. Am I dressed OK for dinner with your family?"

Jacob took in her simple flowered skirt and white blouse. "You look like springtime."

"Is it too much for Sunday dinner with your family? Or too plain?"

"You're perfect."

Judith's gaze connected with his and color

bloomed in her cheeks.

"I mean...uh...you're dressed just fine." His attraction to Judith was unlike anything he'd experienced. It was quick and deep, like a sapling root searching for water. Jacob took several steps away from her and changed the subject. "Drop your keys in that slot on the door and we'll get going." Jacob opened the passenger side door for her.

"I met my neighbors," she said as she climbed into her seat.

"Your closest neighbor would be Beverly Lewis," he said as he drove out of the lot. "Is that who you mean?"

"That's right. Her daughter, Keneisha, woke me up the other morning."

A slow grin crossed Jacob's face. "Keneisha is one of those people who will never meet a stranger."

"No kidding," Judith answered. "And Beverly gave me a cooking lesson."

Jacob gave a nod of approval. "Beverly Lewis is one of the best cooks around. She makes a sweet potato pie that's so good it would make a man propose."

"Oh, really? Does Beverly know you feel that way?"

"She does. But she won't marry me, and she won't give my mom the recipe."

"She certainly seems like a nice woman, but she's under the impression I've already agreed to let Rev. Washington use my grandfather's church."

Perhaps he should tell her what the FBI agent had said. But nothing was definite yet. If Henry's group started meeting in Isaiah's old church, then Jacob would make sure Judith took precautions. "Henry told me that he and some men from his congregation are coming tomorrow afternoon to look at it. But no matter how much work that old place needs, he's determined to make it useable. If you're not going to allow him to use it, best say so."

Judith didn't respond.

They rode in silence until he parked on the street outside a large brick house.

"Here we are. Everybody's dying to meet you."

"Who's everybody?" Judith asked when Jacob opened her door.

"You'll see."

He held out his hand to help her out of the truck and she took it, sliding off the seat with grace. Then she dropped her hand to smooth her skirt.

"Ready to go in?"

Judith tucked a loose curl behind her ear. "I'm anxious to meet your mother. I'd like to hear about how she knew my mom. But..."

Jacob cocked his head to one side, waiting for her to finish.

"But I'm not that crazy about meeting your whole family. Two brothers and two sisters?"

"And their husbands, wives, and children."

"How will I ever remember everyone's name?"

"Don't worry, I'll stay close to you. If you forget somebody's name, just ask."

Judith bit her bottom lip and looked at the house.

"Tell you what, Judith. Anytime you want to leave, just tell me and I'll take you back to the cabin right away. Deal?"

Judith took a deep breath and let it out. Her gaze shifted from the house to Jacob and back again. She was definitely weighing her options.

Was there something more he could do to reassure

her? Jacob held out his hand. "It's only an invitation to Sunday dinner, Judith. But if there's some reason you don't want to meet my family, then you and I can go somewhere else. Maybe you'd like to go for a drive."

Judith looked at his outstretched palm. She closed her eyes briefly, and then slid her hand into his. "I'm ready. I just needed to say a quick prayer."

Jacob squeezed her hand. "Nothing wrong with that." He led her down the driveway towards the back of the house and entered through the kitchen door.

"Mom?" Jacob called over the noise of his family. "Judith's here."

His announcement was met with abrupt silence as all heads turned their way.

Behind his back, Judith rose to her toes and whispered, "I'm ready to go."

Jacob looked down at her and smiled. "Look, there's the Davidsons. You know them."

The lawyer and his wife approached, beaming smiles of welcome.

"How's it going?" Walter Davidson asked.

"Fine," Judith murmured.

"So nice to see you again," Dorothy Davidson said, taking Judith's arm and leading her away from the door. "Did you know Emma and I grew up with your mother?"

"Emma?"

"My mother," Jacob explained.

"That's me." Jacob's mother stepped away from the oven and took both of Judith's hands. "I'm so glad you've come."

"Thank you," Judith answered politely.

"Jacob," his mother said, "you introduce Judith to everyone while I get the food on the table."

୬୦୫

Judith looked at the expectant faces that crowded the Frasers' kitchen and fought the urge to run.

"Judith Robertson," Jacob began, "this is my sister Hope, her husband Brian, and their daughter, Chloe. Chloe's the niece I told you about, the one who loves to read."

The three of them could have been models for the perfect, healthy, American family. "Nice to meet you," she murmured.

"And this is my other sister, Faith."

Good looks obviously ran in the Fraser family. With her long blond hair, Faith fairly shone. "Hope and Faith," his sister said. "Shouldn't be too hard to remember our names."

"Faith's husband is Ben," Jacob continued, nodding towards a man with a baby on his lap, "and their son is Joshua."

"Cute baby," Judith said.

"He's a keeper," the baby's father said with a wide smile.

"And these are my brothers' wives, Pamela and Martha, and that little beauty is Isabella, Martha's daughter."

They must have had beauty contests before they chose their mates. Jacob's sisters-in-law were every bit as lovely as his sisters.

"Welcome," said one of the beauties.

"Nice to meet you," said the other.

"Where are David and Richard?" Jacob asked.

"In the den with Dad," Hope answered.

"The game must be on," Jacob said. "Come on,

Judith. I'll introduce you to my brothers."

Judith took a fortifying breath and followed Jacob across the hall.

In the den, three men and two boys sat on overstuffed couches and recliners, their attention riveted to the television.

"There you all are," Jacob said as he pulled Judith into the room. "This is Judith Robertson, Isaiah Beecham's granddaughter."

The oldest man muted the television and stood to greet her. "Judith, welcome to our home. I'm John Fraser. So glad you've come."

She'd no more than shaken his hand when the other two men followed his lead.

"These are my brothers, Richard and David," Jacob said.

"Nice to meet you. Glad you could make it," they said in unison.

"Hey, when are you going to turn the sound back on?" the boys asked.

"And those models of politeness are David's twin boys, Ethan and Evan," Jacob explained.

"Do you like baseball, Judith?" Jacob's father asked.

Baseball, football, basketball? They all ran together in Judith's mind under the broad heading of sports she didn't truly understand. "Sure," she said. "Go ahead and turn the game on."

"Finally," one of the twins muttered and returned his attention to the television.

Within seconds, Jacob's attention was lost in the bewildering noise of professional baseball.

Judith found a seat on the couch and gathered her thoughts. Why wouldn't her stomach stop somersaulting? No one here was going to harm her. No one wanted anything from her that she wasn't willing to give.

Mrs. Fraser stuck her head through the doorway. "Dinner's ready," she announced. "Turn off that TV and come eat."

"Ah, man," the twins whined in stereo.

"Off it goes," John Fraser instructed. "What Grandma Emma says is the law around here."

The boys hung their heads and shuffled towards the dining room.

Jacob turned to Judith. "Ready to eat?"

Although she barely knew him, Jacob had become her anchor in this sea of strangers. She'd been afraid of him the first time they'd met, but now she counted on him to ease her way. Maybe she'd made a friend. She stood and walked to his side. "I'm ready."

"Chloe," Jacob's mother said, "Judith is our guest today. Let her have your seat beside Jacob."

The child gazed at Judith. From the obstinate set of Chloe's mouth and the glare in her blue eyes, it was obvious the girl was not pleased to give up her usual chair.

"Please don't make Chloe move," Judith said. "I'll sit anywhere."

Chloe slid into the chair as if to claim it before someone else attempted to take her place.

When Jacob caught Judith's gaze and winked at her, she relaxed a few degrees. Perhaps she could fit in with this noisy family. If only she hadn't had to meet them all at once.

"OK, everybody," John Fraser said. "Quiet down for the blessing. Judith, would you like to sit by me?"

"Sure," Judith answered as she found her place.

Jacob's father bowed his head and a calm silence enveloped the group. "Thank you, Lord for this food and for the loving hands that prepared it. Thank You for our health and for our family. Watch over us this week, Lord, and help us remember to listen for Your will. Amen."

A chorus of amen's sounded from the family, followed by the clamor of dishes and children's voices.

Jacob's father passed her a plate of yeast rolls. Judith took one, but didn't bite into it. The way her stomach jumped, eating was out of the question.

"How are you doing out there in Isaiah's cabin?" John Fraser asked.

"Fine."

"Keeping yourself busy?"

"Judith's an artist, Dad." Jacob spoke up. "Her paintings are so lifelike, I thought they were photographs."

"What are you working on now?" Emma asked.

"I'm illustrating a book about fairies."

"Fairies?" Ethan said.

"You mean like the tooth fairy?" Evan asked.

"Or Tinkerbell?" his brother chimed.

The twins elbowed each other, congratulating themselves on their joke.

"That's enough, you two," Jacob's brother warned.

"Hey," Ethan said, "could you paint a picture of Evan and make him look like a fairy?"

"I think you forgot you're his twin," Jacob said. "What's to keep Evan from saying it's a picture of you?"

"Yeah." Evan giggled.

"I like fairies," Chloe said. "If I was a fairy, I could fly. I'd fly around the flowers with the bees."

"Until somebody smashed you like a bug," Evan said, smashing his hand against the table for effect.

"Or sprayed you with bug killer," Ethan added, his hands around his throat as if choking.

Their father's patience was wearing thin. "Will you two get your minds off fairies?"

"Yeah, Evan," Ethan taunted. "Get your mind off fairies."

Evan drew his fist back in warning.

His father caught Evan's fist in his hand. "Last warning, you two jokers. Mind your manners or you'll be washing the dishes by yourselves."

"Oh, man," they whined, but took the threat to heart.

Judith smiled at the boys' antics and took a bite of her roll. She was never nervous around children. Unlike grownups, kids seldom hid their true intentions.

"As soon as we've had dessert," Jacob's mother said, "I'll show you some photos I found of your mother."

"But you have to promise not to laugh," Dorothy Davidson added. "Those old styles look mighty peculiar now."

A piece of carrot flew across the table and landed by Judith's plate.

"Whoa," Evan yelled. "Did you see that? Way to go, Joshua."

The baby giggled in response and threw another carrot.

Faith removed the bowl of food from the high chair tray and offered Joshua a cup of juice.

"Ah, don't do that," Ethan protested. "I want to see what else he can throw."

Jacob caught Judith's gaze across the table and smiled.

Judith grinned in response. Despite her earlier misgivings, she was doing fine with his family. And his family was doing fine with her.

The carousel of conversation continued to swirl around the table.

Judith listened to the family's discussion of distant relatives, upcoming events, and plans for summer vacations. Bit by bit her body relaxed until her shoulders no longer ached and her stomach no longer fluttered. By the time dessert came, she found herself enjoying her slice of pecan pie.

When nothing was left of the pie except crumbs, Faith and Hope volunteered to clean.

"Thank you," Emma Fraser said with exaggerated gratitude. "Judith, you come with me and Dorothy."

Judith left the crowded dining room to follow Emma.

"When Jacob told me you were coming to dinner, Dorothy and I started digging," Emma explained as she led Judith into her bedroom.

There, spread out on a king-sized bed, were yearbooks, several photo albums and plastic storage boxes.

"We've been reliving our younger days," Dorothy added when she joined them.

The two women sat in the middle of the bed and pulled the albums into their laps. "Kick off your shoes and climb up here," Emma instructed Judith. "Good thing you wore that full skirt."

The two women seemed warm and sincere in their welcome, but was Judith really supposed to climb onto the bed with them? Wasn't that too familiar?

Dorothy opened an album, but Emma looked at Judith expectantly. "Is something wrong, Judith?"

Everyone was asking her that question today. She didn't want to insult Jacob's mother, but she didn't know the right thing to do.

"This is the earliest picture of Rachel we could find," Dorothy held out an album for Judith.

Judith eased onto the edge of the bed and took the album from Dorothy's outstretched hands.

Three young girls dressed in high heels, hats, and sunglasses smiled out at Judith.

Emma scooted to the edge of the bed until she was sitting next to Judith. "We were playing dress up. That's me," she said, pointing to the blonde girl, "that's Rachel with the big hat, and that's Dorothy."

"We couldn't have been more than six years old," Dorothy explained. "Weren't we just too cute for words?"

Dorothy and Emma laughed, but Judith's attention was fixed on the photo. Dressed in someone's old prom dress and pursing her red lips in a magnified pucker, Judith's mother looked every inch the impish girl she must have been. Judith glanced up from the photo at the middle-aged women who continued to chat. Not only had they known her mother, they'd been childhood playmates.

"Where did my mother live when—"

Before she could finish her question, a yearbook was placed on top of the album. "Now this was our freshman year in high school. Will you just look at those glasses?" Dorothy said with a chuckle. "I'm glad I got rid of those."

"And here we are going to the homecoming dance," Emma said, thrusting a photograph in Judith's face.

"Oh, Emma," Dorothy continued. "Look at this one. That's you and John, isn't it?"

Photos followed in quick succession as the older women recalled each event.

Soon, Judith's head spun with details of county fairs, dances, and school plays. She tried to keep up, but Emma and Dorothy spoke in half-sentences and giggles. She tried to ask questions, but one memory triggered another and soon the two older women were in a world of their own.

Judith needed to sit with the photos. If only she could examine them the same way she examined the intricate cross-hatching on an acorn's cap. If only she could climb into the photos and talk to her mother.

A familiar pain stabbed Judith's heart. Her mother had been so full of life. Even in the still photographs, she seemed to glisten with vitality. A vitality that had been stolen from her when Judith had let a killer in the house. Judith's stomach churned as the memory of her mother's blood on the kitchen tile invaded her thoughts. "Excuse me," Judith muttered as she pushed off the bed. "I'm going to find a restroom."

"Use mine," Emma called after her.

But Judith trotted up the stairs. Just a few minutes to catch her breath and she'd return to the bedroom. Just a few minutes to talk herself down from the panic those memories instigated.

At the top of the stairs, she leaned against the wall and took several deep breaths. She wouldn't cry. Tears only weakened her resolve to challenge the fear that had kept her hostage. She needed to step away from the photos, to put some distance between herself and the memory.

Judith heard a child's voice coming from the room at the end of the hall. Someone was reading aloud. She followed the sound into a small bedroom where Chloe sat on the floor in a puddle of afternoon sunlight.

Judith tapped lightly at the door and the blonde head swung up. Wide blue eyes focused on her. "Hi. You're Chloe, right?"

The girl nodded, her unwavering blue gaze never leaving Judith's face.

"May I join you?"

Chloe nodded again and Judith eased down beside her. "You've got a lot of books up here. Jacob told me you liked to read."

"This is my room when I visit Grandma Emma," Chloe explained.

"What are you reading?"

Chloe lifted the book from the floor to show Judith the cover.

"Cats. Funny you should be reading that. A friend just gave me a kitten and I don't know how to take care of it."

A spark of interest lit Chloe's eyes. "Really? Can I see it? I want a cat but my mommy says I can't have one because we already have two dogs that my daddy uses when he goes hunting. Dogs are OK, I guess, but I want a little kitten that will stay in my room and sleep with me at night."

"My cat's name is Pumpkin and so far all she does is hide under the couch." Judith rifled through the closest pile of books and withdrew one. "Do you like this book?"

Chloe's eyes grew wide and serious. "That book is awesome. It has the best pictures of dragons I ever saw."

"Why, thank you. I painted the pictures."

Chloe's brows drew together in suspicion. "You?"

"Believe it or not. See?" Judith flipped to the back cover where her photo was featured alongside the author's. "That's me."

Chloe's studious gaze shifted from the book to Judith's face several times before she spoke. "That's really you?"

"It really is. Want to see my driver's license?"

Chloe giggled.

"Give me a piece of paper and a pencil," Judith said, "and I'll draw a dragon just for you."

Chloe scrambled to her feet and returned seconds later with the requested items. Judith spread the paper on the book for stability and began to sketch. The girl craned her neck to see Judith's work, but being dissatisfied with the view, leaned against Judith's shoulder, nearly pushing Judith to the floor.

"Hold on, Chloe. Let's get situated here." Judith spread her skirt and crossed her legs. "Come sit in my lap."

Chloe didn't hesitate to accept the invitation and a few seconds later, the book and paper were in Chloe's lap while Judith continued her sketch.

"I was wondering where you went." A deep voice interrupted their concentration.

Chloe and Judith jerked in surprise.

Chloe jumped out of Judith's lap and went to her uncle. "Come see, Jacob. She's drawing a dragon for me."

Jacob grinned and joined her on the floor. "May I see?"

"No," Judith announced, holding the book and paper against her chest. "It's not finished yet."

"You have to wait," Chloe admonished him. Then she turned to Judith. "You'll show him when it's finished, won't you?"

"Only if he behaves."

"Oh, he will," Chloe vouched. "He's a very good uncle."

Chloe resumed her seat in Judith's lap. A few minutes later, Judith put down the pencil. "I think that about does it. What do you think, Chloe?"

"Oh," Chloe whispered. "That's a beautiful dragon. I'm going to name it Serena. Can I show Jacob now?"

"It's your picture. You can do anything you want with it."

Chloe squirmed out of her lap and handed the paper to Jacob. "If you're nice to Judith, she'll make a picture for you, too."

"Oh, I plan to be nice to Judith. Don't worry about that," Jacob answered with a wink to his niece. "You ready to go home, Judith?"

"I'm not finished talking to your mother and Dorothy."

"Mr. and Mrs. Davidson went home, but my mom's downstairs." Jacob stood and offered his hand to help Judith to her feet.

Judith took Jacob's hand, stood, and turned to Chloe. "Thanks for showing me your books."

"When can I see your kitten? Does she like to play with toys? I could bring her a cat toy."

"You can visit whenever it's OK with your mom. But I'm warning you, my cat is very shy. She might not want to play with you right away."

"I'm going to ask Mom now," Chloe announced as she skipped out of the room.

Judith followed Chloe downstairs, only to find Jacob's mother storing the boxes of photos in a hall closet. "Oh," Judith said, "I was hoping—"

"I just can't get over it." Emma wrapped her arms around Judith's shoulders. "Rachel's little girl right here in my house. You must come back. Come next Sunday, or drop in any time. No need to wait for an invitation."

Judith savored Emma's tender hug. If her mother had lived, surely her hugs would have felt like this. Judith squeezed Emma gently and let the loving warmth seep into her heart. "Thank you for inviting me," Judith said as she released Emma. "And thanks for showing me the photos. I'd like to make copies if that's all right with you."

"Of course. I'll get them together for you."

"Ready to go?" Jacob called from the kitchen.

Emma laughed softly. "My youngest son is not the most patient of my children. But if you'd like to stay longer..."

"No, but thanks for everything. I'm really glad I got to meet you."

"Anytime, Judith. I hope we'll see a lot of you."

৵৵

"My family liked you," Jacob said once they were on the highway.

"I was nervous at first, but they all made me feel welcome." Judith scooted down in her seat and let her head rest on the back.

Jacob saw that her eyes were closed. She couldn't be asleep, could she? "Judith?" he said in a soft voice.

"Hmm?"

"Are you all right?"

"Yes. Just thinking."

"About?"

"Your mother and my mother. Can you believe they actually went to school together? They even played together when they were girls."

She'd fit in well with his family. The way Judith had respected Chloe's claim on his attention had been especially endearing. So many grownups discounted children's feelings.

"I'm anxious to make copies of your mother's photographs," Judith said.

"Want to come to lunch again next Sunday? Or maybe you'd like to go into the city for dinner."

"With your mother?"

"No. With me."

Judith sat up.

He'd obviously surprised her with his invitation, but a date was the next logical step in getting to know her better.

Judith's voice sounded distant when she finally answered. "I guess it'd be OK."

Jacob couldn't keep from smiling at her halfhearted acceptance. "I've got a busy week ahead of me. Would next week be OK?"

Silent seconds ticked by as he waited. Maybe he should retract the invitation.

She finally answered. "That'll be fine."

What was it about dinner with him that made her hesitate?

Jacob stopped his truck in front of the cabin. "You know, if you'd rather not go to dinner—"

"No," she said with surprising force. She tucked her hair behind her ear and folded her arms across her waist. "I mean, dinner will be fine. It's just dinner. Right?"

There it was again. Her courage had defeated whatever it was that had made her hesitate.

"Right," he said with a smile as he walked around and opened her door.

"Thanks for bringing me home," she said as she slid out of the truck. "I enjoyed meeting your family. It must have been something growing up with all of those brothers and sisters."

Jacob held out his palm as an invitation for Judith to slip her hand into his. She looked at his palm for several seconds before setting her fingertips on the edge of his hand. Jacob lightly closed his fingers around hers and made his voice as carefree as possible. "Oh, it was something all right. My brothers and sisters always made fun of me for being the baby. But for all the teasing I got, they also looked out for me."

She pulled her hand free as she stepped onto the porch.

Jacob stood before her, searching her face for a hint of what she was thinking. But the only clue she gave him was a wide yawn she hid with her hand.

"Call me crazy, but I think you're tired."

"Sorry. My brain's on overload. I've got so much to think about, so much to decide on."

"So, I'll see you soon?"

She smiled in reply. "Sure."

Why was it so difficult to leave? He should just step off the porch, get in his truck and drive away. What was he hoping to accomplish by remaining there?

A gentle breeze blew a dark curl across her cheek and Jacob used his fingertips to brush it away. "Any place special you'd like to eat?"

Judith stepped away from him. "I don't know what's around here, but I'm not a picky eater. Anything will be fine."

Even his slightest touch seemed to make her uneasy. But he'd earn her trust. Someday he wanted to rub his cheek against her head and feel her beautiful curls against his face.

"I guess I'll go in now," Judith said.

Jacob dropped his hand and stepped back quickly, surprised at where his imagination had led. "OK," he said as he walked towards his truck. "I'll be in touch."

He glanced in the rearview mirror as he steered his truck down the dirt road away from the cabin.

Judith Robertson was growing on him, and he didn't mind one bit.

6

Judith was deep in the woods when she recognized Rev. Washington's booming voice. She'd left the cabin at dawn, intent on capturing scenes of the forest as it greeted the new day, and, as usual, she'd lost herself in the sketches. A quick glance at her watch confirmed she'd been working for nearly three hours.

The voices grew louder as Judith made her way through the forest towards the clearing where the old church sat.

"What do you think about the windows?" Henry called to someone. "How rotten is the wood?"

"It would be best to replace the frames," another man's voice answered. "But we can use pieces of scrap for that."

"And the wiring?" Rev. Washington called again. "What about that, Brother George?"

"It's in bad shape," a different voice answered. "It would be best to replace as much of it as possible."

At the edge of the tree line, Judith stopped to watch the men.

One walked on the steeply pitched roof as confidently as a bird on a telephone wire, another scraped at the window frames with a chisel.

The morning sun cast long shadows as the men moved around the area, the timbre of their voices changing from concern to excitement as they worked. There was no doubt Henry and his friends would approach her soon, asking for permission to use her grandfather's church. After seeing the delight in their faces and hearing the enthusiasm in their voices, it would be hard to deny them.

A familiar truck pulled up beside the church.

Judith bit back the involuntary smile. Jacob Fraser was becoming much too important to her.

Of course she'd noticed how attentive he'd been at his parents' house—holding her hand, not letting her get lost in the jubilant chaos of his family.

But her reaction to all that attention was alarming. It just wasn't normal for her heart to race at the sound of his voice, or to have her stomach do flip-flops at the sight of him. There was always the possibility he was being nice to her just so she'd sell her grandfather's timber to him, but he didn't seem the type.

She took her sketchbook from her satchel, quickly turned to a fresh page and began to sketch. Jacob had the most amazing profile—strong chin, a firm cheek line and eyes as sharp as a falcon's. His plain t-shirt and jeans molded his physique and Judith concentrated on the lines his muscles made beneath his clothing.

Henry greeted Jacob with an enthusiastic handshake, and then led him into the building.

Judith hurried to finish the rough sketch, tucked the book under one arm, and ambled into the clearing with what she hoped passed as nonchalance.

"Brother Henry!" the man on the roof called out. "Mr. Isaiah's granddaughter is here!"

"Good morning." She shaded her eyes and called up to him. "Are you OK up there?"

"No need to worry. I spend almost every day on a roof somewhere in town." He walked towards a ladder and made his way down.

Henry Washington stepped out of the church to greet her. "Mornin', Miss Judith. So good to see you."

"How's everything going, Rev. Washington?"

Before Henry could answer, Jacob joined him. "Hey, Judith. What are you up to this morning?"

"Making more sketches," Judith answered, trying to speak over the fluttery feeling in her throat. "How's it going in there?"

"Nothing a little hard work and some building supplies can't fix," Henry answered. Then he clapped a hand on Jacob's shoulder. "And Jacob here has come to our rescue."

Jacob waved away the words as if they were pesky flies. "Now, Henry, all I did was talk to my minister."

"And all your minister did was call the other ministers in town," Henry said. "It's just wonderful, Judith. The other churches around here are going to take up a special collection to go towards what we need. If you give us the go-ahead, we can start the work right away."

Judith caught Jacob's attention. "Will you excuse us, Rev. Washington? I'd like to talk to Jacob for a minute."

"Of course. But I'll be praying for the answer I want to hear."

Judith led Jacob to the edge of the clearing. Once they were out of earshot, she turned and looked up at him. "You're the one who said I needed to be careful about loaning my grandfather's church. Now you've gone and arranged for help. Are you trying to confuse me?"

Jacob braced one arm against a tree trunk and leaned in. "I was thinking about Henry's church, not yours. Letting his congregation meet here could mean trouble."

"Trouble from the arsonists?"

"Yep. For the most part, people around here get along. I'm not saying it's perfect, no place is. But apparently there are some who feed on hate."

Judith looked over Jacob's shoulder at Henry and the men who had gathered around him. "I don't want to disappoint Rev. Washington or Beverly Lewis. How long will it take them to get my grandfather's church in shape?"

"A week or two."

"And Rev. Washington's church? That has to be built from the ground up, doesn't it?"

"Yeah. And that will take a minimum of three months. Probably longer."

Judith frowned in concentration. She'd vowed to keep her grandfather's church safe, but how could she deny the people who needed it? The arsonists' most potent weapon wasn't fire, it was fear. If she kept her grandfather's church closed, she'd be giving in to that fear.

"What are you thinking, Judith?"

"I know I may be putting my grandfather's church in danger, but how can I refuse to lend it? This old church has been empty too long." She stepped away from Jacob and strode towards the church. "OK, Rev. Washington. The church is yours to use."

Henry clapped his hands in joy. "Thank you, Jesus."

"But there's one condition," Judith hastened to add. "I'm only letting you use it for six months. During that time, I expect you to do whatever you can to rebuild your own church."

"Oh, bless you, Judith. Bless you, bless you. We never intended to be here permanently. Mr. Isaiah's church is like a tabernacle in the wilderness. Praise God's holy name!"

"Amen," the men around him responded.

Judith offered her hand. "It's a deal, then?"

Henry slid his hand into hers. "It's a deal."

"Thank you, Miss Judith," the men said, each shaking her hand in turn.

"Did you hear that, Jacob?" Henry called to him.

Jacob stepped beside Judith and laid a hand on her shoulder. "I heard. Sounds like you'll be busy for the next few months."

"As it says in the Book of Romans, 'We know that all things work together for good to those who love God, to those who are called according to His purpose.' We'll be busy doing the Lord's work."

❧

As Henry and his friends drove away from the old church, Jacob fell in step with Judith. "What have you got planned for today?"

"Working. Why?"

"Thought you might like to do some exploring."

"Exploring of what?"

"Your new property. I bet you didn't know there were orchids growing nearby."

"Orchids? I thought they only grew in the rainforest."

"These aren't the big, showy flowers you may have seen at the florist's shop, but they're orchids all right. The species that grows around here is called Ladies' Tresses."

"I'd like to see that. Come on up to the cabin and I'll get ready."

As they stepped onto the porch, an orange blur shot across Jacob's boots.

"What in the world?"

"That's my cat," Judith said between laughs. "She never walks anywhere. She disappears for hours on end, and then I'll find her food dish empty."

"So, you're doing OK out here?" Jacob asked as he followed her into the cabin.

Judith laid her sketchbook on the kitchen table. "Yeah, everything's been fine. I won't lie and say it wasn't hard at first, but now I'm used to the night noises. Well, most of them."

"Like what?"

"Like the bullfrog that spends the night right under my bedroom floor. The first time I heard that I nearly jumped out of my skin. And the owls. Now I know why they call them screech owls."

Concern tugged at his heart. He tilted his head and looked at her. "So, you've been scared out here?"

"No, of course not, I just..." Judith looked away from him. "Well, I'm not scared anymore."

His concern disappeared as he wrapped his arms around Judith's shoulders and pulled her into an embrace. "Anytime you feel frightened, I hope you'll call me."

Judith stilled in his arms. "I just need more time to adjust, Mr. Fraser."

Jacob tightened his arms around her. "Oh, no. Not Mr. Fraser again. I thought you'd given that up."

Judith smiled up at him. "Why, Mr. Fraser, what are you talking about?"

"Are you always this stubborn?"

"Who? Me?"

She felt good in his arms. A perfect fit. He smiled down at her, enjoying the sparkle of mischief in her eyes. Was it too soon to kiss her?

Before he could test the answer to his question, Judith stepped away from his embrace.

"How long will be we walking?"

"About half an hour." Jacob picked up Judith's sketchbook and flipped through the pages. "What have you been working on?"

"Birds mostly. I got the idea that fairies might train birds so that they could ride on them."

"Wait a minute, who's this?"

Judith's eyes grew wide with alarm. "Give me that."

"I'd swear this was a picture of me."

Judith grabbed for the sketchbook.

"Hold on there," Jacob said, holding the book high above his head. "Why were you drawing pictures of me? You're not going to make me a fairy, are you?"

Judith stretched to her tiptoes and reached for the book again. "Give me that. It's mine."

"I'll give it to you, but you have to do something first."

Judith stepped away from him and crossed her arms in front of her chest. "What?" she asked with a scowl.

"First, no more Mr. Fraser."

"Fine."

"So, what's my name?"

"Jacob. Now give me my book."

"Second," Jacob continued as if he hadn't heard her, "you have to give me a kiss."

"A kick? I'll be glad to give you a kick. And I

know just where I'd like to aim it."

"No, no," Jacob said between chuckles. "You know what I said. A kiss."

Judith narrowed her eyes and pursed her lips tightly.

Holding her sketchbook high over his head, Jacob thumbed through the pages. "Now, where was my picture?"

He felt the briefest of kisses on his cheek and turned quickly to catch her in another embrace.

But she was quicker. With a move that would have made Pumpkin proud, Judith snatched the book out of Jacob's hand and scurried through the back door.

"Judith?" Jacob called as he stepped outside. "That's not exactly what I'd call a—"

Beverly Lewis's lively black eyes grinned up at him. "Hey, Jacob. What are you doing here?"

Jacob caught the warning glance Judith threw his way and bit back a grin. "Oh, just visiting. What about you?"

"I brought Judith some of my peach cobbler." Beverly nodded towards the foil-covered dish in Judith's hands. "Brother Henry came by to give me the good news, and I just had to come over and thank my new neighbor."

"Peach cobbler?" Jacob asked. "Beverly, when are you going to marry me?"

Beverly clapped her hands and gave a peal of delighted laughter. "You know you're too ugly for me, Jacob Fraser. Besides, you just like my cooking."

Jacob took the dish from Judith's hands and peeked under the foil. "And that's a problem?"

"Come on in, Beverly," Judith invited. "If we don't eat some cobbler now, I might not get any."

Beverly laughed again. "Jacob here, he does have a sweet tooth. I can testify to that."

❧❧

Judith chuckled quietly as she found bowls and spoons. How liberating it was to indulge in good-natured teasing with a man, rather than doubt his every move. Jacob and Beverly sat at the small round kitchen table.

"You know, Beverly," Judith began, "I only gave permission for Rev. Washington to use my grandfather's church for six months."

"That's what he told me," Beverly answered as she heaped the peach cobbler into the bowls. "That'll work out fine. We'll do the repairs that are needed on Mr. Isaiah's church, and then get started rebuilding our own. We've got all the labor, just need the materials."

Jacob was spooning the cobbler into his mouth.

"And Jacob's going to see to that," Judith said.

"Don't I know it? Brother Henry told me all about it. My, Jacob. I'm going to have to make you one of my sweet potato pies if you keep this up."

Jacob dropped his spoon into the bowl and shot an accusing look at Judith. The pink tinge on his cheeks told Judith her tactic had been successful. "I didn't do anything," he protested.

"No use trying to be modest," Beverly said. "We all know how you helped. Yes, sir. I'd better buy some sweet potatoes next time I go to the store."

Maybe Judith shouldn't cause Jacob such uneasiness. But she was having so much fun. "It wouldn't surprise me," she added, "if Jacob showed up to work on my grandfather's church. Everyone says what a great friend he is."

"That does it," Jacob said, the blush stretching from his face to his neck. "Time for me to go."

Beverly and Judith exchanged glances, and then Beverly let out a squeal of laughter. "Don't tell me you're embarrassed."

"I'm not embarrassed," Jacob protested. "But I will take the rest of this cobbler with me. Judith, I'll see you later."

Before Judith could answer, Jacob swept up the dish of cobbler and darted out the front door. As the screen door banged behind him, she and Beverly looked at each other and burst into laughter.

"Oh," Beverly said, holding her sides. "We shouldn't have teased him. I didn't know he was so shy."

"Don't worry about Jacob," Judith answered. "Trust me. He deserved it."

7

The rain started on Friday morning. What began as a gentle summer shower soon threatened Piney Meadow with ominous thunder and intense flashes of lightning.

Judith huddled inside, trying to ignore the rushing wind that bowed pine saplings and whistled around the corners of the cabin. But when she heard the church's bell clanging with the powerful gusts, ringing as if calling for worshipers to huddle inside its walls and find refuge from the storm, a shiver ran down her spine.

She was in the deep end now. Not only had she left her fortified condominium to live in a secluded cabin that didn't even have a lock on the door, she'd willingly endangered her grandfather's church. Was it worth the risk?

No matter how high her anxiety soared, the answer to that question was obvious. It was better to risk the old church than to leave it safe, but empty. Without the love of a congregation, her grandfather's church was an empty shell, devoid of life and missing the energy that only the Holy Spirit could supply.

But wasn't Judith inviting violence by loaning the church to Henry's congregation? She'd structured her life so that the monster would never again find her. She'd hidden from danger and threats of danger until she existed in a sheltered cocoon.

But had that really been living? She'd tried to become invisible, to be only as noticeable as paint on the walls. And she'd paid a high price for her safety.

She'd given up friends and sacrificed her future by surrendering to fear. Had her grandfather known that? Maybe he'd known the land would tempt her out of hiding.

The memory of Granddad's warm hugs put a smile on Judith's face. He'd loved her even though she'd been too afraid to travel the distance to see him. Maybe it was too little, too late, but she couldn't allow herself to back down now. It felt as if the whole universe was pushing her to see it through.

A crash of thunder startled her, causing the paintbrush to skid across a fairy's face. She groaned in frustration and reached for a rag. Then the lights blinked out.

Judith sat back in the darkness and sighed. So much for finishing the painting today. She lit a candle and set aside the paints. As she cleaned her brushes, the image of her mother's face floated to the front of her mind.

Rachel Beecham. Judith's memories of her mother had little to do with how she'd looked. The scent of lilies could bring back the remembrance of her mother's perfume and, even after decades of being without her, Judith could close her eyes and remember the feel of her mother's hand on her brow, checking for a fever, or brushing bangs out of her eyes.

Mother. The word was so packed with emotional power that Judith never said it without a tightness coiling in her chest.

As soon as she mailed the fairy paintings, Judith would paint her mother's portraits. By using the old photos, she could document her mother's growth from girlhood to teenager to young woman. Given enough time, she could begin to know the person her mother had been. Given the opportunity, she could mine the rich memories of her mother's friends until she had a deeper understanding.

Since she had no light with which to work, Judith decided to call Emma Fraser and arrange another visit. But she groaned with frustration when the words *No Service* appeared on the cell phone's display. She hesitated a moment, and then remembered Emma's standing invitation. Hopefully, the phrase "come by anytime" wasn't just politeness, because that's exactly what Judith planned to do. Without another moment's consideration, she grabbed an umbrella and headed for her car.

As the roadster's wheels splashed through puddles along the dirt road, it soon became clear that Jacob's earlier warning had not been exaggerated. While her sports car had been nothing but fun to drive on the paved streets of Dallas, Jacob had been right about the rural roads of Piney Meadow.

Less than a mile away from the cabin, her BMW sank up to its axles in oozing red mud. Her tires spun uselessly, spraying muck behind the rear wheels as she dug the car even deeper.

Muttering under her breath, she retrieved her cell phone and auto club card from her purse. But when she remembered the thunderstorm had blocked her cell phone service, the muttering grew into a low growl of frustration.

Now what? The choices were limited. Either sit in the car until the storm passed or walk back to the cabin.

Judith eased the car door open and looked into the deep puddle that skirted the edge of the door. No telling how long the rain would last. She'd have to walk.

She grabbed the umbrella and then, stretching her legs as far as possible, bracketed the puddle and pushed herself out of the car. "Yes!" she shouted.

Feeling every inch the victor, she kicked the door shut and promptly slipped, bottom first, into the muck.

Caked with mud from the back pockets of her jeans to her sneakers, Judith squished her way towards the cabin. The rain intensified, threatening her flimsy umbrella. She fought the wind for a few minutes, turning the umbrella against the gusts like a swordsman parrying attacks from an invisible foe, until one mighty blast tore the umbrella from her hands and carried it into the woods. She eyed the umbrella, lodged halfway up a tall pine, and ground her teeth.

Cold, stinging rain bit at her face, dripped down her back and chilled her to the bone. Her clothes clung, sopping wet and heavy, adding to the difficulty of her trek. Shivering, but determined, Judith trudged on, counting the steps to her grandfather's cabin as a way to occupy her mind. It was better than going over the mistakes that led her to her current condition. Just when she was sure things couldn't get worse, they did.

Jacob Fraser pulled up beside her, driving her grandfather's truck.

᧖᧗

"Judith?" Jacob called.

Judith covered her face and shook her head.

"Are you all right?" he called again.

She stopped, fisted her hands on her hips, and glared at him. Hair was plastered to her face and drops of water fell from the end of her nose.

She was beautiful.

"I'm fine. What's the matter, don't I look fine?"

Jacob knew she was embarrassed, but it was all he could do not to break into laughter. "Get in the truck, Judith. I'll give you a ride the rest of the way."

"I don't need a ride."

"Uh-huh. I can see that."

She stomped a few more paces.

Jacob eased the truck forward to keep up with her. "I saw your car in the road."

She didn't answer, just kept her gaze straight ahead as she splashed through the puddles.

"Want me to call the tow truck for you?"

"No."

"I went by the mechanic's to check on Isaiah's truck, and it was ready. I thought I'd bring it out, and then you could drive me back to town."

"Uh-huh."

"Are you sure you wouldn't like to ride the rest of the way?"

"I'm sure."

It was amazing how Judith could look so good, even with her backside covered in mud. Jacob coasted beside her a few more feet until he saw the cabin in the distance.

"Judith," he tried again. "Being stubborn isn't getting you anywhere. Now climb in."

Judith whirled. "Are you deaf or something? I *said* I don't need a ride. Just go on."

Jacob shook his head slowly from side to side.

Stubborn didn't even begin to describe the kind of woman who would rather walk in mud and rain than ride in a warm, dry pickup.

But tagging along wouldn't change her mind and might make things worse. He drove on, parked in front of the cabin and stepped onto the porch to watch for her.

A few minutes later, Judith came around the curve and into view—wet, muddy, and so angry he wouldn't have been surprised to see steam rising off her.

Just as she reached the front porch, the rain stopped. Judith tilted her head back, said something to the sky, and then headed towards the back of the cabin.

Jacob walked through the cabin and opened the back door for her.

"No!" she shouted, holding her hand out, palm facing him.

"No, what?"

"Don't come out here. In fact, go back to the front porch and stay there until I tell you it's OK to come in."

"Why?"

Judith's voice took on a more desperate edge. "Because I want you to. Isn't that a good enough reason?"

"No need to bite my head off."

Judith's fists perched on her hips as she leaned forward to drive her point home. "I can take care of myself, you know."

Jacob leaned towards her to make his own point. "Just because you can doesn't mean you have to."

Judith paced a few yards, her sneakers squishing with every step. Finally, she swung around to face him. "I'd like to take my clothes off out here, you big doofus. But I can't very well do that with you staring at me, can I?"

Jacob crossed his arms in front of his chest and leaned on the doorjamb. "Now that would be something to see."

She stomped up the back steps and shoved at his chest. "Front porch, mister. Now. Or you can walk back to town."

"OK, OK," Jacob said, throwing up his hands in mock surrender. "First, let me get you a towel. Then I'll wait for you on the porch."

He stepped back inside to hide his laugh. She sure was cute when she was mad.

❧❧

"Would you like to have lunch?" Jacob asked as the truck fishtailed onto the main highway.

"With you?"

"That's the idea."

Judith fingered her damp hair. Although she'd pulled it into a ponytail, tiny ringlets escaped to curl at the nape of her neck. "I guess so."

"We'll get something to eat, and then you can drive me to the mechanic's. Is that a problem?"

Judith decided to change the subject. "I haven't heard anything from Rev. Washington. Do you know if he's going to do any repair work on the old church?"

"As a matter of fact, I'll be out tomorrow to help Henry. We were going to start today but the rain delayed us."

"How much work do they intend to do?"

"Since the arrangement's temporary, we'll only do what has to be done. Beverly and the other ladies are coming to start the cleaning."

"Have you talked her into cooking something else for you?"

"No, but if she was to offer, I wouldn't turn it down. By the way, my niece, Chloe, is dying to visit. Is it OK if I bring her tomorrow?"

"Sure. But I think it's my cat she wants to see."

Jacob swung into the parking lot of the Timber Land Diner. A huddle of muddy pickup trucks were parked in front and as soon as Judith and Jacob stepped through the door, several voices hailed him.

While Jacob shook hands with the men at the counter, Judith squeezed into the one empty booth at the back of the crowded restaurant and looked over the laminated menu.

"Hey there, Judith." Jo Nell set napkin-wrapped silverware on the table. "Nice to see you again. Want another iced tea?"

Before she could answer, Jacob appeared at the table. "I'll be out in the parking lot for a few minutes, Judith. One of the local landowners has some pesticides in his truck he'd like me to look at."

"OK," she answered.

"You want the usual, Jacob?" Jo Nell called after him.

"You know it," he called as he stepped outside.

"I'll bring you a glass of tea," Jo Nell said to Judith, and then left to check on another table.

Since she was having iced tea whether she wanted it or not, Judith returned her attention to the menu. She was deciding between fried catfish or a club sandwich when a man slid onto the bench across from her. Her silent alarm rang, but she ignored it for the moment.

He was dressed in a business suit and tie, the same

uniform her father wore to work every day.

"Hey there," he said genially. "I saw you get out of Isaiah Beecham's truck. You must be the granddaughter everybody's talking about."

He grinned and Judith's apprehension lessened. He was just being friendly, like everyone else she'd met in Piney Meadow. "That's right. I'm Judith Robertson."

"That's a pretty name," he said while shaking her hand. "My name's Dwight Thompson."

"Nice to meet you. Do you come here often?"

"Almost every day. My brothers and I meet here for lunch. Those are my brothers over there," Dwight said, pointing to two hefty men at a nearby table. They both wore white shirts and ties, but unlike Dwight, they weren't smiling.

Judith tried to dismiss their scowls and suppress her anxiety. "What's good to eat here?" she asked, gesturing to the menu.

"Oh, just about everything," Dwight answered. "Course, they don't have anything like watermelon or chitlins."

Judith struggled to understand. "What's a chitlin?"

"You don't know?" Dwight continued. "I figured you liked soul food." A sly smile crept across his mouth.

"What makes you think that?"

"Because you're friendly with Henry Washington and his crowd."

Judith frowned, not quite understanding what this odd conversation was all about. "Do you know him?"

"I know him." The man's smile slipped, and then reasserted itself. "It sure was a shame what happened to his church. It would be just awful if the same thing happened to that old church on your grandfather's property."

Now the alarm wasn't because of fear. The distasteful truth of what Dwight had been talking about solidified in Judith's gut. "Are you saying my grandfather's church is in danger?"

"If you help Henry Washington and his bunch, you might find yourself in a heap of trouble. I'd think twice before letting Henry use that old church."

Judith took a deep breath and pushed her back against the seat. There was a small chance Dwight was trying to give her a friendly warning, but she didn't think so. "I've already told Rev. Washington he can use the church. I don't go back on my word."

"I know you're new in town, but you need to be careful who you align yourself with. If you start getting all friendly with the blacks, someone will have to remind you which side you're on."

"And what side would that be?"

Dwight studied Judith for several moments before he spoke. "Do I have to spell it out for you?" When she didn't answer, he continued. "People like us have to stick together."

The words he didn't say, "white people," were loud and clear. In an instant, all of Judith's fears and anxieties were gone. In their place, an unfamiliar anger took root. Her nails bit into her palms as irate words formed on her tongue of their own accord. "I'd rather stick with porcupines and skunks than with people like you."

Dwight's eyebrows shot to his hairline. "No need to climb up on your high horse. I'm just giving you a friendly reminder. Like I said, it would be a shame if fire destroyed Isaiah's church, too."

Judith gripped the edge of the table, her rage quickly reaching the point of no return. "You don't scare me."

"I don't?" Dwight laughed, and then quickly changed his tone. "I think you're lying."

Judith slid from the booth, rested her palms on the table and leaned towards Dwight. "Listen to me, you moron. What I do with my grandfather's church is my business. You can take your threats somewhere else."

"Is there a problem?" Jacob's deep voice cut across the tension that arced between Judith and Dwight.

"Threats?" Dwight echoed. "Who said anything about threats?" He pushed himself out of the booth and stood toe-to-toe with her. "I hope you're being careful out there, Judith. If anything were to happen to you, there'd be nobody around to help."

"And just what does that mean?"

Dwight smiled indulgently at Judith, the kind of smile people give to naïve children.

Then he clapped Jacob on the shoulder. "No problem, Jacob. I was just introducing myself to Isaiah's granddaughter. She's quite a little firecracker, isn't she?"

"Listen, you baboon," Judith continued. "If I ever see you or your brothers on my property, I'll—"

"You'll what, Judith?" Dwight mocked. "Gonna beat us up? A little bit of nothing like you?" He laughed and turned his back to her. Then he raised his voice, calling the attention of the people in the diner. "Did you hear that everybody? This little lady wants to beat me up."

The faces of the diners turned towards Judith and the noise of the lunch crowd faded away.

"You must have misunderstood me," Dwight said, his voice ripe with conciliation. "Or do you always fly off the handle this easily?"

His remark about her temper dug into her like talons. First he'd threatened her, and then made it look as if she'd blown her top for no good reason. "Misunderstood my—"

"People are watching you, Judith. Mind what you say." Jacob's voice was calm, but commanding.

Oblivious to the townspeople who had witnessed her outburst, Judith shifted her anger to Jacob. "Are you telling me to be quiet?"

Several beats of silence passed as Jacob studied her without a reply.

"That does it." Judith strode through the pack of curious onlookers towards the front entrance.

∽∾

Jacob watched Judith stomp through the diner, then pulled the truck keys from his pocket. She wouldn't get far without them.

Dwight joined his brothers, and the diners went back to their meals.

Jo Nell approached carrying two glasses of iced tea. "Is Judith coming back?" she asked.

"I don't think so," Jacob answered.

Jo Nell set the glasses on the table. "Got your hands full with that one."

"I think you're right. I've never seen anybody get so mad so fast."

Jo Nell's voice lowered to a whisper as she leaned towards him. "I saw Dwight Thompson sitting with her, but I couldn't overhear what he was saying."

The faded bruise on Della Thompson's cheek flashed into Jacob's mind. The thought of Dwight hurting Judith shot a chill straight to his heart. "Do you think Dwight said something he shouldn't have?"

"I'm not sure," Jo Nell answered, "but I don't doubt it. Dwight can be quite the bully." She looked through the diner's plate glass windows to where Judith sat behind the steering wheel of her grandfather's truck. "Why is she just sitting out there?"

Jacob held up the keys.

"Oh. How long are you going to make her wait?"

"Until she calms down. Wouldn't be safe for her, or anybody else, if she took off while she was still angry."

At that moment, Judith got out of the truck, slammed the door and began walking away from the diner.

"Uh-oh." Jo Nell said. "Looks like she's hoofing it."

Jacob shook his head in disbelief. "Maybe the walk will help her calm down."

"Maybe," Jo Nell agreed. "But it's a long walk to Isaiah's cabin. Want me to box up your food?"

"Guess so."

Jacob met Jo Nell at the counter and paid for his food, and then drove to where Judith was walking along the shoulder of the highway. He stopped a few yards in front of her, got out of the truck and stepped back to where she'd stopped.

"Get in the truck, Judith."

"Are you still telling me what to do?"

"What happened back there?" Jacob asked with a nod towards the diner. "Did Dwight hurt you?"

"Now you're interested in my side of the story?

You sure weren't very interested in what I had to say a few minutes ago."

"You were in a diner full of people, every one of them listening to you badmouthing Dwight. In a small town like this, it's not smart to let people know your business."

Judith shot one stiff arm towards the diner. "That jerk threatened me. Told me I'd better not help Rev. Washington or my grandfather's church might go up in flames."

A current of unease slithered through Jacob's gut. "I don't doubt Dwight was out of line, but I'm more concerned about your safety." He placed the truck's keys in her palm. "Promise you'll be careful. I'll get somebody in the diner to give me a ride to the mechanic's."

He walked away, not sure if her silence meant she was shooting imaginary darts in his back, or if she was just too angry for words.

His life was getting more complicated by the minute and complications were one thing he tried to avoid. He heard the truck drive away, but didn't turn around.

Judith was as angry as two bulls in the same pasture. Maybe some time alone would help her cool down.

But what if Dwight acted on his threats? Dwight was trying to con him into raising the offer for the land and Jacob suspected Dwight of hitting his wife. But Dwight's involvement with the church burnings seemed farfetched. The Thompsons attended Jacob's church. They prayed and tithed and sang along with everyone else.

Was it possible Dwight was actually a criminal?

An arsonist who targeted African-American churches? Should Jacob inform the FBI agents about Judith's argument with him?

Mark Grey was sure to tell him that raised voices weren't proof. It was possible Della's bruise hadn't come from her husband's fist, and there was no evidence Dwight was involved in the burnings. But if Dwight hurt Judith...

Jacob came to an abrupt halt as that thought crossed his mind. A vision of Judith sleeping in her grandfather's cabin, blissfully unaware of a serpent-like fire creeping towards her, made his stomach clutch.

He couldn't let her be harmed. Best if he stayed closer to Judith for the time being.

8

Judith packed the last of the fairy paintings and taped the box. She'd ship the pictures and wait for her editor's call. She was ahead of deadline, always a nice place to be, and now had time to spend on her mother's portraits. If only she could get those photos from Emma Fraser. After yesterday's outburst, she'd never made it to Jacob's parents' house.

She still couldn't believe how furious she'd gotten. Whenever she'd felt threatened before, she'd retreated into her self-protective shell. But yesterday was different. Dwight hadn't just threatened her, he'd threatened her friends and her grandfather's church. She hadn't been angry for herself as much as for those she cared about.

Her usual timidity had evaporated in the heat of that fury. She'd felt like a lioness protecting her cubs, empowered by anger and willing to attack. For the first time in a long time, she wasn't cowering in the corner, afraid of someone's cross words. Now she was striding onto the battle field, her shield and sword at the ready.

But she'd been wrong to let her anger splash on Jacob. Jacob hadn't heard Dwight's racial slurs or his barely veiled threats. Jacob had only seen her in that out-of-control state where rage had pushed her. Not that Dwight hadn't had it coming. But turning her anger on Jacob had been wrong. Just plain wrong.

Her kitten jumped on the kitchen counter and

sniffed the butter Judith was spreading on a biscuit. "OK. You're hungry. But first get off the counter."

She lifted the kitten and cuddled it against her chest with one hand while she poured dry cat food into a bowl with the other.

Pumpkin rewarded her with a low purr that reverberated against Judith's chest.

"OK, sweet cat. It's coming, it's coming." Before Judith could place the bowl on the floor, the kitten dug its claws into Judith's shirt and let out a loud screech.

"Ouch!" Judith yelled. "What in the world?"

The kitten darted out of the kitchen just as someone knocked on the cabin's front door.

Rubbing the sore spot where the kitten's claws had drawn blood, Judith opened the door to see Chloe standing alone on the porch. "Well, good morning."

Chloe's face brightened. "I came to see your cat. Is it inside or outside?"

"It's inside, but it's probably hiding by now. Where's your uncle?"

"Right here," Jacob's deep voice answered as he stepped onto the porch. "How are you, Judith? Feeling better?"

Chloe pushed her way into the cabin. "Here, Pumpkin. Here, kitty kitty."

Judith stepped outside to join Jacob on the porch. "I owe you an apology," she began.

"Oh yeah?" he asked with a quick smile and a sparkle in his eyes.

"Yeah. I'm sorry for yelling at you yesterday."

Jacob gave a small shrug. "It's all right."

"I've never lost my temper like that before. I usually just shove everything into a dark corner and brood about it. But yesterday...the things Dwight said…I let him push me right over the edge."

Jacob paused a few moments, as if considering her explanation. "Tell you what, Judith. If that's as bad as your anger gets, I think I'll survive." He stepped to the edge of the porch and scanned the nearby forest. "It you're in danger, maybe you should reconsider letting Henry's congregation use the church."

"I can't believe you said that!" As if the irate words had flown from Judith's lips of their own volition, she clamped a hand over her mouth. She took a deep breath and let it out. Then took two more. "Sorry," she said with an apologetic smile. "The thing is, Dwight has only stiffened my resolve. There's no way I'd let that bully change my mind."

Jacob nodded slowly. "OK. As long as you remember to be careful. I don't want anything bad to happen to you."

"I found Pumpkin!" Chloe screeched as she sped through the door. "But she's under the bed and I can't reach her. Can you come?"

"Judith will have to help you with that," Jacob said. "I've got to get started on the church. Henry's expecting me." He gave Judith one last smile and stepped off the porch.

"Come on, Judith." Chloe pulled her hand to urge her along. "I want to play with Pumpkin. Then, will you teach me how to draw a dragon?"

Judith glanced back at Jacob, saw him strap a tool belt around his lean hips, and felt that peculiar lurch in her stomach again. "We'll be down to see you later."

"Looking forward to it," Jacob called as he headed down the path towards the church.

∽∾

A few hours later, Keneisha's boisterous laugh sent Pumpkin scurrying out of Chloe's lap. "Hey, Miss Judith! You in there?"

Before Judith could make it to the front door, the girl bounded into the front room where Judith had been giving Chloe her first art lesson. "Whoa there, Keneisha," Judith said between laughs. "If you don't slow down, you'll be out the back door before I get to say hello."

"Hey, Chloe," Keneisha said. "Whatcha doing?"

"Painting. Want to see?" Chloe held up the watercolor tablet.

"Ooh," cooed Keneisha appreciatively. "That's a girl dragon, isn't it?"

"I painted it the same color as Pumpkin. Do you like it?"

Keneisha gazed at Judith. "Did you teach Chloe how to do that?"

"I did."

"You gonna teach me, too?"

"If you want."

"Hot dog! When you gonna teach me?"

"Now's a good time."

"Yeah, but my momma sent me to get you. She said you were supposed to come down to the church right now, and that I wasn't supposed to take no for an answer. So...you coming?"

"What do you think, Chloe?" Judith asked.

Chloe smiled broadly. "I want to show Jacob my picture."

"Then I guess we're going."

Keneisha and Chloe ran down the path, the sound of their laughter floating back like dandelion seeds in the wind.

Judith followed the girls until the forest path opened to the large clearing where the church stood.

Six long tables covered with bright, colorful cloths and laden with food sat in front of the church. Men, women, and children stood in small groups, as if waiting for a signal to begin eating.

"Here she is, Momma!" Keneisha shouted.

"About time," Beverly said as she stepped forward and took Judith's arm. "Miss Judith, this here is the congregation of the All Saints Community Church. We've been working all morning, and now it's time to give thanks and enjoy a meal together."

Henry Washington stepped forward. "But we couldn't begin without our guest of honor."

Judith stared at him. She was the guest of honor?

"You're about to eat some of the best food in Texas," Beverly crowed.

"But first we'll give thanks to our Lord God," Henry added. The group quieted and Henry lifted his face towards the sky.

Judith bowed her head and closed her eyes. When she felt a familiar hand slide into hers, she eagerly interlaced her fingers with Jacob's.

"We give thanks to you, O Lord!" Henry shouted.

"Amen!" shouted the band of men and women.

"Where there was hatred, You brought love."

"Yes, Lord!"

"Where there were those who would destroy, You built us up!"

"Praise the Lord!"

"Where there was wickedness and deceit, You sent us generosity and help!"

"Hallelujah!"

"Thank you, Jesus! Your Name be praised!"

A last round of praises echoed through the woods.

Judith opened her eyes to see Jacob smiling down at her.

Chloe wedged herself between them. "Look, Uncle Jacob. I painted a dragon."

Jacob pulled out Judith's chair and waited for her to sit, then lowered himself into a chair and set Chloe on his knee. "Let me have a look at that," he said. He unfolded the paper and examined Chloe's artwork. "I think you're pulling my leg. Judith drew this. Not you."

"Tell him, Judith," Chloe demanded. "Tell him that's my dragon."

"I give you my word." Judith held up her right hand. "That is a Chloe original."

Jacob gave a low whistle of appreciation. "That's one fine dragon, Chloe. Just wait until your mother sees it."

"I know," Chloe answered in a serious whisper. "Can I go play with Keneisha now?"

"Sure," Jacob answered, allowing her to wriggle off his lap.

Judith watched her hurry away to join the other children. "You sure are good with kids."

"You're not so bad yourself. Ever thought of having some?"

"Some what?"

"Kids."

Judith choked on her lemonade. Where had that question come from? Of course, she'd thought about having children. But that was one of the many hopes she'd given up in exchange for safety.

Jacob clapped her on the back and grinned. "Does

the mention of kids always affect you this way?"

"Of course not."

"So…have you?"

"Ever thought about having kids? Sure."

Why was he talking about this?

Beverly slid into the chair on the other side of Judith. "There's a lot of people here who want to meet you, Judith. You ready?"

"Do I have a choice?" Judith asked so quietly that only Jacob could hear.

He slid an arm across the back of her chair and leaned close. "They want to thank you. That's all."

A dark-skinned woman beamed as she thrust a plate in front of Judith. "Hey there, Miss Judith. You ready to taste the best fried chicken in Texas?"

"You hush," another woman said as she elbowed the first one out of the way. "Everybody knows you make the best fried chicken, but I make the best candied yams. Here, Miss Judith, you take some of this."

A third woman used her ample hips to nudge away the first two. "Hold on there, Miss Judith. Don't eat so much chicken and candied yams you don't have room for my strawberry cake."

Person after person paid their respects, bestowing plates of food on Judith until the table overflowed with aromatic dishes.

Judith scooped up a bite of food and leaned towards Jacob's ear. "You've got to help me eat some of this food."

Jacob chuckled in a low and intimate way. "I'm willing to give it my best effort, but it looks like you've got enough to feed the Texas National Guard. By the way, you look a lot better than you did yesterday."

Yesterday? If only she could erase the entire day. "Are you referring to when I was covered in mud?"

A slow smile crept across Jacob's face. "Seeing you wet and muddy was a revelation."

A revelation of just how stubborn she could be. Judith decided to play it safe. "How's that?"

"The first time I saw you, I thought you were pretty, but probably not my type. But when I saw you yesterday, slogging your way down that muddy road bound and determined not to accept help from me, I got to see a whole different side of you."

"Yeah. The muddy, wet, stubborn side."

"And that was the revelation."

"That I look good in east Texas mud?"

"No. That I'd seen the worst you could be."

"Wow, Jacob," Judith said drolly. "Stop before you embarrass me with all this sweet talk."

He laughed. "You see, the girls I've dated all start out the same. They're sweet and obliging, never complain about a thing. But then, after a month or so, their true natures come through."

Judith jumped on her chance to change the subject. "You've dated a lot of the local girls?"

"Oh, one or two."

"That's all?"

"What about you? Have you ever had a steady boyfriend?"

"We were talking about you."

"So we were."

"And you were going to tell me about true nature."

"I was going to tell you about your true nature."

There was no talking her way out of this. "According to you, my true nature is quick-tempered and stubborn?"

"Yep. And kind to children, generous to strangers, and courageous."

Courageous? She'd spent most of her life hiding from real and imagined dangers. No one had ever described her as courageous. Perhaps the change the Holy Spirit was shaping in her was beginning to be apparent. But talking about herself made her uncomfortable. It was time to change the subject. "What about you?"

"What about me?" Jacob asked.

"What's the worst thing about you?"

"Hmmm. I'm not sure. Maybe there isn't one."

"Maybe I should interview those old girlfriends."

Jacob paled slightly at that suggestion, but was saved by Henry's timely arrival. "Are you going to sit in the shade for the rest of the day, Jacob, or do you still have some work left in you?"

"Henry, my friend, you couldn't have asked at a better time."

༺❦༻

Jacob ambled away from the table. His walk was loose-gaited and easy, his stride carefree. It would be difficult to paint such a walk, to capture the loose animation in a frozen moment, but Jacob's walk said he was confident in his body, at home in his skin. He exuded masculine poise with every stride.

In contrast, she must look like a scared chicken, running from every raindrop, sure the sky was falling. Except Jacob had described her as courageous. Maybe he saw something in her that she couldn't see in herself.

Jacob climbed a ladder to the roof. His muscles rippled with power as he swung himself onto the top of the building. How deftly he used his tools. His hammer flashed with each strike, his body able to answer whatever demand he put on it. He was a man comfortable with hard labor, well-acquainted to the rigors of work.

Judith had never known a man who used his body with such power. The only man she'd ever been physically close to was her father, and he worked at a bank. But she couldn't imagine Jacob working in an office, wearing a suit and tie every day.

When Jacob's gaze connected with hers, Judith's knees weakened. This, too, was a new emotion. She'd never felt so strongly attracted to a man as she did to the tall, handsome male who smiled down at her. She returned his smile and felt her face warm from his attention. So many things had happened since she'd followed the Holy Spirit's prompting and faced her many fears. Could meeting Jacob be one of the things God had planned for her?

She wasn't ready for more than friendship. But it was true she felt things for him she'd never felt for any other man.

"What are you staring at, Judith?" Beverly's voice startled Judith.

"What? Oh...uh, nothing. Just watching the men work on the roof."

Beverly followed Judith's line of sight, and then smiled. "Oh, I see how it is. Jacob's making eyes at you."

Judith ducked her head and stood. "Let me help you clean up this leftover food."

Beverly clapped her hands together and laughed.

"That's all right, honey. I met my husband at a church picnic and we did some flirting of our own. Nothing wrong with looking."

Judith could try to disagree, but Beverly had seen the truth. Denying what had probably been plainly evident would be futile. "Hand me a trash bag and I'll get started."

"Not going to talk about it, huh? Well, that's all right, Miss Judith. Just as long as I'm invited to the wedding."

Judith removed a trash bag from the box in Beverly's hand and began discarding the used paper plates and cups. The sooner she got away from the topic of romance, the better for herself and her blushing face. "Have you seen Chloe?"

"She's playing with my girl. They know not to go too far away."

Judith cinched the trash bag and carried it to one of the large waste receptacles behind the church. "What else can I do to help you?"

"We're about done with the cleaning. Do you want to work on the parking lot or paint the woodwork?"

Judith looked at the asphalt covered lot. Workers were cutting weeds and repainting the lines that marked the spaces. "If it doesn't make any difference, I'd rather paint the woodwork."

"Makes no difference at all. Come on, friend, and I'll introduce you to the man with the paint."

Judith spent the rest of the afternoon painting the new wood the workmen had used to replace the rotten boards. She listened to the camaraderie of the workers, their good-natured teasing and exchange of family news. These people cared for each other. Christian fellowship sustained and nourished them. Many years ago, her grandfather had built a church for the benefit of one congregation. Now, she continued his legacy by lending it to other worshippers. Henry, Beverly, and the rest of the congregation depended on her. She would need every ounce of courage she had to see this through to the end.

When the last of the work had been finished, Judith stepped outside and took a deep breath of the fragrant early evening air. Sunlight streamed through the lower branches of the pines as the workmen and their families packed their belongings.

Jacob ambled towards her, his tool belt slung over one shoulder. A breeze fluttered his sandy hair and the fading sunlight haloed his form. He was all man, strong, yet gentle, determined, yet patient. Jacob smiled at her, a slow, good-to-see-you-again smile, and she imagined running to him, wrapping her arms around his chest and holding on.

Her heart jumped in surprise. She'd done no more than hold his hand a few times, yet the need to be closer to him was nearly overwhelming. Who was this man that he could affect her so deeply?

"Ready to go home?"

Her throat was too dry to answer. She nodded.

"Where's Chloe?"

Before Judith could answer, Beverly closed the trunk of her car and shouted. "Keneisha! Chloe! Time to go home!"

Jacob and Judith walked to Beverly's side and waited for the girls.

"Where'd they go?" Jacob asked.

"I told them not to go too far," Beverly answered. "Keneisha! Chloe! Y'all come on!"

Cicada song was the only sound that answered.

"I'll go look for them," Jacob answered.

But before he'd taken two steps, they heard squeals from the nearby forest. The two wide-eyed girls ran out of the woods, their fright-filled screams piercing the otherwise placid evening.

"Hold on there," Jacob said as he caught the youngsters. "What's going on?"

Keneisha had tears in her eyes and both girls were breathless. "There's a man," Keneisha began.

"He told us..." Chloe said between pants.

Keneisha wiped her tears on the sleeve of her blouse. "And then we..."

Jacob squatted to Chloe's eye level and she wrapped her arms around his neck.

"I didn't know if..."

Jacob's brow darkened as the girls tried to tell their story.

Judith's heart raced as the many dreadful possibilities flew through her mind.

Beverly opened two bottles of water and handed them to the girls. "Drink this. Calm down and catch your breath. Then tell us what happened."

"Evening, folks."

In the twilight, Judith hadn't seen the man approach. Her stomach clenched when she recognized the face. Dwight Thompson. What was he doing here?

Jacob stood and positioned Chloe behind him. "Evening, Dwight. What brings you out here?"

Keneisha buried her face in her mother's stomach and Beverly put two protective arms around her daughter.

Dwight smiled. "I was just out driving when I saw these two little girls playing in the woods. I thought they might be lost, but when I went to see if they needed help, they ran away. Sorry if I scared them."

Jacob looked back at Judith, and then shifted his gaze to Beverly. "No harm done."

Dwight eyed the church building. "Is this the church Henry Washington's group is going to use?"

Anger drove out all of Judith's fears. She stepped to Jacob's side, not bothering with any pretense of friendliness. "Why are you asking?"

Dwight laughed softly. "There you go again, jumping down my throat for asking a simple question."

"I'm going to take Keneisha home," Beverly said.

"Good idea," Jacob said.

Beverly guided Keneisha to her car and drove away.

Jacob faced Dwight. "Was there something else on your mind?"

"No, I'll be on my way. That little girl hiding behind your back, she's your niece, isn't she?"

Jacob's voice was impassive. "That's right."

"Your sister Hope's daughter?"

"Right again."

"Does your sister know you let her play with black children?"

Judith's restraint snapped. She took an angry step towards Dwight. "You're on my property, and I want you to leave."

"You're as prickly as a razorback, little lady. Well, keep your pants on, I'm leaving." Dwight turned and sauntered back towards the woods. A few steps later, he turned and called back. "It'll be an awful shame if this church burns, too. All that hard work up in flames."

Jacob nudged Chloe towards Judith, and then

stepped closer to Dwight. "I hope that's not a threat."

Dwight held up his hands, palms out. "Not from me, friend, not from me. But we both know it's a possibility. All I'm saying is it would be a shame if it happened again."

The muscles in Jacob's jaw tensed. "It's time for you to go, Dwight."

Dwight smiled broadly. "You're right about that. My wife will have dinner waiting for me." He lifted a hand to wave goodbye and disappeared into the foliage.

Judith wanted to spit out the sour taste in her mouth, but she settled for a long drink from a bottle of water. Her stomach churned with an insidious blend of anger and fear. One part of her wanted to chase after Dwight and force him to listen to her irate words. Another part wanted to grab Chloe and run to the nearest safe place. She put a hand on Chloe's shoulder. "Did that man hurt you, Chloe?"

Chloe shook her head. "He just scared us. That's all. Me and Keneisha were playing hide and seek and suddenly there he was. We both took off running."

Judith gathered the little girl close. "It's OK, now. He's gone and you're safe."

Chloe turned to Jacob. "Can we go home now?"

"Sure," Jacob said. "Is it OK if I carry you?"

"I'm too big to be carried."

"I know. But I'd like to, anyway." Jacob swung the girl onto his hip and reached his free hand towards Judith.

Chloe was fine, Judith told herself as she took Jacob's hand. Despite her fears, nothing bad had happened to the child. Chloe rested her head on Jacob's shoulder and closed her eyes, safe in her uncle's arms. Although Judith would never prevent Chloe from receiving the reassurance she needed, she wished she could take the little girl's place.

❦

Judith sat on the cabin's front porch and watched the tail lights of Jacob's truck disappear. The summer light did not surrender easily to darkness and she'd have at least an hour before the fireflies began to blink their secret messages throughout the night.

Jacob hadn't wanted to leave her alone, but Judith refused to spend the night at his mother's house. She'd won every battle against her fears so far. No way would she let Dwight's threats get the better of her.

Judith closed her eyes, took a deep breath, and slowly exhaled. The wind rustled through the lofty tree tops, making the surrounding forest whisper its eternal praise. This was her favorite time of day to pray.

Thank you, Lord. Gratitude swelled in her heart as she thought about Chloe and Keneisha. Dwight hadn't hurt the girls, but Judith still didn't trust him.

Watch over those I care about. Judith had always asked the Lord to keep her father safe, but tonight she included Henry Washington and the members of his church.

She'd spent most of her life hiding, but the members of the All Saints Community Church had faced their fears. They weren't about to let the threat of arson keep them from rebuilding their church. What did a Christian do when hatred destroyed what they'd have built? They prayed for the wrongdoer and rebuilt.

Help me to know Your will. The Lord had been preparing her for this moment, and here she was, ready to answer His call. What more could the Lord have in store for her?

It was a good evening to read a Psalm, but as Judith reached for her Bible, headlights shone around the curve leading to her cabin. An unfamiliar black sedan pulled to a stop, and a forty-something man, tall and distinguished looking, got out of the car.

"Miss Robertson?" he asked.

Judith swallowed the hint of panic that rose in her throat. Just because he was a stranger didn't mean he intended to harm her. She stood and wrapped her hands around the post that supported the porch's roof. "Yes?"

"I'm Special Agent Mark Grey with the FBI." He slipped on a charcoal-colored jacket that matched his slacks and showed her his identification. "If you have a few minutes, I'd like to speak to you."

What did the FBI want with her? Her knees trembled as she walked down the steps and checked his I.D. "What brings you all the way out here?"

"Sheriff Miller asked the Bureau to help with his investigation of the church arsons. I understand you've agreed to lend a meeting place for Henry Washington's congregation."

Judith's worry faded. The FBI was in Piney Meadow because of the arsons. That had to be a good thing. "It's an abandoned church my grandfather built many years ago. It's a temporary home until Rev. Washington can rebuild. Would you like to see it?"

"If it's not too much trouble."

"Let me get a flashlight."

"I've got one in the car." Mark retrieved the flashlight and fell into step beside Judith. "How many people are in Rev. Washington's congregation?"

Judith led him along the narrow pathway. "I don't know for sure. My best guess would be about fifty."

"That's the same for all the churches that have been destroyed. Small groups of people who gather for mutual support and casual worship."

"And all African-American."

"Right."

"Any idea who's behind the fires?"

"We've got a few leads."

"Here we are." Judith stepped inside the church and flipped on the lights. The sanctuary had been transformed. Vases of fresh flowers decorated the cloth-covered altar and the spotless windows reflected the light.

Mark switched off the flashlight. "Someone's been hard at work."

"They sure have. Even though I told Rev. Washington he could use the church for only six months, his group still fixed it up."

"Goes to show how much they value the place." Mark walked down the center aisle, his fingers skimming the tops of the pews and his footsteps echoing throughout the empty church. "You know, Miss Robertson, there's a chance this place could end up in flames."

"I believe it's worth the risk."

Mark returned to the spot where she waited. He leaned against the back of a pew and gazed at her, as though assessing her character.

Judith felt her skin warm under his inspection and fought back the urge to confess something. "I hope you find the people behind the arson."

"We will. It takes time, but we'll find them. Actually, that's one reason I dropped by to see you tonight."

Mark's smile reminded Judith of a magician. He had something up his sleeve. "What's on your mind?"

"The sheriff's office and I would like to rig several security cameras around your church. In a way, you and Rev. Washington's congregation are daring the arsonists to strike again. If they do, I'd love to have it all recorded."

"Is that the best protection you can offer?"

Mark crossed his arms. "Yes, it is. Like most police departments, Sheriff Miller simply doesn't have the manpower he needs."

Her grandfather's church would be as tempting as a big piece of cheese in a rat trap. But if it would catch the rat who'd destroyed four churches, it would be worth it. "You can put up cameras. Since I live nearby, I'll be able to keep an eye on the place, too."

Mark's face took on a serious expression. "Being this far from the main road puts you at a disadvantage, Miss Robertson. It'll take a long time for anyone to get out here. Have you had any threatening phone calls or letters?"

Judith bit her bottom lip. "Sort of. At the diner yesterday I met a man named Dwight Thompson. He warned me about letting Rev. Washington use the church. He was here earlier today. I was suspicious, but Dwight said he was just driving around. I think he was checking out the location."

"I don't suppose he made any specific threats."

"In a way. He said it would be a shame if the church burned and that it was dangerous for me to stay here alone.""

"Any witnesses?"

"Jacob Fraser. Do you know him?"

"I met him a few days ago. He's been a big help."

Jacob was helping the FBI?

"I'll check out Dwight Thompson," the agent said. "If he's got a record, it may point me in the right direction." Mark reached into the inside pocket of his jacket and retrieved a business card. "If anyone else makes a threat or if you need to get in touch with me, call my cell phone."

Judith took the card from his outstretched fingers. "Thanks. Are you going to hide the cameras?"

"Why do you ask?"

"If it's well-known we've got security cameras around the church, the arsonists might leave it alone."

"Maybe. But criminals aren't usually the sharpest tools in the shed. More often than not, they think they can disable the cameras or outsmart them."

Judith took one last look at the sanctuary before turning off the light and closing the door. If only she could put some type of fireproof bubble around this dear little church. If only there was some way to stop the arson without risking what her grandfather had put in her care.

9

It wasn't bird song that roused Judith on Sunday morning, but human voices raised in joyful songs of praise. As the sunlight streamed through the open bedroom window, she strained to make out the words that drifted from her grandfather's church on the summer breeze.

"*No matter what,*" a woman's voice sang out.

"*You are with me,*" the choir added.

"*Even in the depths of despair.*"

"*You are with me.*"

Could her grandfather hear those happy voices lifting their song to heaven? That old church had seemed so desolate when she'd first seen it, long silent as the years passed. But now it was bursting with music and praise, the people inside charging it with new vigor.

"*No matter what I face.*"

"*You are with me.*"

The song ended with a flourish of shouts and clapping, only to be followed by a deep baritone beginning a new song.

Drawn by the music, Judith dressed, grabbed her sketchbook, and set off for the church. She slipped into the building as quietly as possible, an act that was surprisingly easy to accomplish since the entire congregation had joined in the song. She found a folding chair and scooted into a corner, intent on viewing the scene without calling notice to herself, and flipped to a blank page. Within seconds, she was drawing. First, the baby peeking at her over its father's shoulder, then a profile of the grandmother who sat nearby, swaying in time to the music, but not singing.

She worked excitedly as her gaze flitted from one joyful face to another. These people had something Judith had often seen in her home church. Fellowship. Assurance. Bliss.

When the song came to an end, Rev. Washington stepped up to the plain pulpit and held up his Bible. "Brothers and sisters!" he called across the small church. "Are you ready to hear the word of the Lord?"

As the church members echoed their answer, Judith turned her attention to Henry. He was no longer the soft-spoken, middle-aged man she'd met. Something had transformed him, as though he'd tapped into a boundless source of energy. His dark eyes shone and his voice intensified as he spoke.

"Today friends, our lesson comes from the Book of First Peter."

The congregation quieted, but Rev. Washington did not open his Bible. Instead he recited from memory. "'And who is he who will harm you if you become followers of what is good? But even if you should suffer for righteousness' sake, you are blessed. And do not be afraid of their threats, nor be troubled. But sanctify the Lord God in your hearts and always be ready to give a defense to everyone who asks you a reason for the hope that is in you, with meekness and fear; having a good conscience, that when they defame you as evildoers, those who revile your good conduct in Christ may be ashamed. For it is better, if it is the will of God, to suffer for doing good than for doing evil.'"

Judith's pencil dashed across the page as she tried to capture the fervor in Henry's eyes. Concern and worry fell away from his face as he spoke, making way for a genuine zeal.

"It is better to suffer for doing good," Rev. Washington repeated, "than to do evil."

These people certainly knew about suffering, Judith thought. Hadn't they lost their church because of evil?

Dwight Thompson's threats came to mind. He must have had something to do with the burning of the All Saints Community Church. Why else would he have warned her against getting involved?

Rev. Washington's choice of scripture was right on the mark.

She would not allow herself to be troubled by Dwight's threats.

"We can seek revenge," Henry continued, "or we can seek the path of love."

Judith scowled as she sketched, remembering how Dwight had advised her to remember which side she was on. As if she'd ever ally herself with his brand of hate.

"Because God is with us," Henry concluded. "God was with us in the past. God is with us now and God will be with us in the future."

The congregation shot to its feet, shouting in accord, and the music started again.

Time for Judith to go.

She slipped through the door and walked away unnoticed, but just before she stepped into the woods, she glanced behind her to catch one last look at the church. The music was so loud, the people inside so exultant, it seemed as though the church itself was dancing with joy. Of course, her grandfather would have approved her decision to lend the church to Henry Washington. How could anyone who witnessed the devotion of the All Saints Community Church ever doubt it?

Judith's spirits were so high as she strolled back to her cabin, not even the sight of Jacob's mother sitting on her porch could lessen them.

"There you are," Emma Fraser smiled in greeting. "I knew you'd show up sooner or later."

Judith dropped into the empty chair. "Been waiting long?"

"Not at all. Besides, I've been enjoying the music."

"Isn't it wonderful? I woke up to that glorious sound and just had to see for myself."

"You went to Henry's church service this morning?"

"For a little while. I wanted to make some sketches."

"May I see?"

"Of course. Come on in." Judith propped the screen door open with her foot and followed Emma into the cabin. "Can I offer you a soft drink?"

"That would be perfect. Thanks."

Judith opened her sketchbook to her most recent drawings and passed it to Emma.

"Oh, Judith," Emma gasped. "These are amazing. Look at Henry's eyes! I've never seen him preach before."

"He became a different person. Almost as if someone had plugged him in." Judith set two glasses of cola on the kitchen table and eased into the empty chair. "So, Mrs. Fraser, what brings you out to visit?"

"Call me Emma, won't you? I have a feeling we're going to become great friends." She passed a large clasp envelope across the table. "I brought the photos you wanted to borrow."

Judith held her breath as she withdrew the precious pictures. "Thanks. I'll make copies and get the originals back to you."

"Take your time. Are you making an album?"

"Maybe," Judith answered absent-mindedly, her attention riveted on the photos. "But right now I plan to use them to paint some portraits of my mother." Judith fingered the pictures carefully, mentally cataloging them in chronological order.

"Why?"

"Why what?"

Emma's silence brought Judith's attention back to the woman sitting across from her. "Why do you want to paint portraits of your mother? Aren't the photos enough?"

Realizing she'd been unintentionally rude to her guest, Judith replaced the pictures inside the envelope and concentrated on Emma. "Drawing and painting are my ways of understanding a person. I study an object or an image so closely that, after a while, I begin to get inside it. To notice things nobody else has ever seen. Then I show the rest of the world."

"Like the fire in Henry Washington's eyes," Emma said.

"Exactly."

"It's funny, isn't it? How you've come back to Piney Meadow so many years after your mother left. Rachel and I promised we'd keep in touch, but after she moved away…"

Judith watched Emma's eyes as they focused on

something too far in the past for Judith to follow. "I don't know where my parents were married. Was their wedding in Piney Meadow?"

"Right up that path," Emma replied with a fond smile and a nod towards the church. "We decorated that old church with white ribbons and fresh flowers. Even had a little canopy of pine boughs that your parents stood under to say their vows. When Aaron saw Rachel coming down the aisle, I thought he would burst with happiness."

Judith had seen the photos of her parents' wedding, but Emma's words brought the vision to life. Her parents had married in the church her grandfather had built. A church that was now her responsibility. "Was it hard for my mother to leave Piney Meadow to move to Dallas?"

"Heavens, no. She was so much in love with your father she would have gone to the moon with that man."

"What about my grandfather? He must have been sad to see her go."

"No doubt," Emma answered with a nod. "But that's the thing about being a parent. If you do your job well, your children will be healthy and happy enough to leave you." Emma shifted in her chair and leaned closer to Judith. "Have you decided what to do with your inheritance?"

The answer came to Judith like sunshine breaking through a cloudy sky. "From what you've just told me, I'm more certain than ever I won't sell. Jacob talked to me about leasing the land. If I hire Fraser Lumber to manage it, they'll be able to take some of the timber and I'll still get to keep the land. That way everyone gets what they want. Right?"

"Talk to Jacob about it. He'll do what's best. He always has." Emma drained her glass and pushed away from the table. "I'd better get going. Hope and Chloe are waiting for me at the house. We need to make final plans for Chloe's birthday party. Guess what she wants for the theme."

"Don't tell me. Dragons?"

"You know it. We're going to have the party in our back yard. But where I'm going to get dragon-themed party decorations is beyond me."

"Since I got you into this mess, why don't I take care of the decorations? I could paint some murals and some paper tablecloths."

"Would you? Really?"

"It sounds like fun. Chloe can help."

"Oh, Judith. You're a lifesaver! Just wait until I tell my daughter."

Emma stood and Judith walked with her onto the front porch. "Thanks again for the photographs. I'll take good care of them."

Emma slid an arm across Judith's shoulders. "It's so good to know you're here. Rachel left, but you've come back. It feels like a complete circle."

∽⌒

The following night, Judith brushed out her hair and studied the dress laid across her bed. She still couldn't believe she'd actually shopped for her date with Jacob. But she'd brought only casual clothes from Dallas. Plus, she had no idea where Jacob was taking her. A new dress was definitely called for.

The fact that she'd driven to the nearby city and looked in three stores before she found the right color didn't necessarily mean she was buying it just for Jacob. She knew from experience that royal blue looked best with her dark hair and eyes.

She examined the new shoes she'd bought and wondered if Jacob was as excited about the date. They hadn't really spent much time alone together, and tonight it would be just the two of them.

But it was just dinner, she reminded herself. Just dinner with a friend. Getting excited about seeing him was foolish. Not that he wasn't good looking. That handsome face had probably netted him more than a few feminine hearts. And he moved with easy confidence, a type of masculine grace that spoke of strength and power. But she had a life in Dallas, and once she'd finished her business in Piney Meadow, she intended to go back to it.

Still, it would be nice to spend time with him. As long as she remembered his friendship was all she was interested in.

∂∾∽

Jacob pulled up in front of Judith's cabin, checked his appearance in the rearview mirror, and slid out of his truck. Just as he stepped onto the porch, Judith came through the screen door. He gave a low whistle of approval. "Nice," he said.

Her cheeks grew pink under his inspection. "What?" she asked. "This old dress? I wear it whenever I don't care how I look." She gave him a playful grin.

He slid his hands into the pockets of his dress slacks and leaned against the post. "Now, why don't I believe that?"

She stepped off the porch and made her way to the truck. "You look pretty nice yourself. You don't strike me as the type of man who wears a tie very often."

"You're right about that," he answered, falling into step behind her. "But I've been known to put one on for church and other special occasions."

"So tonight's a special occasion? Where are we going?"

"Thought we might go into the city for Chinese food. That OK with you?"

"Sure."

Jacob opened the passenger side door and Judith moved to climb into his truck. She let out a low grumble of frustration, turned her back towards the seat and tried to boost herself up. Unable to lift herself, she blew out a breath and faced Jacob. "I have a problem."

"What's wrong?"

"Your truck's too high."

The last thing Jacob wanted to be was the type of dense male his sisters were always complaining about, but he didn't have the slightest idea what Judith was talking about.

She set her purse on the truck seat and faced him. "I don't suppose you have a stepladder."

A ladder? She'd been in and out of his truck plenty of times. Why would she need a ladder now? "What are you talking about, Judith?"

She rolled her eyes and a pang of uneasiness settled in his stomach. Despite his best intentions, Jacob was being one of those dense males.

"My dress," she said. "Stupid me bought a dress that's too narrow to climb into your truck."

"Oh," Jacob answered, smiling with relief that her

eye roll hadn't been directed at him.

"If you'll wait here," she said, "I'll go change."

"Nah, that's not necessary." Jacob placed his hands on either side of her waist and lifted her onto the seat.

"Oh!" she gasped. "You made that look easy."

"It was easy. You don't weigh more than a sack full of feathers."

"Oh, Jacob," she said with a laugh. "You sure know the right thing to say to a girl."

He closed her door, circled the front of the truck, and climbed behind the wheel. He'd known his first date with Judith would be different than any other. So far, he was right on the money. Plus, once they got to the restaurant, she'd need help getting down. As he drove away from the cabin, Jacob began to formulate a plan for how to use that to his advantage.

৵৽

Judith fastened her seatbelt and relaxed. "I had a visit from the FBI."

"Oh, yeah? Was it about loaning your church?"

"Yep. An agent named Mark Grey came to see the place. He wants to put up security cameras so he can record any suspicious actions."

"You agreed to that?"

"I know I'm putting my grandfather's church at risk, but the way I see it, it's better to risk the building in order to do something good than to play it safe."

"I like that about you." Jacob stretched his right arm across the back of the truck's bench seat, rested his fingertips against Judith's shoulder, and then glanced at her.

Just a little touch. His fingers barely skimmed the fabric of her dress, yet his touch sent ripples of excitement down her arm.

She started a new conversation. "Tell me about your family."

"What do you want to know?"

"I can't imagine what it must be like to grow up with that many brothers and sisters. Did you like it?"

"Didn't have much choice. I had a friend when I was a kid. He was like you, an only child, and I used to love to go over to his house. He didn't have any big brothers beating up on him or big sisters teasing him."

"That sounds awful."

"But the thing is, he always wanted to come to my house to play. He loved hanging around with my big brothers and he had a crush on both of my sisters."

"Is this a story about the grass always being greener?"

"My point is we don't have any choice about what kind of family we're raised in. I was lucky though. My parents loved each of us, taught us right from wrong and provided an education."

"And now you work in the family business."

"Yep. It's my father, my two brothers, and me."

"No sisters? Your mother doesn't work?"

"My mother worked with my dad before I was born and, although they could work in the business if they wanted to, my sisters chose other things."

"Dorothy Davidson told me you used to be a police officer."

"That's right."

"Where?"

"Houston."

"I didn't take you for a big city kind of guy."

"I enjoyed living in the city."

"Why'd you move back?"

"That's a long story. Look, here's the restaurant. You hungry?"

There was something Jacob wasn't telling her, but Judith decided to let it go. They were just getting to know one another, and their friendship would come to a dead end if she pushed for secrets he wasn't ready to tell.

Jacob stopped the car in a far corner. Just as Judith was devising a complicated plan that involved sliding out of her seat and straightening her legs at just the right moment in order to land on her feet, Jacob opened her door and held out his arms.

Judith smiled at her rescuer and placed her hands on his shoulders. Once she was on solid ground, he stepped closer, putting them toe-to-toe.

"Whenever I get close to you, I smell gardenias," he said in a low voice. "Perfume?"

"Just soap." She took a deep breath, inhaling his pleasant, masculine scent. "You smell pretty nice yourself."

He fingered a strand of her hair. "Your hair has a mind of its own, doesn't it?"

Judith stifled a groan, hating to hear the same critical words hair stylists had always used to describe her unruly hair.

"I like it," Jacob added.

Judith jerked her head up to look into his eyes. Was he kidding?

He placed his hands on the nape of her neck and fanned her hair through his fingers. "It's so soft. It curls around my finger like grape vine." He wasn't kidding.

If Judith hadn't liked him before, she definitely

liked him now.

❧

Jacob leaned across the table and looked at Judith. "Now it's your turn to tell me about your family."

Judith took a sip of hot tea and shrugged one shoulder. "There's not much to tell. There's just my father and me."

"What was it like growing up like that?"

"Quiet."

"And lonely?"

"Sometimes." Judith set the teacup on the table and slowly ran her finger around the rim. "But as long as I had a pencil and a piece of paper I was happy."

"You could draw even when you were a little girl?"

"Couldn't stop drawing. I'd see something and just have to put it on paper. I ran across one of my early sketchbooks when I was packing to come here. Let's just say, I've improved since then."

He'd love to see those early drawings. He wanted to know everything about her. "Did you go to college?"

"Art school. In Chicago."

"And after art school, you moved back to Dallas?"

"Right. I landed a few illustrating jobs while I was still in school, and they led to more. I worked for several years at an advertising agency, then quit that job and started freelancing. My father thought quitting was a terrible mistake, but I've been much happier working on projects I choose."

"Like children's books."

"They've been an interesting challenge. I have to

make the author's words come to life in a way children will understand. Sparking a child's imagination is the best part of the job."

"Like fairies living in tree trunks."

"You remember."

"What's your next project?"

"My editor has been talking about a book on mermaids, but, so far, there's nothing definite."

"How does one research mermaids?" Jacob closed his eyes and placed two fingers on his forehead. "I see a trip to the beach in your future."

Judith laughed at his feigned attempt at fortune telling. "There's nothing definite yet. Although I wouldn't mind a trip to the beach."

"When I lived in Houston I went to Galveston every chance I got. I love walking along the beach in the evening."

"How long did you live in Houston?"

"Three years. I've been back in Piney Meadow for two."

"Do you miss it?"

The corners of Jacob's mouth turned down in a thoughtful frown. "Not really. Being a police officer was more exciting than acquiring and managing land, but it's good to be back with my family. When I needed them, they welcomed me back with open arms."

There it was again, that hint of something bad that had happened in Houston. Judith thought of her own tragedy. Should she tell Jacob about her mother's death? Maybe he already knew. "Did your mother ever tell you how my mother died?"

Jacob reached across the table and took Judith's hand. "Mom told me your mother was murdered. I'm so sorry you had to go through that."

It was the perfect thing to say. No empty platitudes or awkward pity. Just a simple statement of his feelings.

"Did your mother also tell you I was the one who let the murderer into the house?"

Jacob tightened his hold on her hand. "I don't know the circumstances of your mother's death, but I do know you wouldn't ever let anyone hurt her. A few days ago, you were ready to punch Dwight Thompson for simply saying hateful words. You've got a protective streak in you that's wider than a redwood."

Could Jacob Fraser get any more perfect?

Judith opened her mouth to thank him, but emotion choked her voice. She took another sip of tea and focused her gaze on the flickering candle in the center of the table.

It was time to tell the story to her new friend. "My mom hired a man to take care of our yard. He came one day, just like he did every week, and cut the grass. Mom always gave him a glass of cold water when she paid him, so when he rang the bell, I opened the door and let him in." Judith glanced at Jacob.

He leaned forward in his chair and focused on her, waiting patiently for her to continue. He was listening, she realized. Simply listening. Judith's heart eased. Jacob wouldn't judge her harshly for the mistake she'd made so long ago.

Judith tucked her hair behind her ear and continued. "I saw our neighbor's cocker spaniel running loose. That dog was always escaping, so I went outside to catch it. When I went back into our house, my mom was on the kitchen floor. Her throat was cut and she was bleeding to death."

Jacob's brows drew together in a concerned frown. "How old were you?"

"Eight."

He shook his head slowly. "And you still blame yourself?"

"No. I mean…well, I try not to."

"If you hadn't been there that day, your mother would have probably let the killer in, anyway. That was her routine, wasn't it?"

"I guess so. I opened the door, called to my mom that the yard man was there, and ran outside. But maybe my mother would have seen something in his face that warned her. Maybe she wouldn't have let him in that day."

"That's a lot of maybes, Judith."

Judith's gaze connected with Jacob's. His dark blue eyes showed no hint of duplicity. She found no hint of censure or blame in his face, only sympathy and understanding.

"Chloe's going to be eight years old in a few days." Jacob was changing the subject? Perhaps he couldn't bear to listen to more.

Judith smiled back at him and shifted in her chair. "I know. I volunteered to help with the decorations."

"So if Chloe did something similar, would you blame her?"

Tears sprang to Judith's eyes. Chloe. Innocent, effervescent Chloe. May the Lord protect the child from such horror. "No, of course not. She's just a little girl."

"And so were you, Judith. Just a little girl."

Judith brushed away tears with the fingers of her free hand. She'd heard those same words many times before. She'd been a child, blameless and unable to know what the killer had in mind. So why had the words held so much more power when Jacob said them?

Because of Chloe, of course. Chloe was as guileless as a puppy and Judith cared for the child. For the first time, she truly understood how innocent she'd been at the age of eight.

Judith smiled at Jacob through her tears. "Thank you," she said in a hoarse whisper. "How'd you know the right thing to say?"

He pulled her hand to his lips and kissed her fingers. "I've got my secrets, too."

"You don't have to tell me."

"I know, but...I want to tell you why I left the Houston P.D."

Judith propped her elbow on the table and rested her chin in her hand. She'd listen without judging, just as he had.

Jacob let go of her hand, took a deep breath and let it out. He shifted his gaze from hers and looked out the restaurant's window. "I was on patrol one night when we got a call for a robbery in progress at a warehouse. That wasn't usually a dangerous call, but the dispatcher said 'possible hostages' and that got the attention of several squad cars. My partner and I were first on the scene. We started taking fire almost immediately."

A sharp pain darted through Judith's chest at the thought of Jacob being in danger, but she didn't speak.

"It was so dark that night," he continued. "The robbers had shot out the security lights, and the lights from the squad car weren't helping much. We took cover behind our car and decided to wait for backup."

Jacob leaned back in his chair and clasped his

hands in front of his stomach. He still hadn't made eye contact. He continued to stare out the darkened windows as though he was viewing the scene. "We didn't know where the suspects were, but I thought we were relatively safe behind the car. But during the next round of fire, my partner got hit in the right shoulder. For a second I didn't know what to do. Should I tend to my partner's wound or try to locate the shooters? Just then a man stepped out of the shadows, his arms raised in front of his chest and his hands clasped together."

Jacob imitated the shooting stance. "My partner yelled at me to shoot, but I couldn't see a gun. I'd heard about dead kids who'd been carrying toy guns and I didn't want to make that kind of mistake. But as the man came nearer, I could make out a dark shape behind him. Two men were walking together, but I still couldn't see a gun. Finally, they got close enough for me to see what was going on. The guy in the back had a gun up against the ribs of a teenager in the front."

Jacob quieted then, his gaze locked on the windows. His breathing remained steady and his face placid, but a muscle flexed in his jaw.

Judith cleared her throat. "So the hostage was a human shield?"

Something flickered in Jacob's eyes, as though her voice had brought him back from the memory. "Right, but more than that, the perpetrator was forcing the hostage to take a firing position so it would look like he was the one who had the gun." Jacob's voice drifted into silence again.

Should Judith wait until Jacob's attention came back to the present or should she prompt him to finish the story? He'd obviously survived the incident, but something had convinced him that a life in law enforcement wasn't for him. Judith touched his arm, drawing his attention from the windows and back to her. "What happened, Jacob?"

"I fired at the guy in the back, but I wasn't fast enough. The robber shot the hostage a split second before I shot him."

Judith closed her eyes and let the pain pass through her. She knew what it was like to feel responsible for someone else's death. She wanted to gather Jacob into her arms and hold him. She wanted to kiss his brow and reassure him. "The man you shot, did he die?"

"No. Last I heard he and the other robbers are still in prison."

"And the hostage?"

"Dead. A teenage boy who'd been helping his father and uncle with inventory."

She drew her hand away and leaned back in her chair. They sat for a few quiet seconds while sorrow worked its way through her soul. The pain on Jacob's face was plain, and Judith longed to comfort him.

The waiter came and went, but still they remained silent.

It was Jacob who finally spoke. "Did the police ever catch your mother's killer?"

"They found him dead in the trailer where he lived. He'd killed himself."

Jacob grimaced and shook his head slowly. "There's all kinds of crazy in the world."

"Did anyone blame you for the hostage's death?"

"No. No one, but me."

"I don't think you did anything wrong. You were in an impossible position."

"I hesitated, Judith. If I'd shot the robber a few seconds earlier, a teenager's life would have been saved. One second, maybe two, made the difference. I couldn't stomach the idea of picking up a gun again, knowing the price of making a mistake. Being a cop lost all of its attraction."

And if Judith hadn't opened the door that day, if she'd stayed by her mother instead of running outside, maybe she could have prevented her mother's death. "We both wish we could go back and do things differently."

"But we can't. Besides," Jacob said as he clasped his arms behind his head, "returning to Piney Meadow turned out to be a good decision. One of the reasons I moved to Houston was to prove I could make it on my own, but I missed my family." He flashed a mischievous smile. "Please don't tell my brothers and sisters I said that. I get enough teasing as it is."

Jacob's joke signaled it was time to put their tragedies behind them.

Judith smiled in relief and drew an imaginary X over her heart. "Your secret's safe with me."

෨෧

They rode back to Piney Meadow in an easy silence.

But when Jacob parked the truck in front of the cabin and turned off the engine, the silence was suddenly uncomfortable.

Judith knew she could invite him in, but what would they do? She was all talked out, and she wasn't ready to do more than talk. Jacob probably wanted a goodnight kiss, but Judith didn't want their first kiss to be in the truck.

However, she couldn't get out of the truck by herself unless she was willing to split the seam of her skirt. She eased the truck door open and Jacob sprang out to meet her on the passenger side.

He fixed his hands around her waist but didn't lift her down. Instead he studied her face in the soft light from the truck, their eyes level for once.

"Thank you for dinner," Judith said.

A small smile crossed his lips. "You're welcome."

He continued to watch Judith for a few seconds, not saying a word, not moving in for a goodnight kiss.

"Are you going to help me down?" Judith asked.

"No. I like the way you look there. Can't get out without my help, can't get around me, either."

Judith knew when she was being teased. "You don't scare me."

"Good. That's not my intention."

"What is your intention?"

"Haven't decided. I was considering a kiss, but somehow it doesn't seem like the right time. Not yet, anyway."

"So, I'm stuck here until you decide?"

"Have you ever been on a moonlight hike?"

"No, and I'm not interested in one now."

"What are you interested in, Judith?"

"First, to get out of this truck. Second, to go inside."

"That's all?"

"For now, Jacob. That's all for now."

He nodded his understanding and lifted her onto the ground. Without saying another word, she stepped onto the porch, opened the front door of the cabin and flicked on the light. Then she turned back to Jacob.

He waited beside his truck, his profile lit by the light from the cab.

"Goodnight," Judith said.

"Oh, I almost forgot," he said with a snap of his fingers. "I'm supposed to ask if Chloe can come tomorrow to work on birthday party decorations."

"Sure. But make it after lunch. I have to go into town and buy supplies."

They stood watching each other. Judith didn't want him to leave and she didn't want him to stay. She longed for him to hold her in his arms, but didn't trust herself to touch him. For the first time in her life, her body seemed to be divorced from her mind.

This is the man for you, her senses yelled.

Too much, too soon, her mind answered.

A vision of herself jumping off the porch and throwing herself into his arms formed in Judith's mind. The desire to feel his lips against hers was nearly overwhelming.

But Jacob saved her from herself. "Take care," he said as he returned to the truck and started the motor.

Judith raised a hand in goodbye and watched the taillights disappear down the dirt road. Someday she'd be happy he'd left. But she wasn't so sure at that moment.

10

Jacob's heart lifted as he turned down the dirt road that led to the cabin the following day. When he'd eagerly volunteered to pick up his niece after her art lesson, his sister had winked at him and smiled.

"Just you try getting Chloe to leave," Hope had said. "She's crazy about Judith."

Chloe wasn't the only one, Jacob thought. In the weeks he'd spent with Judith, she'd gone from being a pretty stranger to holding a special place in his heart. His father had always told Jacob that when he met the right one, he'd know it, and there was no denying the lightness he felt whenever he was close to her.

There was something special about her - a strength that made him proud and a vulnerability that made him protective. Jacob rounded the last curve and saw Judith hanging sheets of paper from an old clothesline. She smiled when he approached, a warm welcome that encouraged his thoughts about making Judith more than a friend.

"Those look great." Jacob said.

"Thanks." She fastened the last clothespin. "Chloe loves to use water colors."

"Where is Chloe?"

"Playing over at Beverly's house. Hope that's OK."

"Sure. Keneisha's got so many cats, Chloe will be happy all day." Surprised, but grateful to find Judith alone, Jacob drew Judith into an embrace. She eased in his arms and rested her head on his shoulder. "Did you sleep well?" he asked.

"Not really," she said in a soft voice.

"Why not? Something on your mind?"

"What about you? Did you sleep well?"

"Tossed and turned all night."

"Did you have something on your mind?"

"Just a pretty girl with curly dark hair and beautiful eyes."

He felt her lips curve against his shoulder.

"What are you doing for the rest of the day?"

"Nothing special."

"If you're still interested, I could show you where to find those orchids." And if she wasn't interested, he'd find another reason to spend the day with her.

"Sure. Just let me get my sketchbook, and then I'm all yours."

He liked the sound of that. Making Judith all his was becoming more attractive every day.

Judith disappeared into the cabin and returned a few minutes later. She tucked a sketchbook and pencils into a satchel and draped the strap over her head. "How far is it?"

"Not too far. We'll follow this trail for a way, and then cut across a meadow to the marshy area."

They walked for several long minutes, Jacob a few paces ahead, clearing the undergrowth with his footsteps and holding back the branches to ease her passage. They were at the meadow before he broke the comfortable silence. "You've got a really nice piece of land here, Judith. Isaiah left you many blessings."

Judith eased onto a fallen log and removed a bottle of water from her satchel. "Selling this land would be like rejecting my grandfather's gift. Did your mother tell you I decided to lease the land to your family?"

Jacob blew out a breath of relief and said a silent thanks to the Lord. At last, he'd have good news to share with his father. "No, she didn't."

"I don't know the first thing about owning a forest," Judith continued. "I thought it would be best to simply leave it alone and let nature take over."

"Not if you want to really take care of it."

After taking a long drink, she passed the bottle to Jacob. "What does that mean?"

"Forest management includes inspecting the timber stands and keeping an eye on the wildlife populations. Especially if we find endangered species." Jacob drank the cool water, glad she'd thought to bring some.

Judith accepted the bottle, capped it and returned it to the satchel. She wrapped her arms around her knees and sat in silence, scanning the surrounding area. "Will your family harvest the timber?"

"Some of it," Jacob answered, lowering beside her. "But with four hundred acres, you could harvest trees every year and never really see a difference. Remember, a lumberman wants to protect the forest more than anyone else. Conservation doesn't mean leaving a site untouched. It means using the site in the best way possible."

"How long have the Frasers been in the lumber business?"

"My grandfather started the lumber mill. Now my father oversees the mill and my brothers each specialize in different aspects of the business. I'm the forester, David is in charge of finding the best market for the timber, and Richard operates the building supply."

"What does a forester do?"

"Scout for new property and manage the land we own. That's how I renewed my acquaintance with your grandfather."

"You liked him, didn't you?"

Jacob braced his hands on the log and stretched his long legs. "I liked him a lot. Isaiah lived a simple life. We'd usually meet for coffee in the morning, and then we'd drive out to inspect some part of the property. He talked a lot about how the community had changed since he was a boy, but that the forest had been the one constant in his life. Seemed to me as though he'd grown roots as deep as a red oak."

Judith stood and stretched. "Do we have much farther to go?"

"No," Jacob said, rising. "Just across this meadow to where that stand of yaupon is growing." He nodded towards the shrubs.

"I'll just follow you," she said.

"Good enough," Jacob answered with a grin and led the way. "My sister, Hope, told me to make sure you were coming to Chloe's birthday party."

"Will your whole family be there?"

At the other side of the meadow, Jacob stopped and turned to face her. "You sound like the turkey that was invited to Thanksgiving dinner."

"Remember, I grew up with just my father. Two quiet people in one big house. I liked your family, but when I first met them I felt like my underwear was showing."

The thought flashed across Jacob's mind, but he quickly whisked it away. Those kinds of thoughts would only lead to trouble. "Think you could get used to my big family?"

"Why would I want to?"

"Well, Judith, as should be obvious by now, I'm seriously considering courting you."

"Courting?"

The tips of his fingers touched hers, and then he pulled her hand into his. "Don't you know what courting is?"

Judith didn't withdraw her hand. "Let's pretend I don't."

"Well, first I ask you out on a series of dates, and we spend a lot of time together. Then, after a few dates, I start buying you presents."

"Presents, huh? I like that part." Her eyes twinkled.

"Then, after you fall in love with me, I buy you an engagement ring."

Color flooded Judith's cheeks, but her voice remained playful. "Awfully sure of yourself."

"Not really." Jacob slid his calloused hands along Judith's soft cheeks and tilted her face up to his. "I'm going to kiss you now, Judith. If you don't want my kiss, you'd better say something."

Jacob waited for her consent, his gaze intent as he struggled to read her thoughts. But before he could decode her reaction, she raised on tiptoe and gently laid her lips on his.

Jacob deepened the kiss. At last, she was in his arms, kissing him as freely as he kissed her.

How wondrously pure she tasted, as warm and sweet as the first spring morning after a hard winter. How perfectly she fit in his arms, her tall, slender body a perfect match for his. Could she really be the one? The one God had made for him?

When at last they broke apart, Jacob cradled her

head against his shoulder with one hand and wrapped his other arm tightly around her. "Oh, Judith. I'm so glad you came to Piney Meadow. So glad." His lips brushed against her hair, her forehead, her temple. "I've been waiting for you for a long time."

Judith raised her head, wrapped her arms around his neck, and smiled.

Jacob encircled her waist and lifted her off her feet, melding his lips with hers. She laughed as their mouths touched, and Jacob swallowed her laughter, taking it inside until his heart shone with the burgeoning love he felt. He lowered her and stepped away. "We'd better stop this now, Judith, before I forget I'm a gentleman."

She brushed her lips across his knuckles. "I'm glad you're a gentleman."

Oh, yes. He would do whatever he could to win this woman. But time to step away before temptation grew too strong. "Besides," he said, striving to make his voice sound casual, "I still have to collect Chloe."

"But the orchids," Judith said with a frown. "You never showed them to me."

Jacob pointed to the ground. "See those dark green leaves growing around that brown stalk? That's the orchids. They bloom in the fall."

Judith swatted his arm. "Did you bring me out here on false pretenses?"

"Nope. I always planned to get you alone where I could talk to you without interruptions. The forest is the perfect place for that."

Judith tried to feign annoyance, but she couldn't stop her grin from spreading to a full-blown smile. "Next fall, huh?"

"Yep. Think you'll be around to see them?"

"Maybe. All I need is a reason to stay."

"Oh, I plan to give you a reason," Jacob said, taking her hand and pulling her back towards the trail. "You can count on it."

〜◦◦〜

He'd kissed her.

Judith held Jacob's hand as they walked towards Beverly's house, her heart smiling at the memory of his kiss, and his words fluttering in her chest.

Could he really want to marry her? So soon? No man would decide such a thing on a whim. Would he?

Everything told her that he was a thoughtful, responsible kind of man. Not one to throw proposals around. If he was serious, she'd have to give an answer. Did she want to marry him? Judith rubbed her temples to quiet the questions.

"You're awfully quiet. Something on your mind?"

"Are you serious about wanting to court me?"

"Is that a problem?"

Yes. No. She looked into his eyes, to see the mix of concern and hope that flickered there. She pulled her hand free and took a few steps to distance herself. "I need time to pray about it, Jacob."

"Take your time, sweetheart. I have faith in our future, so I can wait until you feel the same."

"How can…why do you…" Judith slapped her hands against her thighs in frustration.

He held her so closely she could feel his heart beat. She tipped her face up and he lightly touched his lips to hers. "I know I caught you by surprise, but you're the woman for me. Don't you feel it, too?"

Judith's knees weakened from the gentleness of his

lips and the strength of his embrace. Warmth bloomed from her heart to every part of her body until she was sure she'd collapse from the overwhelming feeling of being loved.

Had he asked her a question? With his lips moving so tenderly over her face, all rational thought evaporated. She curled her fingers into his shirt and gave in to the astonishing sensations surging through her.

A voice came from somewhere outside the cocoon of tenderness he'd created, and Judith struggled to focus on something other than Jacob. He abruptly let go, leaving her mind reeling in a muddle of sensations and oblivion.

Chloe was there, dancing around Jacob and chattering about Keneisha.

Awareness slowly fought its way into Judith's brain. Chloe. They'd come to Beverly's house to pick up Chloe.

"Keneisha's momma took us to her new church. Keneisha wants me to go to church with her. Can I?"

"That's a question for your mom and dad," Jacob answered.

Judith watched Jacob and Chloe walk down the red dirt road, realizing that she should follow them, but unable to move.

"Something wrong, Judith?"

No, for the first time in her life, something was very right. She walked quickly to catch up.

Jacob turned his attention back to his niece. "How do you like Keneisha's new church?"

"It's OK," Chloe answered, swinging Jacob's hand. "But it's not big like our church. And it's made of wood instead of bricks. And it doesn't have pretty windows like our church."

"It's not size, or bricks, or stained glass windows that make a church, Chloe."

"It's not?"

"A church is made of people who love the Lord, no matter where they meet," he explained.

Chloe shifted her interest to Judith. "What's your church look like?"

"It's a big, brick building with a huge cross planted right in front of it."

"Does it have colored windows?"

"Oh, yes. Right above the front door, there's a stained glass window that shows Jesus calming the storm at sea."

"Is He walking on the water?"

"Yes."

"I'd like to see that. I think church is lots of fun," Chloe continued. "The people are nice and they always have doughnuts."

"Tell you what, Chloe," Jacob said. "Let's invite Judith to visit our church."

"Want to come on Sunday?" Chloe asked. "The children's choir is going to sing."

"I'll come," Judith promised. "I'd love to hear you sing."

Satisfied with that answer, Chloe skipped away and Judith and Jacob resumed their slow pace.

"I'm glad to know you go to church every week." Judith said.

"Been going almost every Sunday for as long as I can remember. My whole family goes. We meet at the church, always sit in the same spot, and then go to my parents' house afterwards. The responsibility of living my life so that others can see Christ in me has been challenging, but that's who I am. Having a relationship with God is as important to me as breathing."

Judith closed her eyes and sent a prayer of thanks heavenward. The Lord had sent her a man of faith.

"Chloe!" Jacob called. "What do you think you're doing?"

Chloe and Keneisha were climbing up the low branches of a tree.

"We're rescuing a kitten!" Chloe called back.

"That cat'll come down when it's good and ready," Jacob said, lifting first Chloe, and then Keneisha out of the tree.

"But it's just a little kitten," Chloe argued. "What if it can't get down?"

"I'll keep an eye on her," Judith assured.

"Time for us to go," Jacob said. "Say goodbye to Beverly and thank her for letting you play."

"OK," Chloe answered as she grabbed Keneisha's hand and ran into Beverly's house.

Jacob slid one arm around Judith's shoulders. "I have to go out of town tomorrow. Can I see you when I get back?"

"Of course."

He brushed his lips across her forehead. "I'm going to miss you while I'm gone."

"I can live with that."

"Think you'll miss me?"

"Nope. I'll be too busy dating all the other men who want to court me."

"I don't like the sound of that."

Judith slipped her arms around his neck. "You're the first, Jacob. Don't you know that?"

"Doesn't matter if I'm the first, as long as I'm the last."

Judith saw affection and warmth when she looked into Jacob's cobalt eyes. She laid her lips on his, delighted to feel his arms slip around her back and press her body close. She never would have met Jacob if she hadn't decided to conquer her fears. Answering the Lord's call to move out of her sterile cocoon had definitely been the right choice.

11

"You in there, Miss Judith?" Keneisha called.

Judith saw the girl's smiling face pressed against the screen door. "Come on in."

"What you doing?"

"Come see."

Keneisha skipped into the small living room where Judith had set up her workspace. One glance at the canvas had her eyes round with wonder. "Is that who I think it is?" she whispered.

"That depends," Judith whispered back. "Do you think it's Rev. Washington?"

Keneisha nodded, her pigtails bouncing with the movement.

"Then you're right."

"Sometimes, when Brother Henry looks like that, he scares me."

"Why?"

"See his eyes? How they get all bright like that? It makes me think that God is speaking."

"And that scares you?"

"Heck yeah, that scares me. Doesn't it scare you?"

"Not really. But he definitely made an impression on me."

Keneisha stepped back from the easel. "You're not gonna give this picture to my momma, are you?"

"Think she'd like to have it?"

"I don't know, but I sure don't want it in my

house. Every time I'd look at it, I'd have to say the forgiveness prayer."

"The forgiveness prayer? What's that?"

Keneisha folded her hands in prayer and cast her dark eyes towards the ceiling. "Dear Lord, please forgive me for all the sins I committed today. I'm really sorry. Amen."

"Covering all your bases, huh?"

"Yep. My momma said I was supposed to list all the sins I could think of, but there was so many, I decided to just lump them all together."

Judith covered her mouth to hide her smile. "But what does this picture have to do with the forgiveness prayer?"

"If that picture was in my house, it'd be like Brother Henry was preaching to me every day. And Miss Judith, nobody needs that."

Judith turned away and bit back her giggle. "So what do you think I should do with it?"

"You could give it to Brother Henry," Keneisha answered seriously. "He could take photos of it and pass them out to all the sinners."

Judith's sides ached from trying not to laugh at Keneisha's nine-year-old theology. If she didn't change the subject, the dam would burst. "What brings you over today? Did you come to play with Pumpkin?"

"No. My momma sent me. She says if you're gonna go into town, can she have a ride to the grocery store 'cause our car won't start."

"Of course. Just give me a few minutes to clean up this mess."

෧෧

"Are you ever going to get your car pulled out of that mud puddle?" Beverly asked as they bounced past Judith's BMW.

"As a matter of fact, the tow truck's coming tomorrow."

"Why'd you wait so long?"

"To teach myself a lesson."

Keneisha frowned. "What kind of lesson?"

"To remind myself that being stubborn can lead to some uncomfortable situations."

"Oh, my," Beverly said. "I bet there's a story in there somewhere."

"Tell me the story," Keneisha demanded.

"Let's just say that on that particular day, I ended up wet and muddy because I was too stubborn to accept help when it was offered."

"Is that all you're going to tell?" Beverly asked.

"For now. What's wrong with your car?" Judith asked in an artful change of subject.

"Dead battery. My son's coming tomorrow to put in a new one, but I needed to get to the store tonight. I promised a banana pudding for a potluck lunch we're having tomorrow at Brother Henry's house. You ought to come."

As Judith headed west into town, she held up one palm to ward off the invitation. "No thanks. That much attention makes me nervous."

"Is that why you snuck into church last Sunday? Like a scared rabbit afraid the fox was around the corner?"

"You saw me?"

"Of course I saw you. What were you so scared of, anyway? Didn't you know you'd be welcome? We would've given you the place of honor."

Lending her grandfather's church had been easy, but accepting all of the gratitude that followed was turning out to be much more difficult.

"You should see the picture Miss Judith's painting," Keneisha said.

"Is that right?" Beverly asked. "What's she painting now?"

"I'm not gonna tell you," Keneisha answered with a mischievous grin. "It's a surprise. Right, Judith?"

"If you want it to be a surprise, I won't tell."

Keneisha slipped her arm through her mother's and giggled. "When it's finished, Judith might give it to Brother Henry. For the new church."

"Any idea when the new church will be ready?" Judith asked.

"That's why we're meeting tomorrow," Beverly replied. "The donations have started coming in and we need to draw up some plans. If everything goes all right, we'll be holding the harvest festival in a brand new church."

Keneisha and her mother talked about the new church and whether or not there would be any banana pudding left over.

Judith noticed an old, rusty pickup pull off the road, wait for her to pass, and then come up behind her. The speed at which the truck approached her rear bumper shot a barb of fear straight through Judith's heart. She took a quick glance at her passengers.

Keneisha and Beverly were laughing, unaware of the oncoming menace.

Perhaps it was simply someone in a hurry. Judith took her foot off the accelerator and gradually slowed down so the guy behind her could pass.

But he didn't.

Judith's apprehension reached new heights. The vehicle was riding her bumper, only inches from ramming her. She squinted into the rear view mirror, trying to see the driver's face, but with the sun visor tipped down, she could only see a bearded chin and a hard-set mouth. Another man sat in the passenger's seat, his face similarly blocked from view.

There was no shoulder on this stretch of road and the truck was still too close for her to brake. She pushed the accelerator to the floor. They were at least five miles from the highway. Five miles of a little-traveled country road bordered by forest on both sides. What in the world did the other driver want?

"Beverly," Judith said in the most casual voice she could muster. "Will you check in my purse for my cell phone?"

"Sure," Beverly answered, pulling Judith's bag from the floorboard. "Want me to dial it for you?"

"Good idea." Judith continued to let the truck slow, her gaze darting from the rear view mirror to the curving road.

"OK," Beverly said, holding up the phone for Judith to see. "What's the number?"

Judith tightened her hands on the steering wheel. "Nine, one, one."

"What's the matter?" Keneisha looked at Judith.

"I think I might be having a little car trouble, that's all." Then Judith caught Beverly's attention. She gestured with her head towards the back window.

Beverly dialed the phone, and then glanced through the back window. "Oh, Lord. What in the world does that fellow think he's doing?"

"Trying to scare us?"

"You'd best speed up, Judith. Don't let him get so

close."

"I'm already over the speed limit."

"You need to get on the main highway. There's nobody around here for miles."

Judith took Beverly's advice. She shifted into high gear and pulled away from her pursuer. But only for an instant.

Within seconds, the other truck slammed into the rear of her pickup.

Judith's body jolted, straining against the seatbelt. Adrenaline laced with fear shook her. Struggling to maintain control, she shot a worried glance at Beverly as the truck veered towards the edge of the narrow road

Beverly spoke into the phone, giving their location to the operator.

Judith righted the vehicle and pushed the old pickup for every ounce of speed it had. It was only two miles to the two-lane highway with the nice wide shoulders. If she could keep control that far, she and her passengers would be safe.

She spared a quick glance at Keneisha.

Beverly had one arm wrapped tightly around her daughter's small body.

The road straightened. It was a beeline to the highway from that point on. Almost there.

Beverly continued to talk into the phone, her voice calm despite the situation. "No, I can't see any license plate. It's too close to us. You'd better send a police car."

Judith glanced into the rearview mirror again. The rusty pickup was gone. But before she could take a breath, she saw it shooting out of her blind spot.

The other vehicle swerved, barreling into their

side. The next second, Judith's truck vaulted over the edge of the road and headed straight for the forest.

Beverly screamed and wrapped both arms around Keneisha.

Judith pushed on the brake with both feet as they bounced past the tree line, branches slapping at the windshield as she fought with the steering wheel.

Judith's head knocked against the window and a sharp pain shot through her left shoulder as the pickup finally came to rest, wedged between two sturdy pines.

Beverly and Keneisha huddled against the passenger side door, terrified, but intact.

An eerie silence followed, as if the world was holding its breath.

Judith pried her fingers from the steering wheel and looked at her passengers. "Are you all right?"

Beverly inspected Keneisha. "You OK? Does anything hurt?"

"I'm OK. Are you OK, Momma?"

"I'm OK. How about you, Judith? Are you hurt?"

A sharp pain pierced her left shoulder and her head ached. "I'm fine," Judith lied through a tremulous smile. "Just need to catch my breath."

"Are you sure you're all right?" Beverly's voice ripened with concern.

"Just a headache," Judith answered. But she could not deny the blackness at the edge of her consciousness that lured her towards oblivion. "I'm going to close my eyes and rest for a few minutes."

"Judith!" Beverly shouted, and then shook her shoulder. "You wake up right now!"

Judith struggled to answer, but only managed an unintelligible mutter as the pain pulled her into nothingness.

ڶۦ

Judith became aware slowly. Her head throbbed. A blur of light.

Keneisha's dark eyes were intently watching her. "She's awake," the girl announced.

"'Bout time, Judith." Beverly hovered over her. "You've been out for almost three hours."

"Where am I?" Judith mumbled, her voice a hoarse mixture of grogginess and pain.

"The emergency room. Got yourself a cracked collarbone and a minor concussion."

Judith blinked, trying to focus on her surroundings. Pain radiated from her head, down her left shoulder, and on to every joint of her body. She was lying on a hospital bed, her left arm in a sling. "What time is it?"

"Almost seven o'clock," Beverly answered, arranging the blanket around Judith's shoulders. "My son's here to take me home, but I'm not leaving until I know you're all right."

"I'm so sorry about the wreck."

"Sorry? Wasn't your fault. The way I see it, if you hadn't been on your toes we could have ended up a lot worse. We could have turned over or something."

Judith rubbed her eyes in an attempt to stay awake. "How'd I get here?"

"The ambulance, of course. The doctor said you're going to stay here for the night. I'll be back tomorrow to check on you." Beverly left Judith's side to gather her purse. "And I called your father."

"What? How?"

"I used your cell phone. He said he'd be here as

soon as he could." Beverly laid a hand on her arm and squeezed gently. "I talked to the police. I described that old jalopy the best I could, but told them we couldn't see who was driving. They'll be around to talk to you, too."

Judith nodded and another sharp pain flashed through her head. She raised her right hand to her forehead.

"Still in pain, aren't you?" Beverly asked. But she didn't wait for an answer. "Is there anyone else I should call for you?"

"No," Judith said around a yawn. "I'm going to rest here and wait for my father." She cupped Keneisha's worried face in her hand. "I'm sure glad you weren't hurt. Will you look after Pumpkin while I'm in the hospital?"

The girl's face brightened. "Sure I will, Miss Judith. Me and Pumpkin, we get along fine. And when you get home, I'll come by and help you."

"It's a deal," Judith replied.

❧

The cold hand of panic gripped Jacob's heart as he darted into the hospital emergency room. Of all the days to be out of town.

Judith had been in an accident.

A soft hand on his back caused him to pivot. Beverly slipped one arm around his waist. "Judith's in room twenty-three, just down the hall."

"She's all right?"

"She's a might banged up, but she'll be fine."

"You and Keneisha?"

"We're both good."

167

"Thanks for calling me."

Beverly smiled like a child with a secret. "I figured you'd want to know. You're a might sweet on our Judith, aren't you?"

"I guess it shows."

"Like Rudolph's red nose." Beverly chuckled and squeezed Jacob's waist. "My oldest boy's waiting outside. You go on and see our friend."

Jacob hurried down the short hallway. He entered and peered down at Judith's sleeping figure. Her pale face was small and fragile in the dimly lit room, like a translucent pearl in the moonlight. A dark bruise shadowed her forehead and her left arm was in a sling. Brushing a curl of dark hair away from her face, he laid his lips gently on her forehead. "Thank you, Lord," he whispered into her hair.

Judith's eyelids fluttered open. "Jacob?" her voice was a raspy whisper.

His hand immediately found hers amid the tangle of sheets. "I'm here. How are you feeling?"

"I'm OK. What are you doing here?"

"Beverly called me."

"Someone ran us off the road." Judith shifted. "I was so scared Keneisha or Beverly would be hurt."

Jacob brushed his lips over her knuckles. "Shh," he whispered. "It will be all right now. Everyone's praying for you."

"Will you take me home?"

Jacob gingerly touched the bruise on her forehead and ran his fingers through her hair. "Not until I talk to your doctor. He may want you to stay in the hospital for several days."

"I'm not going to stay here."

Jacob released some of his anxiety.

Judith must be feeling better if she was putting up a wall of stubbornness.

"Well, like it or not, the doctor is the boss. At least, for now."

"Will you be back in the morning?" Judith murmured as her eyelids closed.

Since he hadn't planned on leaving her side until she was well enough to go home, his answer came easily. "I'll be here."

∂∞⌐

Jacob yawned and stretched in the chair. The smell of coffee on the patients' breakfast trays tempted him. He'd had little sleep the night before and a shot of caffeine would be a perfect antidote to his fuzzy mind. But not even the best coffee on the planet could pry him from Judith's side.

Special Agent Mark Grey entered Judith's room, two cups of coffee in his hands. "Morning, Jacob. I thought you could use this about now."

"You're a mind reader."

"Not hardly, but my job would be easier if I were." Mark reached into his pockets and withdrew packets of sugar and creamer. "How's Judith this morning?"

"Still sleeping. Let's step into the hall so we don't wake her."

"I need to talk to Judith about the accident."

Jacob took a deep drink of coffee. Judith hadn't slept well during the night, and he didn't want Mark to wake her. "Have you spoken to Beverly Lewis? She was in the truck with Judith."

"Yes, I talked to her late last night. Mrs. Lewis is certain it wasn't an accident."

Jacob's gut tightened. "But why would someone run them off the road on purpose?"

"Probably trying to scare her. We've got a strong lead on a group that's calling itself Hunters United."

"Never heard of them, but there are lots of hunters around here."

"These guys aren't hunting wildlife."

He sagged against the wall as Mark's meaning sank in. Jacob had always felt secure in his home town. He'd traveled the back roads of surrounding counties, gone wherever he'd wanted without fear or caution. But apparently, the same was not true for his neighbors. "Are the members of this group from this county?"

"We're not sure yet. As far as we can tell, they operate mainly in Shelby and Sabine Counties. Sheriff Miller is coordinating his investigation with the authorities there."

"Have there been any church fires in those counties?"

"As a matter of fact, yes. During the last eighteen months, there have been two fires in Shelby County and one in Sabine."

"All of them arson?"

"Yep. Very similar methods of combustion."

"And you think they've branched out to San Augustine County."

"More like recruitment. It could be that burning an African-American church is a type of initiation into the group."

Jacob shook his head in disgust. Burning a church was like spitting in God's eye. "What does this group have to do with Judith's accident?"

"Try to look at it from their point of view. They

burn down a church, and then a well-meaning person helps the displaced congregation. That's like nullifying their actions. Makes them look weak in front of the group."

"So they tried to scare her into not helping Henry's group."

"That's what I think. Judith told me about her run-in with Dwight Thompson. I checked out him and his brothers, but they've got nothing worse than speeding tickets."

"Judith told me you want to set up cameras around her church."

"Right. My partner is taking care of that today."

"Do you still think someone will try to burn down her church?"

"It's possible. If I could get it on video, that would be gold. Do you know when Judith's going to be released?"

"No. Why do you ask?"

"It would be best if she didn't stay in that cabin alone. If someone is trying to scare her, they probably won't quit harassing her until she stops helping Rev. Washington."

"Don't worry about Judith being alone. I don't intend to let her out of my sight until you find the people behind running her off the road and the arson."

Mark reached into his jacket pocket and removed a small notebook. "I do have one lead you could help me with." He opened the notebook and scanned the information. "Sheriff Miller told me about a family named Buchanan. The grandfather has a history of passing out hate literature."

Jacob's stomach tightened at the mention of the Buchanans. "That's Lee Buchanan. He's not liable to talk to anyone in uniform, or to the FBI."

"We'll see about that." Mark stepped closer and lowered his voice. "Nothing personal, Jacob, but you look like somebody ran over you with a two-mule team. Any chance you'll get some rest?"

"I'll go home once I'm sure Judith's all right."

"Fair enough." Mark shook Jacob's hand. "I'll be back this afternoon."

After Mark left, Jacob returned to Judith's bedside.

Would she change her mind about lending her grandfather's church? Risking the building was one thing, but risking her was too much.

Jacob propped his elbows on the bed, and bowed his head. "Father," he prayed, "what is Your will?" Allowing Henry's congregation to meet in the old church couldn't be wrong. Surely, the Lord would bless anyone who stood up for fellow Christians.

Jacob thought of the service revolver he'd tucked away in a lock box when he'd resigned from the force. Was it time to start carrying it again? He could feel the gun's cold metal in his hand, the heaviness of the pistol matched by the weight of his mistake. After what had happened in Houston, would he be able to shoot someone?

Invisible bands of steel tightened around Jacob's chest as he thought of the very real possibility of having to protect someone he loved. The warrior in him was ready to battle Dwight Thompson, or anyone else who threatened Judith or his family. But his mistake was a shadowy monster lurking in dark doorways. Maybe it was time to face that monster.

Jacob rested his chin on his hands. He'd believed a career in law enforcement had been the Lord's will for him, but his failure had led to years of doubt. Could he ever go back? "Lead me, Master. Help me to know the right thing to do."

Judith stirred, opened her eyes, and smiled at him. She reached her right hand towards him and he held it against his chest. Then she closed her eyes and returned to sleep. Would Jacob shoot someone who endangered Judith?

Oh, yes. He might live to regret it, but he'd protect the woman he loved.

12

"What do you mean you're not ready to go back to Dallas?" Judith's father was clearly concerned. Ever since his arrival, he'd been trying to convince her to leave Piney Meadow.

"I'm not hurt seriously, Dad, and I've got things I want to do here."

"With a fractured collarbone? You won't be able to take care of yourself."

"Judith is always welcome to stay at my parents' house," Jacob volunteered. "My mother would love to have her."

Judith waved her right arm. "I still have one arm that works just fine. I can take care of myself."

"Judith, this is not the time to be stubborn. Your health is at stake. Come to Dallas with me. After you're completely healed, you can come back for a visit."

But she couldn't leave Jacob now. Not when their relationship was just beginning. "I'll be fine in the cabin, Dad. Beverly's only a phone call away."

"And I intend to keep a close eye on her," Jacob added.

Her father paced the length of the hospital room. "Sometimes I wish you were still a kid. Back then you had to listen to me."

Judith reached out a hand and he quickly closed the space between them. "Dad, you're worrying for nothing. I'll be fine."

"Being run off the road isn't 'nothing', Judith. If you won't come home, at least stop living out in the middle of nowhere by yourself."

Maybe her father had a point. Someone had run her off the road, and whether it was a prank or malice, the results could have been much worse.

"How about a compromise?" she asked. "If I stay with Jacob's parents until I'm recovered, would you feel better then?"

"What are the chances of getting you to come home to Dallas without a fight?"

Judith had always been an obedient daughter, but she needed to stay in Piney Meadow. "I don't want to fight with you, Dad. But I hope you'll understand why staying here is important to me."

Her father's face was impassive as he looked from Judith to Jacob. "All right," he said after a long pause, "it's a deal. But as soon as I'm finished with the merger I'm working on, I'll be back in Piney Meadow to check on you."

❧❦

Once he was satisfied that Judith was safely tucked away in his parents' guest room, Jacob joined her father at the kitchen table.

"What do you think about Judith's accident?" Aaron Robertson was not a man who minced words.

"Both Judith and the woman riding with her say it was no accident."

"Has anyone been bothering her?"

"Judith had a dust up with a local businessman named Dwight Thompson. Judith said he threatened her."

"What kind of threat?"

Jacob got a bottle of water from the refrigerator, purposely delaying his answer. Judith's father had a right to know what his daughter had been up to, but, at the same time, Jacob felt a loyalty towards the woman he cared for. "Did you meet Beverly Lewis or Henry Washington?"

"Yes," Aaron answered. "I met them at the hospital. What do they have to do with Judith's accident?"

"Nothing directly." Jacob leaned against the kitchen counter and considered the events of the past few weeks. "Henry's church was destroyed by fire. It was a clear case of arson, and the local churches have all pitched in to help rebuild, but Judith allowed Henry's congregation to use her grandfather's church in the meantime."

"I remember that old church. I married Judith's mother there. I can't believe it's in good enough shape to use."

"It needed some repairs but those were accomplished easily enough." Jacob took another long drink of water. "There's a possibility that someone— maybe Dwight Thompson—is trying to pressure Judith to stop helping Henry's group."

"Let me see if I've got this straight. Henry Washington's church was burned and now the arsonists are threatening my daughter?"

"I intend to keep a close eye on Judith. She won't be staying alone in her grandfather's cabin anymore."

Aaron crossed his arms and raised one eyebrow. "Sounds as though you've got more than a passing interest in my daughter."

"Yes, sir. You may as well know I intend to marry

her."

"Marry?" Aaron shook his head in obvious disbelief. "You've only known her for a few weeks."

Jacob held out his palms in a gesture of conciliation. "I'm not saying the wedding's going to be any time soon. I'll give her all the time she needs. But I know she's the one."

"I'm not sure anybody's good enough for my girl, but I'll have to give you the benefit of the doubt. To tell you the truth, I felt the same way about her mother. I saw Rachel walking across a courtyard and knew instantly she was the girl for me. We dated for four years before we married, but she was worth the wait."

"I've been waiting for Judith. And now that she's here, I don't intend to let her get away."

"Well," Aaron said as he sagged into a chair, "this certainly changes things. And here I was thinking she'd be coming home soon. I bet Rachel's father is up in heaven having a good laugh at me."

"How's that?"

"I took his daughter away from Piney Meadow, and you're going to bring his granddaughter back."

෨ஒ

A few days later, Jacob was helping his brother fill an order when he spotted Dwight in the lumberyard. "Do we have an order for Dwight Thompson?" Jacob asked Richard.

"Not that I know of," Richard answered. "Why?"

Jacob didn't bother to answer.

Richard's nose was buried in a stack of papers, his attention lost in order forms and bills of lading.

Jacob ambled over to where Dwight casually

inspected a load of siding.

"Morning, Jacob," he hailed.

Jacob shook the hand Dwight offered. "Morning. What brings you out to this way?"

"Oh, just looking. I'm thinking about building an addition to my garage and wanted to get some prices."

"I'm sure we've got everything you'll need. Let me call somebody to help you." Jacob stepped away, but Dwight fell into step beside him.

"How's your family?" Dwight asked, his tone friendly and good-natured.

"Everybody's doing fine. How about you?"

"Oh, good enough. I was sorry to hear about what happened to your friend."

"Who's that?"

"Isaiah Beecham's granddaughter. What's her name? Julie?"

"Judith."

"That's right. Judith. Serious name for a little bit of nothing like her." Dwight had something on his mind.

Jacob waited.

"I heard she had an accident while driving Isaiah's truck," Dwight continued. "I guess that old truck was too much for her."

"It wasn't an accident."

"What do you mean?"

"She was run off the road. It was a blessing she wasn't hurt worse than she was."

"That's awful," Dwight said, looking genuinely concerned. "Must have been some kid driving too fast on those back roads. Any idea who it was?"

"Not yet. But both Beverly Lewis and Judith described the vehicle that ran them off the road, so once the sheriff locates it—"

"If the sheriff locates it," Dwight interrupted. "Lots of old, rusty pickups around these parts."

Jacob hadn't described the type of vehicle that had been involved. His suspicions rose by several degrees. "How'd you know it was an old, rusty pickup?"

"Didn't you say that?"

"No."

"Oh…well…must have heard it from somebody."

That was possible.

"I guess Judith will be leaving Piney Meadow soon."

"Why do you think that?" Jacob asked.

"Who could blame her? Getting run off the road isn't exactly my idea of a warm welcome."

Jacob decided to try a different tactic. "I suppose some people would say Judith was asking for it."

A flicker of surprise lit Dwight's eyes. "I suppose you're right. Still, I hate to hear about her getting hurt just 'cause she didn't know who her friends were." Dwight was smooth. He was skating on the edge of condoning what had happened, but he wouldn't flat out state it.

"Her friends?" Jacob asked, his voice struggling to appear indifferent.

"You know what I mean. People in Piney Meadow have always gotten along fine as long as they stay with their own kind. But a city girl like Judith probably didn't know that."

Heat rose in Jacob's face. If Dwight had said these things to Judith in the diner, no wonder she'd lost her temper.

"Another thing to think about," Dwight continued, "is the kind of people who'd burn a church. If their message is ignored, they might not stop at burning empty buildings."

"If you know about the crimes, Dwight—"

Dwight threw up his hands in mock surrender. "Not me, friend. I'm just repeating what I've heard around town." He stepped away from Jacob and glanced at his watch. "I'd best be getting back to the office. I'll come back and check on those prices when I've got more time."

Jacob's suspicions of Dwight Thompson deepened as he watched the man saunter towards the parking lot. But suspicions weren't evidence. Neither Mark Grey nor Sheriff Miller would be able to act on Jacob's misgivings.

Best to keep an eye on Dwight and his brothers. If they had harmed Judith, they wouldn't stop until she backed down.

13

Judith climbed into the passenger's seat of Jacob's truck and waited for him to close her door. Instead, he tossed her travel bag into the bed of the truck and rested against the open door.

"I still don't like this," he said.

"I need to go back to the cabin. Even though your family pampered me better than an heiress at a spa, I want my life back."

"I understand but…"

They'd already talked about the possibility of further violence and she'd agreed to sleep at Beverly's house. She'd keep her end of the bargain, but she couldn't let fear have power over her again.

"If anything happened to you, Judith…"

She caressed his cheek. "I spent many years running from imaginary villains and monsters. In an effort to keep myself safe, I locked myself away from everyone except my father."

Jacob placed his hand over hers.

"But I asked God to give me the strength to conquer my fears. Going back to the cabin is my way of not giving in to those old, familiar anxieties. I want to reclaim my life."

Jacob dropped his gaze. He was thinking things over, or praying. After a few moments of silence, he looked at her and smiled. "I understand. I've always thought you were courageous. Guess I didn't realize just how brave you are."

Judith kissed his cheek. "No one has ever called me courageous before."

"I won't be the last. Now, if you're ready, let's get you home."

A full moon hung low in the sky as Jacob drove out of Piney Meadow and turned onto the main highway. A few miles later, a siren sounded and Jacob slowed his truck to a stop on the shoulder of the road. As the Piney Meadow Volunteer Fire Department engine and a line of pickup trucks passed, he dug his cell phone from his shirt pocket. "Darn it."

"What's wrong?" Judith asked.

"Phone's off. Sorry, but I've got to follow that fire engine. I'm one of the volunteers."

"Of course."

As Jacob joined the caravan and sped down the highway, an uneasy feeling slithered through Judith's gut. Fire had claimed Rev. Washington's church. What if someone had sabotaged the construction of his new building?

"Where is Henry's new church?" she asked.

"On the other side of town, not too far from the lumber mill. Whatever's burning on this side of town, it's not Henry's church."

As the fire engine neared the county road that led to her cabin, one thought echoed through Judith's head.

Don't turn. Don't turn.

The fire engine's brake lights shone like angry eyes as it slowed and turned.

"What's down this road besides my grandfather's property and Beverly's house?"

Jacob looked at Judith, his eyes brimming with

concern. "Nothing," he answered.

Judith used her cell phone to call Beverly. The unanswered ring grated against her anxious ear. Snapping the phone shut, she looked at Jacob with a silent plea.

"It could be nothing," Jacob said without conviction. "Maybe just a small grass fire or somebody's campfire got out of control."

But as they rounded a corner, an unnatural glow illuminated the sky. "That's not a small fire," Judith said.

"No," Jacob agreed.

Judith redialed Beverly's phone number and counted the unanswered rings. Did Beverly fail to answer because she wasn't home or was she unable to answer because of the fire? Keneisha's joyful smile and lively dark eyes drifted into Judith's mind. *Please, let them be safe.*

The fire engine turned down the dirt road that led to Judith's cabin.

Not the church! Had someone set fire to her grandfather's church?

As they followed the fire engine the true source of the flames became apparent. Waves of fire surged through her grandfather's barn, the old timber groaning as it suffered the torturous flames.

Jacob's truck skidded to a stop. He shot out of his seat, reached into a toolbox in the truck's bed, pulled out a bulky jacket, and then raced to join the other firefighters.

Judith scrambled out of his truck and made her way to the fire engine.

The barn was beyond rescue. The sheets of metal that had once formed the patchwork roof tumbled to the ground, sending avaricious sparks into the overhanging canopy of pines.

"Judith!"

Judith's ice cold blood warmed at the sound of Beverly's voice. She saw Beverly pushing through the firemen.

The two women embraced.

"Are you OK?" Judith asked. "Where's Keneisha?"

"We're both OK. I called the fire department as soon as I saw the smoke."

A wall of the barn collapsed, sending a wave of heat and smoke towards them.

"Let's get out of the way." Beverly said.

Keneisha was standing on the porch, Pumpkin clutched tightly in her arms.

They went to stand with the little girl.

Judith's heart squeezed at the sight of Keneisha's wide eyes and trembling bottom lip. Judith wrapped her good arm around the girl's shoulders and pulled her close. "It's OK, nobody's hurt."

"But what about Mr. Isaiah's barn?"

"Wasn't much left of it. If the fire hadn't gotten it, the next big wind would have."

The little girl's gaze was transfixed on the blaze.

"Let's go around to the back porch," Judith suggested. "There's no need for Pumpkin to see this."

Judith and Beverly guided the girl to the back of the cabin.

"What's that?" Keneisha asked, pointing to one of the porch posts.

A piece of white paper fluttered in the gusts of heat from the fire. Judith pulled it off a nail and read its chilling message.

You ignored one warning.
Don't ignore the second.
The next fire will hit closer to home.

"What is it?" Beverly asked.

"I have to show this to the fire chief," Judith answered without further explanation. She went back towards the blazing barn.

Where was Jacob? She searched the figures silhouetted by the fire, but couldn't locate him among the other men. The anxiety to see him, to know he was all right, clawed at her throat until it ached from the strain.

A jacketed arm blocked her path. "That's far enough," a man's gruff voice said.

Judith looked into the man's soot-lined face. "I need to see the fire chief."

"That's me," he said. "Emmett Dutton."

"I'm Judith Robertson." A familiar hand touched her shoulder and her anxiety evaporated. She looked up into Jacob's sweaty face. "Are you OK?"

Jacob wiped his face on the sleeve of his jacket. "I'm fine. Sorry we couldn't save the barn."

"The barn is nothing. But I found this on my back porch."

Jacob frowned over the hostile words and passed the note to the chief.

The older man fished a pair of glasses from his pocket and squinted at the paper. "The sheriff should be here in a few minutes. He'll have to look into this, but we'll know more about whether this was arson once the inspector from the state fire marshal's office has a look." He turned to Judith. "Any idea who would want to hurt you?"

"The same people who burned Henry

Washington's church. First, I was told to mind my own business, and then I was run off the road. Now this." Judith gestured towards the ruined barn. "It's Dwight Thompson."

"What do you think?" Chief Dutton looked at Jacob.

"As far as I know, there's no evidence to pin these arsons on Dwight, but he did make some menacing remarks to Judith."

A squad car pulled up behind Jacob's truck.

"Here's the sheriff now," Emmett said. "Thank goodness this is his mess to clear up and not mine."

Mark Grey and Sheriff Miller climbed out of the squad car. Jacob followed Mark to the burn site while the sheriff stopped to talk to Chief Dutton.

When the fire chief handed the paper to the sheriff, the sheriff scowled and returned to his squad car. He retrieved a plastic bag with the word *evidence* written in red block letters across the front and placed the note in the bag. Then he walked to where Judith stood waiting.

"Sorry to see you've lost your barn," Sheriff Miller said.

"Dwight Thompson left that note for me," Judith said.

"How do you know that?"

"He's been threatening me for weeks. It had to be him."

Sheriff Miller scanned the area. "We'll look into it."

He didn't believe her. What would it take to make the sheriff see what was so obvious to her?

Mark Grey approached, his shoes covered with ash. "The arson inspector will be out tomorrow morning, Miss Robertson. Until then, leave everything just the way it is."

"Dwight Thompson left me a note. The sheriff has it."

Mark shifted his gaze from Judith to the sheriff and back to Judith. "We're following every lead, Miss Robertson. But we can't act on hunches and feelings. When we've gathered enough evidence, we'll make an arrest."

"My barn was burned for just one reason. To scare me."

"You're probably right." Mark took a handkerchief from his back pocket and used it to wipe his face. "The security cameras are up and running. If anyone tries to destroy the church, there's a good chance we'll catch him on video. You shouldn't stay out here alone."

"I'm going to stay with Beverly Lewis. Do you know her?"

"Yes, I interviewed her about your car accident." Mark used his chin to point to Judith's arm. "How are you feeling?"

"I'm fine." There were so many more important things to talk about than her health.

"Not scared?"

As she took a quick inventory of her emotions, a revelation astonished her. She felt angry and frustrated, and there were definitely strands of impatience and resentment floating around in her conscious, but she wasn't scared. She'd spent most of her adult life cowering in fear. But she wasn't afraid now.

Beverly and Keneisha walked to Judith's side.

"I'd better call Brother Henry and tell him about this," Beverly said. "C'mon, Keneisha. Time for us to go home."

Keneisha passed the kitten to Judith. "Don't let go of Pumpkin. She's scared of the fire and all those men."

"I'll take care of her. I'll be over to see you later tonight."

"I'll have your room ready," Beverly said.

Judith made her way towards the smoldering ruins of the barn. Just as she rounded the front of the cabin, she saw Jacob shake the sheriff's hand.

Minutes later, the firefighters and the sheriff pulled away, their tail lights forming a long red line in the night.

"What did the sheriff say?" Judith asked as Jacob joined her.

"Says he'll go and question Dwight Thompson. But trust me, Judith. Dwight will have an alibi."

Judith studied Jacob's tired face. "You look worn out. Want to come in for a while?"

"I told the chief I'd stay here to keep an eye on what's left of your barn. I've got to make sure no other fires start. Thank goodness it's not windy tonight."

Judith led him to the cabin. "Can I get you something?"

"How about a gallon of water?" Jacob answered as he laid his heavy jacket over the porch railing and collapsed into one of the rocking chairs. "I'm going to stay out here where I can keep watch."

Judith carried Pumpkin inside the cabin. When she returned with two glasses and a pitcher of ice water, she settled into the rocking chair next to him.

"When are you going over to Beverly's?" Jacob asked.

"When you leave, I'll go."

They sat in silence for several minutes as the night

closed around them.

Jacob rested their joined hands on the arm of the rocking chair and closed his eyes.

Just when Judith suspected he'd fallen asleep, he drank the rest of his water and passed the empty glass to her. "Can I have some more?"

"Of course," she answered. But when she returned to the porch with a full glass, he was no longer stretched out in the chair. She set the glass on the porch railing and trailed him to the ruins of the barn.

He glanced up as she approached, and then continued raking the hot coals and spraying them with the water hose. Plumes of ash and cinders hovered over the site, burning her throat with acrid smoke. "Won't be much longer before this fire's completely dead. Then I'll take you over to Beverly's."

"I can drive myself. I'll get my bag out of your truck."

"Judith?"

She turned and waited for him to continue.

"I'm worried about you."

Judith slid her good arm around his waist and nestled her head against his shoulder. He smelled of smoke and sweat, but she relished the feel of his strength. If only she could ease his worry—go back to his parents' house or let him stay with her—but she wouldn't give in to fear. She'd come too far to let fear beat her down again.

"I know God will protect you," Jacob said. "But relying on faith is hard. I'd feel a lot better if I could be with you."

She rose to brush her lips against his.

Jacob deepened the kiss.

This man loved her, wanted to protect her, and

although she was far from certain about their future together, she was falling in love with him. She encircled his neck with her arm and gave herself to his kiss.

Once things got back to normal, when Henry's congregation was in its own church and Dwight Thompson's hate group was dealt with, she would savor the time she had with Jacob. They would spend hours together, just talking. *Just falling in love.*

Jacob ended the kiss and nudged her back. "Time for you to go."

"Why?"

"Because I know where kissing you might lead. Some things should wait until after our wedding."

He loved her so much he'd even protect her from their shared desires.

❧⟡

Sabine County was a long drive for Jacob, but he would go much farther if it meant helping Sheriff Miller or Special Agent Grey. The note Judith had discovered had turned Jacob's blood to ice. Dwight had told him the arsonists might not stop at burning empty buildings and the note had warned that the next attack would hit closer to home. Did that mean Judith's cabin?

She'd been run off the road on purpose and her barn had been torched. There was no doubt she'd been targeted by someone who didn't like the way she was helping Henry's congregation. Jacob admired the way she'd answered Henry's call for help. He even respected her determination to not back down. But did it have to be Judith?

The fact that she was an outsider to Piney Meadow was undoubtedly a factor. If his family had bought the land, and then loaned the church, no one would have threatened them. The Fraser family employed too many people to risk the loss of business because of threats or property damage.

But Judith was a stranger. She didn't have family scattered throughout the county like he did. Judith didn't know who came from honest, hard-working people and who had family trees full of con men and criminals. She'd been as vulnerable as a baby possum at a highway crossing.

But that was before Jacob had fallen in love with her. Now that his plans for the future were pinned on one beautiful woman with brown, curly hair and dark eyes that flashed with mischief, he'd do everything in his power to protect her. Even if that included talking to the Buchanans before the FBI or sheriff did.

Jacob pulled to a stop in front of a padlocked metal gate. There were five no trespassing signs of various sizes nailed to the gate and surrounding trees. Jacob honked the truck horn and waited. Someone would be out eventually.

About five minutes later, Jacob heard the sound of an ATV. Red dust drifted through the air as a man wearing stained overalls and a white tee shirt drove the vehicle down the dirt road. As the man neared the gate, Jacob recognized Lee Buchanan, the oldest member of the family.

The vehicle stopped. "Is that Jacob Fraser?" the man yelled.

Jacob got out of the truck and walked to the gate. "How are you, Lee?"

The older man scratched his white beard and got

off the four-wheeler. "I'll be better if you're here to do business."

"I'd be willing to talk about it. Are you ready to sell some hardwood?"

"I might be. Come on in and we'll talk. I hope you brought your big wallet with you. Hardwood don't come cheap."

Lee unlocked the padlock and opened the gate. Jacob drove through, then waited while the other man closed and relocked the gate. Once the ATV was ahead of him, Jacob followed it to the Buchanans' main house.

Several generations of the family lived in the ramshackle structure. The original cabin had been no more than four rooms, but as each generation was born, additions had been built. One side of the house was brick, the opposite side brown vinyl siding, and a third addition at the rear was covered with outdated asbestos shingles. There were several abandoned cars and two derelict house trailers scattered around the edges.

Jacob parked his pickup under a shady magnolia.

"Now, what can I do for you?" Lee said, as he approached.

"Last time I was here, you indicated you might be willing to sell some oak. What's your thinking on that now?"

"Depends on the price. What's your bottom line?"

Jacob watched Lee's eyes as he named the price. The flash of interest in the older man's gaze was exactly what he'd been hoping for.

Lee scratched his beard and spit a stream of tobacco juice. "You might as well get back in your truck if that's all you're offering. No need to waste your time."

Jacob leaned against the hood. "You know I don't haggle, Lee. That's my top price."

"I heard you were going to pay Dwight Thompson a pretty penny for some of his pine."

"I don't talk about deals I make with other clients."

"Seems to me that if you can pay that much for common pine, you could come up with more for top grade oak."

"I'm already offering you top dollar. My family has to cut the timber, transport it, and mill it. That's a lot of overhead on our part."

Lee sent another stream of tobacco juice into the red dust. "Wait here. I want to talk it over with my sons."

Jacob let down the tailgate, and sat in the truck's bed. No telling how long Lee would make him wait. But it didn't matter. Land owners could hem and haw, negotiate all they wanted, and try to talk him into a higher price, but he never changed his initial offer.

Despite the magnolia's shade, the summer afternoon's heat pressed in on him. A Confederate flag hung limply from the pole attached to the side of the house and flies buzzed around the old oil drums the Buchanans used for garbage. But the most distasteful thing about the place was Lee's sign collection.

One sign propped on an abandoned Chevrolet featured a crude drawing of a man hanging from a noose. The words painted beneath the picture warned of similar fates to anyone who stepped out of line. Racial slurs blighted other signs and one oversized placard proclaimed the divine supremacy of white people.

Jacob's throat tightened as he read the vile messages. After his first visit to this property, he'd told his father about the Buchanans. His father had agreed that such a family was "not worth the aggravation" and had advised Jacob to drop them as potential clients.

But it wasn't timber that had brought Jacob back to this part of the county.

Lee Buchanan strode out, the screen door banging behind him. "I think we're going to pass this time," he said. "But if you can come up with another thousand dollars, we might be interested."

Jacob climbed out of the truck's bed. "That's not going to happen, Lee, but I appreciate you hearing me out." He opened the driver's side door and turned to face the older man. "Before I leave, there's one other thing I'd like to talk to you about."

Lee's bushy, white eyebrows drew together. "What's that?"

"Have you heard about the church burnings in the area?"

"Of course. Why do you ask?"

"I'm one of the volunteer firefighters in Piney Meadow and we had one a few weeks ago."

"So?"

"Have you heard anybody bragging about setting the fire?"

Lee narrowed his eyes. Then his features changed as a broad smile replaced his scowl. "You must think I'm dumber than a sack of marbles." He let out a harsh bark of laughter. "You see my signs and think I must know people who go around burning black people's churches."

Jacob's throat tightened as Lee stepped closer.

"You listen here, Mr. High Horse Fraser." Lee poked Jacob in the chest with one finger. "It's my right as an American citizen to write whatever I want and put my signs on my own property. Just 'cause you don't like what I write don't mean I'm stupid enough to burn down somebody's church."

Jacob brushed Lee's hand away from his chest. "Have you heard of a group called Hunters United?"

Lee stuck his index finger in his mouth, dug out the plug of tobacco he'd been chewing, and threw it on the ground. He spit a few times before looking back at Jacob. "Yeah, I heard of them. Why?"

"Any chance they're behind the church fires?"

"Of course there's a chance, but I don't have nothing to do with those idiots. Bunch of rednecks who never met a beer they didn't like. Is that why you came to see me? Trying to find out if I can lead you to Hunters United?"

"Can you?"

"What do you think, that people in this county don't know who you are? We know who the almighty Frasers are. We know all about how you used to be a big time police officer until you killed somebody. Nobody around here is going to say one word to you about anything other than money. You want to buy some timber? Then get out that fat wallet and start peeling off the hundred dollar bills. But other than that, you might as well talk to the outhouse." Lee cursed, straddled the ATV, and headed down the dirt road towards the gate.

Jacob shook his head and kicked the pickup's tire. How could he have failed again? Not only had Lee refused to give him any information, but Jacob had alienated him.

ও◦ও

Judith was standing in Beverly's kitchen, drying the last of the breakfast dishes, when she heard Henry Washington's booming voice.

"Hey there, Keneisha. How are you this fine morning?"

"Fine," the girl answered in an uncharacteristically timid voice.

Judith opened the front screen door. "Morning, Rev. Washington. Care to come in for a cup of coffee?"

"Morning, Miss Judith. So nice to see you looking well. How's that shoulder of yours?"

"Much better. Come on in."

Beverly bustled into the kitchen and joined Henry at the table. "Mornin', Brother Henry. So glad you could make time for a visit."

"Yes, Saturdays are the days I visit the sick. Thought it best if I came to see you first."

As Judith poured the coffee, she glanced through the kitchen window and grinned at the sight of Keneisha crouched behind an azalea bush. The girl might be shy around Henry, but she still wanted to know what was going on.

"I sure was sorry to hear about your barn," Henry said, "but thankful no one was hurt."

"The barn is no great loss," Judith said as she set cups of coffee on the table and sat between her friends. "But we need to talk about my grandfather's church."

Beverly and Henry exchanged a look, but waited for Judith to continue.

"I'm afraid for you and your congregation," Judith continued. "What if these people try to do more than damage property?"

"Do you want us to stop using Mr. Isaiah's church?" Henry asked.

"Heavens, no. In fact, I plan on attending your services."

Beverly laid a hand on Judith's arm. "You're always welcome, you know that. But it's time for you to think about your own safety. There's no doubt someone's trying to scare you off."

"That's true," Henry added. "A car wreck and a fire would make most people think twice."

"Don't tell me you want me to back down."

"Our new church building will be finished in about three months," Henry said. "That's a long time to fight this much hate."

"I don't care if it takes three years," Judith replied. "I won't let hate win. How could you even consider it?"

Henry blew out a long breath. "You know, Miss Judith, Sister Beverly and I know a lot more about fighting hate than you ever will. And one thing we've learned is that the only successful weapon against hate is love."

"Love your enemies and pray for those who harm you," Judith said. "That's probably the hardest demand the Lord makes of us."

"But a powerful one. When we pray for our enemies, we take back the strength they tried to steal from us. The people who burned our church believe fear will keep us down, but no matter how many times they destroy the building, they'll never destroy the love that binds us together."

Judith had never prayed for the man who'd killed her mother. Could she pray for him now? "What about you, Rev. Washington? Are you afraid?"

"I've been afraid plenty. But I remember the hundreds of times the Lord has walked beside me, lifting me up and holding me close when I needed comforting. It's easy to look back and see His hand guiding me towards the right path."

"I wish I could be more like you. I've been scared most of my life."

"You don't seem like it to me," Beverly said. "Nobody who's scared could live alone in Mr. Isaiah's cabin. Not to mention the way you kicked sand in the bully's face by loaning your church to us."

"Do you think the violence will get worse?"

"Probably so, Miss Judith," Henry answered in a grave tone. "No one will think less of you if you change your mind."

But Judith would think less of herself. "Several months ago, I asked the Lord to help me overcome my fears. I'll admit that part of me is afraid of what Dwight Thompson and others like him will do, but I'm trying to live by faith. If I give in to threats, if I take away my grandfather's church and run back to Dallas, I'd feel like I didn't trust the Lord to bring me through this."

Henry reached across the table and squeezed Judith's forearm. "I believe it's way past time for us to have a moment of silent prayer." He stretched his other hand towards Beverly and the two of them bowed their heads.

Judith closed her eyes and tried to quiet her mind. If only she was as stalwart as Henry and Beverly. They went about their lives with the threat of violence nipping at their heels, yet remained steadfast in their beliefs.

Judith wanted to believe she wouldn't run away or turn her back on those who needed her, but the temptation to capitulate to fear was always there.

14

With only one working hand, painting was an awkward endeavor. As Judith tried to capture the zeal in Henry's eyes, her mind was occupied with thoughts of Jacob. He'd been busy since the night of the barn fire, and she'd seen little of him. She missed his hugs and kisses. She longed to see his smile and the look of admiration in his eye when he gazed at her.

Pumpkin stretched lazily on the windowsill near the easel. Even her skittish kitten had learned to relax in its new home. But the sound of a car approaching the cabin caused Pumpkin's fur to rise.

Had Jacob arrived for an unexpected visit? Judith's heart leaped at the possibility. But it was an unfamiliar SUV that rounded the corner and pulled to a stop. Two ladies dressed in capri pants and flowered blouses got out of the car. They both wore large straw hats decorated with flowers and ribbon. One carried a camera, the other an oversized straw bag.

Were they lost, or had they driven twelve miles off the highway for a reason?

"Hello there," the taller of the women said with a friendly wave. "My name's Lily White and this is my sister, Rose."

That couldn't be the woman's real name, could it? Who would name their child Lily White? Judith glimpsed the wedding band on the woman's finger. She must've married a man named White. "Hello."

"Are you Judith Robertson?" the shorter woman asked.

"Yes. What can I do for you?"

The women smiled warmly and walked up the porch steps.

"We live in the neighboring county and we're members of the local historical society," Lily said. "We've heard you've got an old church on your property that was built by a local congregation."

Rose shielded her eyes and stepped closer to Judith. "Would it be possible for us to see the church and maybe take a few photos?"

Judith eyed the two women. They both had streaks of gray in their hair and wide, friendly smiles. There was absolutely nothing alarming about their appearance or their manner. So why did her stomach feel as though a miniature kangaroo were trying to escape? "I'm afraid you're mistaken, ladies. There is an old church nearby but it's hardly historical. It's only a few decades old and there's nothing architecturally interesting about the structure."

"Oh." Rose laid a hand on her chest and looked at her sister. "What do you think, Lily?"

"We'd still like to see the place," Lily answered. "We've driven so far and if you'll just point us in the right direction, we won't bother you any longer. You can go back to what you were doing, and we'll explore on our own."

Why were Judith's silent alarms ringing? It had to be her old fears, sounding their habitual warning. But she wouldn't let fear dictate her life any more. These two ladies were as threatening as two spring bunnies. "How did you hear about the church?"

"From our pastor," Rose answered. "He told us

about the terrible arsons that have been happening in this county and how one congregation was able to meet in an abandoned church building."

"That got our curiosity up," Lily continued. "If there's an old church we don't know about it may be an important historical site. So much history happened in this part of the state, and so little is known about it. We stopped at the diner on the highway, and the waitress told us how to find you."

Rose laid her hand on Judith's forearm. "Have we caught you at a bad time?"

"We can come back if you insist," Lily said, "but we do live an hour away."

Judith looked at the kind faces of the two sisters. She was over-reacting. She'd lived in fear for so long any stranger alarmed her, even two middle-aged church ladies. "It's all right. I'll show you where it is."

Judith stepped off the porch and walked to the side of the cabin. "The church is about a hundred yards down this path."

Rose followed Judith closely. "Oh, thank you. You don't know how much we appreciate this."

"My sister and I love the old places," Lily explained. "Our husbands don't understand, but we've always had a fascination with the past."

"Do you know when the church was built?" Rose asked.

"Not exactly," Judith called across her shoulder.

Lily lagged behind her sister. "Has the new congregation made any substantial changes in the structure?"

"No," Judith answered. "They cleaned it up and made some repairs, but it doesn't look much different than when I first saw it."

"Wonderful," Rose said. "That's exactly what we hoped to find."

Judith kept walking while the sisters chattered on about other places they'd discovered. There was nothing about the ladies' words or demeanor to cause the unease that continued to dart through her chest. Would she never be free from fear? Quieting her anxieties would drain her energy unless she learned to ignore their never-ending voices.

She stepped into the clearing where the church patiently waited for its congregation. "This is it, ladies."

Rose and Lily fell silent as they stood in front of the building. Lily raised her camera and began taking photos while Rose walked around the church. When the sisters met at the far end of the building, they put their heads together and talked in low voices. Then Rose walked to where Judith waited.

"May I see inside?" Rose asked. "Lily's going to take some more exterior photos, but I'd love to see how the congregation has fixed up this old place."

Judith watched Lily. The woman had turned her camera away from the church building and was snapping shots of the surrounding area. Why she needed those pictures puzzled Judith.

"Judith?" Rose repeated, "May I see the inside?"

"I guess so," Judith responded. She opened the door for the woman and stepped into the cool interior of the church.

"Isn't this lovely," Rose gushed. "So simple and yet so special." She walked to the altar, and then looked through the recently cleaned windows. "Such a beautiful setting for a church, tucked away in the forest like a secret hideaway. My sister and I are going to have to do some homework and find out more about this place."

The shrill ring of a cell phone disturbed the quiet of the empty church. Rose retrieved the phone from her straw bag. "Yes, Lily? OK, I'll be right out." She ended the call and looked at Judith. "Thank you so much for the tour. My sister says she's taken enough photos and that we'd best get back on the road."

Photos of the outside, but none of the inside?

"Doesn't your sister want any interior pictures?"

"What? Oh, I guess not." Rose seemed to be in a hurry to get back to her sister. She hustled out of the church as though the devil was at her heels.

Lily was waiting at the head of the trail that led back to the cabin. "Thank you for showing us the way," she said with a broad smile. "I think this old place is simply charming. Don't you, Rose?"

"Oh yes," the shorter sister answered. "We'll have to take the photos to our next meeting of the historical society and show them what we've discovered."

The sisters disappeared down the path, but Judith turned for one last look at the old church. Had she done the right thing? Lily and Rose were simply two nice ladies on a scouting expedition for their local historical society. So why did worry gnaw at the edges of Judith's consciousness?

❧

The next day, Jacob guided Judith through the wide doorway of his church and found the pews where the Frasers waited. The lot of them—brothers, sisters, husbands, wives and children—filled two rows. He stopped to kiss his mother and to give his father a masculine hug.

Emma Fraser pulled gently on Judith's arm, drawing her from Jacob. "Jacob told us about Isaiah's barn. Are you all right?"

"I'm fine."

"I've raised five children, Judith. I know when someone's not telling the whole truth."

Judith glanced at Jacob, saw he was conversing with his father, and turned back to Emma. "The fire was another warning."

"You believe someone is trying to keep you from helping Henry Washington."

"Isn't it obvious?"

"What do you plan to do?"

"Exactly what I've been doing. No way will I back away when so many people are counting on me."

"I'm sure Henry doesn't expect you to put yourself or your property in danger."

"That's almost exactly what he said when we talked yesterday. But it's my choice. These church burnings have to stop, even if it means letting my grandfather's church be a trap to catch the arsonists."

Hope beckoned to Judith. "Over here. I've been saving this spot for you."

"We'll talk later," Emma said.

Judith threaded her way through the tangle of feet and squeezed into the spot next to Jacob's sister.

"Chloe's so excited," Hope said. "If you sit by me, she'll be able to see you."

"What about me?" Jacob asked.

As if by unspoken consent, members of the Fraser family shifted until there was enough room for Jacob.

He wedged his wide shoulders between Judith and one of his brothers, and then rested one arm along the pew behind her back. "Where's your husband?" Jacob asked his sister.

"In the balcony with the video camera," Hope answered.

At the sound of organ music, the noisy crowd quieted and faced the altar, and, while she had a few moments to herself, Judith examined the large brick church. A wooden cross hung in the center of the far wall, just as in her grandfather's church, but this church had two pulpits; one on each side of an altar table. Stained glass angels with placid smiles watched over the congregation, as if bestowing a blessing to the worshippers below.

The organ music ended and children wearing red robes with large white collars formed two rows before the altar.

Excited parents and grandparents craned their necks to photograph or wave to their children-turned-celebrities.

"There's Chloe. Can you see her?" Hope grabbed Judith's arm and pointed.

The girl stood at the end of the first row, beaming at the congregation. When she spied the Frasers, her enthusiasm could not be bridled. "Hi, Mom! Hi, Grandma!"

The congregation chuckled in unison, but the choir director gently scolded Chloe. Piano music signaled the beginning of the children's song, and Chloe dutifully shifted her attention.

The children sang, but Judith felt a niggling anxiety at the base of her neck. She glanced around, trying to determine what could possibly cause such apprehension in a church.

Dwight Thompson's gaze was boring straight into

her. Anger and disgust radiated from his face. The menacing look he sent Judith may have been intended to scare her, but it had the opposite effect.

She smiled in return, an action she was certain would rile him even more. Judith glanced at Jacob, hoping he hadn't noticed Dwight's threat.

Jacob only had eyes for his niece.

When the children finished their song, Chloe skipped down the center aisle and wriggled onto her mother's lap. "Did you like it, Judith? Was it good?"

"Couldn't have been better," Judith replied.

Chloe climbed over Judith to find her grandparents while the congregation stood to sing.

Dwight was no longer in the crowd. He was pulling a thin, pale woman through the exit door.

Jacob smiled down at her and pointed to a line of music in the open hymnal.

Judith shifted her attention to the song, putting Dwight and his hostile stare out of her mind for the time being. No matter how edgy she felt around Dwight, she'd never let him know it.

❧❧

After the clamor of the Fraser's Sunday dinner had subsided, Judith sat beside Chloe at the kitchen table, making plans for birthday party decorations.

"Banners would be nice," Judith suggested. "With dragons on either side to hold them up. We could fasten them to the fence."

"What about flags?" Chloe asked. "We could put a different dragon on each flag."

"Where would we hang flags?"

"From the tree branches."

"Oh, I see. That would look great. We could also make tablecloths. They're easy to make out of paper."

Jacob walked into the kitchen and placed a dirty plate in the sink.

"What about napkins?" Chloe asked.

"Painting individual napkins would take a long time," Judith answered. "What do you think about one big centerpiece instead? We could make a 3-D dragon."

"With fire coming out of its mouth?"

"Yellow and orange tissue paper that would look like fire, but not real fire. Not with all that paper."

"What about smoke?"

"Oh, like a fog machine. That might be possible. What a good idea!"

Chloe jumped out of her chair and bounced on her toes. "This is going to be the best party ever!" She dashed out of the room calling for her mother.

Jacob chuckled and sat in Chloe's empty chair. "No wonder Chloe's crazy about you. Sure you're not doing too much?"

"They're just decorations. Besides, it'll be fun."

Jacob slid a hand across her shoulders and pulled her into a one-arm hug. "Chloe's not the only person in this family who's crazy about you."

Judith's cheeks warmed. "Your mother's been unbelievably nice. She treats me like one of the family."

"I wasn't talking about my mother."

"You weren't?"

"It's not my mother who thinks about you night and day, and it's not Chloe who wants to kiss you right now."

Judith lifted her mouth to his. "Someone wants to kiss me?"

Jacob leaned forward. "I think you like my kisses,"

he said, his warm breath tickling her lips.

Judith kissed him, reveling in the softness of his mouth and the secure hold of his arms. She'd never have found Jacob if she hadn't scraped together enough courage to stay in her grandfather's cabin. In his arms, she found love and acceptance, approval and desire. He'd chosen her above all other women, an honor that thrilled her soul. And her heart had chosen him, too.

Jacob leaned back from the kiss and caressed her cheek with the backs of his fingers. "I don't know what I'd do if anything happened to you. Are you sure you're all right out there by yourself?"

"Of course. By the way, I saw Dwight Thompson at church this morning."

"Yeah. His family's been members as long as we have."

"You and Dwight grew up together?"

"He's a few years older than I am. We never went to the same school at the same time."

"Do you think he's capable of burning a church?"

"I don't know. But I do know that until the sheriff can get enough evidence, no one will be arrested."

"Two ladies came by yesterday. They wanted to take pictures of the church for their historical society. The whole time they were there, I kept thinking about how they were photographing something that might not survive."

Jacob frowned. "You were alone?"

"It was nothing to worry about. Just two ladies who wanted to take some photos."

"Still, you shouldn't have been by yourself."

"There's no one nearby except Beverly and Keneisha, and I've already put them in enough danger."

"The truck accident wasn't your fault, Judith. Beverly knows what she's risking."

"I realized that I'd put the church in danger by allowing it to lure the arsonists, but I never thought I'd jeopardize Beverly and Keneisha."

"Do you think Beverly might stay with one of her sons in town until this blows over?"

"I don't know. Why do you think it's necessary?"

He stood and walked to the nearby window, as though he was scouting for enemies in his parents' back yard. "A few days ago, Dwight came by the building supply. We were talking about the fires and Dwight said the arsonists might not stop at burning empty buildings."

"He threatened to hurt Beverly? Or Henry? Surely the sheriff could do something about that."

"He wasn't so blatant. But it did make me think. We've been assuming the church would be burned, but until someone ran you off the road, I never thought you or Beverly could be hurt."

"Jacob, if Beverly and Keneisha are in danger, I'll close up the church. Henry's group can meet somewhere else or wait until their new building is finished. I won't be any part of allowing a child to be injured."

"What do you think Beverly would say?"

"I don't know. She knows I was run off the road on purpose, yet she still lets me spend the night at her house. Seems to me as though she's willing to take the risk." Judith covered her face with her hand and moaned. "Oh Jacob, it would break my heart to leave Piney Meadow now, but maybe it would be for the best if I did."

"You'd leave? For how long?"

"Until the danger's over."

"That kind of danger's never over." Jacob returned to his seat and took Judith's hand. "Do you want to leave?"

"No, but if my presence is endangering Beverly or Keneisha…"

"I'll talk to Beverly when I take you home. For now, I think we should pray about it."

Despite the tension, Judith smiled when she bowed her head. The first thing she'd say in prayer was thanks that the Lord had sent her a man of faith.

❧

A few days later, Beverly surveyed the ingredients Judith had piled on the small kitchen table. "You're sure you want to make chicken and dumplings in your kitchen? Be a lot easier if we did it in mine."

"I need to learn how to use this stove," Judith answered, "and you said my grandfather had everything we'd need."

"That's true. I just feel better in my own kitchen, that's all." Beverly searched through a drawer and passed a knife to Judith. "OK, first step, wash those chicken breasts and cut 'em into small pieces."

Judith cut the chicken as Beverly instructed. "Have you thought any more about staying with your son?"

"I've thought about it, but I'm not going to do it. Keneisha and I will be fine in our little house. I know what it's like to let fear get out of hand, and I'm not about to hide every time somebody says something mean."

"Those men who ran me off the road were after

me, not you. If something happened to either you or Keneisha because of me, I couldn't live with it."

"Oh Judith, you'd be surprised what a person can live with. But you're worrying for nothing. We all know there's a chance your grandfather's church will end up in ashes, but you're in a lot more danger than I am. Now tell me what's been going on with you and Jacob. You two sure have been spending a lot of time together."

"You wouldn't be trying to change the subject would you?"

Beverly grinned broadly. "I've seen the way you look at Jacob when he's not looking, and I've seen the way he looks at you. Doesn't take a psychic to see what's going on. Just when did you fall in love with him?"

Judith's throat tightened at the word. She'd barely admitted her love for Jacob to herself. How did Beverly know?

"That's what I thought," Beverly said, her smile broadening. "Besides, I don't hear you denying it. You love that man, don't you?"

Yes, she loved Jacob. Loved him so much she wanted what was best for him. "After my mother died, I gradually became a prisoner in my own house because I was afraid of everyone and everything. But falling in love with Jacob is one of the scariest things I've ever faced."

"Why's that?"

"If I lost Jacob, or if he changed his mind about me…Oh, Beverly, I don't know what I'd do, then."

"You'd find a way to go on. That's the way life is. People circle in and out of our lives. Some stay longer than others. But there's only one unwavering love."

"Our Father's love."

"You got that right. Now, chop up the celery and onion. And after I peel those carrots, you can chop them up, too."

Judith returned to the cutting board and began to peel and slice the vegetables. She and Beverly worked in silence for several long minutes while Beverly's last challenge bounced through Judith's head. In a way, living her whittled-down version of life had been easier than loving. Easier, but not as fulfilling. And if she was ever going to follow God's will for her life, it was obvious she'd have to continue finding courage.

Beverly passed a peeled carrot to Judith. "Has Jacob mentioned marriage yet?"

Judith's knife clattered on the kitchen floor.

Beverly cackled with laughter. "I see that he has. What did you say?"

Judith picked up the knife and washed it. "He didn't...I mean, he hasn't..."

"My heavens, Judith. Getting information out of you is like trying to get crabgrass out of a patch of lettuce. Am I going to have to find some pliers?"

"Jacob said he wanted to court me, but he didn't propose."

"Uh-huh. But when he gets around to it, you're going to say yes, aren't you?" When Judith didn't immediately answer, Beverly nudged her with a hip. "Aren't you?"

"I don't know. Probably."

"Probably?" The look on Beverly's face clearly communicated her disbelief. "The Lord doesn't make a man any better than Jacob Fraser. Why in the world wouldn't you jump at the chance to marry him?"

"I don't know. I wish this mess with the church

and the hate groups was over. Then I could concentrate on just one thing at a time."

"It'll pass. That's another thing you can count on. Now put the chicken and the celery and onion in that pot with some butter and cook it 'til the chicken turns brown."

Judith moved the ingredients around the bottom of the pot with a long-handled wooden spoon. "Do you think that finding Jacob is part of God's will for my life?"

Beverly turned down the heat under the pot. "Nobody can answer that question except you. What do you think?"

"I'm afraid I'll let him down. Sometimes I think it'd be best if I went back to Dallas, just for a while. Rev. Washington could continue building his new church and Dwight Thompson's hate group would probably back off."

"You know, Miss Judith, I've read my Bible from cover to cover many times, and never once did I see a promise that our lives would be free of strife. You told me you prayed for courage. Well, how do you think you'll get more courage if you don't have times to exercise it?"

"You think courage is like a muscle?"

"Everything in life gets easier the more you do it. You can go on back to Dallas if you want, but that's not going to stop the kind of hate that leads people to burn churches."

"Do you think the sheriff or the FBI will catch the arsonists?"

"Probably. But, Judith, the only thing that stops hate is love. You've got so much love in you it leaks out around the edges. I know one thing for sure, if you don't say yes to Jacob, you'll be grieving for the rest of your days."

Judith knew about living with grief, the way it lodged itself in a dark corner of her heart and refused to leave. "That's some choice you've given me. Marry Jacob and run the risk of letting him down, or don't marry Jacob and grieve for the rest of my days."

"Doesn't seem like too hard a decision to me."

"I'd never want to hurt Jacob."

"And you think that running off to Dallas wouldn't hurt him?"

"Not as much as marrying me and then finding out I can't fit into his life."

"You can't fit into his life or you're scared to try? My word, Judith, you're holding on to this idea so tight, you can't see you're choking yourself."

She wanted to argue, to say just the right thing to make Beverly understand her reasons for hesitating, but it was difficult to quarrel when she knew Beverly was right. The only person stopping her from accepting a life with Jacob was herself.

"Well, enough of this for now," Beverly said, signaling the end of the argument. "Get me some eggs, butter and milk from the refrigerator and I'll show you how to make the dumplings."

Judith fetched the items and watched Beverly mix them with flour. There was only one choice Judith could live with. She'd go forward, trusting in God's plan. But it'd be easier if she had the kind of rock-solid faith Henry and Beverly possessed.

15

The humid summer air pressed close as Jacob drove to the sheriff's office that afternoon. He hadn't heard from the sheriff or Mark Grey since the barn fire, and it was time to get caught up with the investigation.

The men he'd come to see were gathered around a conference table covered with maps and photos. He exchanged greetings and handshakes.

"I don't have to ask what brings you by," Sheriff Miller said. "You want to know if we found anything at the barn."

"And if that threatening note gave you any leads."

Mark poured coffee into a white foam cup and handed it to Jacob. "We didn't find any prints on the paper and the lab is still working on the soil samples we sent in. But the black smoke tells us it was gasoline. That's been the most common accelerant used in the church arsons."

"So you think it's the same people?"

"Maybe. You know how hard it is to build a case based on maybes. What we really need are some eyewitnesses who won't be afraid to testify."

Special Agent Lawson nodded to the maps. "The arsons have all been in a three-county area. That narrows our focus to the hate groups that have home bases nearby."

Jacob sipped the hot, black coffee. "Any more on that group you told me about? Hunters United?"

"No, but they're up to something." Lawson opened a folder and handed a pamphlet to Jacob. "Seems as though Hunters United is proud of their accomplishments. We found these at a bar in Sabine County. As you can see, they have photos of the churches on fire."

Pain darted through Jacob's head as he remembered his futile attempt at getting information from Lee Buchanan. The FBI had managed what he couldn't. "There aren't any firefighters or firefighting equipment in the photos. Could be the arsonists took the pictures before we got there."

"That's what we're thinking," Mark confirmed.

"I've been reviewing the video from the cameras we set up at the Beecham place," Lawson continued. "There's nothing out-of-place except two ladies who visited the church. One of them took some photos and the other went in."

"I need to talk to Miss Robertson about it," Mark said. "She was with the ladies."

"Yeah, Judith told me about them," Jacob said. "They were from some local historical society and they wanted to see the old church."

"Nothing special about that old building." Mark looked at the sheriff. "It doesn't have any historical significance, does it?"

"Not that I know of," Sheriff Miller answered. "It was built about forty years ago. Hardly historical."

Jacob ran his thumb around the rim of his cup. "Have you talked to the ministers of any other African-American congregations?"

"Yes," Mark answered. "Some of them have agreed to meet in other locations until we find the arsonists, but most of them are determined to go on with services as they've always done."

"Any plans to put cameras on those churches?" Jacob asked.

"Already done," Lawson answered. "I review the video as I can, but, like I said, so far nothing's been out of the ordinary."

"So where do we stand?"

"You know how it is, Jacob," Sheriff Miller said. "We gather evidence and wait."

"Lawson and I are here for the long run," Mark added. "The head of our district office has ordered us to stay until we gather enough evidence to make some arrests."

"Do any of you think Judith is in danger?"

"Not any more than she was before," Sheriff Miller answered. "We know the arsons always happen at night and, so far, there's only been property damage."

"But Judith has decided to let Henry Washington's group meet in her grandfather's church despite the destruction of her barn," Jacob said. "Someone wrote 'the next fire will be closer to home'. I think that means Isaiah Beecham's church. Do you agree?"

"It's possible," Mark said. "Miss Robertson's not sleeping out there by herself, is she?"

"No, she's staying with her closest neighbor." Jacob studied the serious faces of the men. "So we just wait for the arsonists to make their next move."

"Unless we get a break on the identity of the members of Hunters United," Lawson said. "We could always bring them in for questioning, but usually the members provide alibis for each other."

"Maybe we'll get lucky with the videos," Sheriff Miller said.

"Or maybe we'll get really lucky and find a

witness," Mark added.

Jacob said his good-byes and headed back to Piney Meadow. He'd found little comfort at the sheriff's office. It was impossible to build a case with so little evidence, but waiting for the arsonists to make a mistake was like waiting for the guillotine to fall.

A few years earlier, his hesitation had caused the death of an innocent hostage. The night replayed in his mind as he drove along the winding highway. He could still see the terror in the teenager's eyes. He remembered with startling clarity how the boy's knees had buckled as his body slumped to the ground. He could still hear the boy's father wailing over his son's limp body.

One second. If Jacob had fired just one second earlier, the boy would still be alive. He'd be in college or dating the girl of his dreams. But one second's hesitation had taken away the boy's future and given his parents a lifetime of grief.

If the sheriff and the FBI needed a witness, he'd provide one. Jacob wouldn't hesitate again.

❦

Jacob grinned at Chloe.

She squirmed with excitement as he drove her to Judith's cabin. She chattered away about birthday cake, presents, and dragons while Jacob thought of just one thing.

Judith.

It seemed as though the Lord was trying to open Jacob's eyes to how life with Judith would be. She was infinitely patient with Keneisha and Chloe, and no one could doubt her courage, but something was holding her back. She took one guarded step at a time, as though testing for hidden traps behind every embrace. Yet every time he kissed her, he felt the rightness of it. Kissing Judith was like a prayer, hopeful and exciting and reassuring at the same time.

As soon as he stopped his truck, Chloe jumped out and ran through the front door. Her squeals of laughter rang through the summer afternoon and Jacob entered to see his niece's arms wrapped around Judith's waist.

"Where's your sling?" he asked Judith.

"Good afternoon to you, too."

She raised her face and Jacob gave her a quick kiss in greeting.

"How are you feeling?"

"Fine. And, to answer your question, I don't need the sling any more. The doctor said I just have to be careful about how I move my shoulder."

"Can we paint now?" Chloe asked.

"You bet. But Keneisha wants to help. Is that OK with you?"

"Can I get her?" Chloe bounced on her toes, unable to contain her excitement. "Can I, Jacob? Can I run and get Keneisha?"

"Sure," he answered, but the word had barely left his mouth before Chloe sped away.

Judith laughed as Jacob gathered her close. "Does your shoulder hurt when I squeeze you like this?"

"No. It doesn't hurt when you kiss me, either."

Jacob knew a hint when he heard one. She sighed when their lips touched and he pulled her even closer. Within a few seconds, he felt his body responding to her nearness and ended the kiss. Some things should wait until they'd committed themselves in marriage. "I sure hope you don't want a long engagement, Judith."

"There you go again. Talking about a wedding like I've agreed to something. I don't remember being asked."

"Oh, I'll get around to asking. Once things have calmed down around here and I've had time to shop for a ring."

She laid her head on his shoulder. "When things calm down? When will that be?"

Jacob didn't have an answer. He knew once Henry's congregation was back in its own church, Judith would stop being a target. Maybe then, she could worry about wedding plans rather than potential arson.

Judith met his gaze. "If the sheriff can't arrest the arsonists, how will the hate crimes ever be stopped?"

Jacob eased her head back onto his shoulder, liking the way she fit so perfectly there. "No matter what happens, the arsonists won't win. They can't stop Henry Washington's congregation and they can't stop the good people in Piney Meadow from helping. I had a talk with the sheriff and the FBI this morning."

Judith looked Jacob in the eye.

"They think your grandfather's church is the next target," he continued.

"I told Henry and Beverly the same thing."

"And we know the fires are always started at night. So," he said, "I've decided to spend the night here for as long as it takes."

"You wouldn't do anything foolish, would you? Like try to catch the bad guys and maybe get hurt?"

Jacob laid his palm on her cheek. "Worried about me?"

A whisper of a grin crossed her mouth. "Who says I'm worried?"

"We can have dinner and breakfast together every day," he said, wrapping his arm around her waist and pulling her close for another kiss.

"Oh?" she asked, with a twinkle in her eye. "You cook?"

"If you marry me for my cooking, you'll be disappointed."

"If I agree to marry you, it'll be for your kisses, not your cooking."

Kisses. There was no doubt Judith liked his kisses. Jacob covered her lips with his, treasuring the way she settled into his embrace.

The sound of giggles broke them apart. One pair of blue eyes and one pair of brown eyes gazed at them in curious wonder.

Jacob froze, searching for an explanation, but Judith appeared unruffled.

With a quick squeeze to his hand, she stepped towards Keneisha and Chloe. "Who's ready to paint?"

❧

Beverly rubbed her daughter's freshly washed body with a towel. "From all the red and yellow paint, I'd say you had a good time today."

Keneisha yawned noisily and nodded.

"Don't worry," Judith said from her place by the sink. "I made sure to buy washable paint. It'll come off her clothes easily."

A soft knock at the front door caused Beverly to frown. "Who in the world could that be? Too late for visitors."

"It's probably Jacob," Judith answered. "Remember? I told you he'd be staying at the cabin."

She struggled not to run as she went to answer the knock. Her heart beat a little faster at the sight of him on Beverly's step. She'd watched him drive away only a few hours earlier, but his smiling face warmed Judith's heart. "Hey, you. What's up?"

"I've got a blanket in the truck that's just big enough for two. I thought you might be interested in some moon gazing."

Judith sighed and imagined melting at his feet, but caught herself before her knees gave out.

"Who is it?" Beverly's concerned voice burst through Judith's fantasy.

"Just me," Jacob said as he stepped inside. "Came to see if I could talk Judith into a walk."

Beverly gazed from Jacob to Judith. "I don't imagine it will take too much persuasion."

"I want to go for a walk," Keneisha said around a wide yawn.

"Oh no," Beverly said with a chuckle. "The only walk you're going on is from the kitchen to the bedroom. You know the way."

"Night, Judith," Keneisha called over her shoulder.

"See you in the morning," Judith answered.

Alone in the brightly lit kitchen, Jacob reached for Judith's hand. "How about it?"

She slipped her hand into his, felt his strength as he tightened his grip, and followed him outside.

As they stepped away from Beverly's house, the summer night enclosed them in a veil of privacy. Jacob retrieved the promised blanket and led Judith into the moonlit forest.

The woods were alive with sound. Crickets and toads sang their timeless melodies while melancholy owls called to each other across treetops.

Jacob led Judith along the silvered pathway.

Her eyes drank in the wonders of moon shadows and spider webs that glowed like luminous lace. Just beyond the illuminated path, nocturnal beings watched with curiosity or caution, but Jacob's hand was strong, his step confident, and Judith followed willingly.

As the pathway narrowed, they stepped out of the dense forest and into a grassy meadow.

Jacob let go of Judith's hand long enough to spread the blanket, and then sat on the soft cloth.

Judith dropped beside him.

"I never knew the moon could be so bright," Judith said.

"Do you know where you are?" Jacob murmured close to her ear.

"Is this the same meadow you showed me before? Where the orchids grow?"

"That's right. We're not far from your cabin."

Judith took in a deep breath and let it out slowly. "I'll never sell this land. My grandfather wanted me to have it and I want to be a good steward."

"To tell you the truth, leasing your land to Fraser Lumber is the answer to one of my prayers."

"How?"

"I won't lie to you, Judith. Bringing in new business is part of my job and I'd hit a dry spell. If I hadn't gotten your property, we'd have been in a bind."

"You should have told me."

"Didn't want to influence you. Plus, some land west of San Augustine has just become available. I have a good chance of getting that. Besides, business decisions should be made with a cool head, not one that's woozy from kissing."

"What makes you think I get woozy?"

"I don't know if it was your glazed eyes or your rapid breathing that gave me the first clue."

"Hmph. You wanted to buy my grandfather's land before you knew I existed. Have you changed your mind?"

"Everything's changed since I met you. There I was, happily going about my work, never knowing you were headed my way. Isaiah gave me much more than a few acres of timber. He gave me you."

Judith's heart quivered with the sweetness of his words. Had anyone ever cherished her the way he did? She touched his cheek with the tips of her fingers and gazed into his eyes. Even in the moonlight, she recognized the sincerity of his words.

Jacob stretched out on the blanket, one hand behind his head, his face towards the full moon.

Judith rolled on her stomach next to him.

"Look," he said, pointing towards the sky. "Can you see the man in the moon?"

Judith flipped over and nestled her head on his shoulder. "No. I've never been able to make out a face. Can you?"

"Not really. When I was a kid, I used to imagine a giant bird. What about you?"

"A woman in an evening dress, stepping out for the night."

"You'll have to draw that for me. No matter how I squint, I can't see a woman."

His lips found hers in the moonlight. The butterfly-wing softness of his kiss drew an ache of longing from her heart. For a moment, all Judith's doubts were eased. Of course she'd marry this man. She wanted to belong to him, to entrust her life and her heart to no one but him.

"I'm thinking about a September wedding," he whispered and kissed her again.

The nearness of Jacob's body, the promise of more kisses, and the enchantment of the moonlit night sheltered her from the misgivings that had troubled her. She could have love with Jacob. A home, a family, and a blessed life were hers for the taking.

⨞⨞

Judith stepped into her cabin the next morning to the smell of fresh coffee and the sound of the shower running. Jacob certainly was making himself at home.

Beverly had sent muffins, and Judith set the foil-wrapped goodies on the kitchen counter before sitting at her work table.

The bathroom door opened and Jacob stepped out wearing a towel around his waist.

Judith took in the sight of his broad shoulders and muscular arms, the light hair that covered his chest.

He was rubbing his head briskly with another towel, but he froze when he saw Judith. "When did you get here?"

"Five minutes ago. Something wrong?"

"Next time, let me know when you come in. I might've walked out completely naked."

An unbidden image formed in Judith's mind and her face grew warm. "It's my cabin, you know."

But Jacob wasn't interested in arguing. He sauntered over to her work table and looked over her shoulder. "I looked at your sketches last night. I can't wait to see how this picture will turn out. By the way, I love that portrait of Henry."

He was too close. The scent of his soap and the way his skin glistened in the sunlight had her heart bouncing. "Don't you need to go to work?"

"Brought my work with me. I'm about a month behind in my paperwork and my brother's been on my case. Thought this would be as good a time as any to get it done. Have you had breakfast?"

"Yes, and you're dripping on my canvas."

"Am not." Jacob braced one arm on the back of Judith's chair and the other on her work table, lowering his face parallel to hers. "What did Beverly fix for breakfast?"

Judith closed her eyes to shut out the sight of his bristly cheek so close to hers. "Eggs and bacon. Why don't you walk over there and ask her to fix you something?"

"You're not trying to get me out of your way, are you?" Jacob asked, his mouth so close she could feel his breath on her ear.

"I've got work to do."

"And I'm distracting you?"

Was he ever.

His low chuckle let her know that he knew exactly what kind of effect he was having. "Are you warm, Judith? Your face is mighty pink."

"That's it," she said as she stood. "Get some clothes on right now, mister."

He made a playful grab in her direction but she sidestepped his reach. "Mess with me and I won't give you the muffins Beverly sent."

Jacob perched his hands on his hips, centering Judith's attention once again on the towel that protected whatever modesty he had. "Did she make the ones with the chocolate chips?"

"No more information until you're wearing clothes."

"All right," he said. "I'll get dressed."

Jacob's smile was playful and confident. He gave her a quick kiss and walked into the bedroom.

Judith blew out a long, unsteady breath. She was either going to have to marry that man or move far away. The temptation alone would kill her.

❧

Jacob was still grinning as he sat at the small kitchen table looking over the unfinished reports. It may have been wrong to tease Judith the way he had, but he'd always been in control. She'd always be safe with him. He would do everything in his power to make sure of it.

She'd been working steadily for several hours, her concentration so fully on the canvas that she didn't seem to be aware of him, or of Pumpkin who dozed on the nearby windowsill.

He'd never seen anyone work with such intensity, frowning over the painting, grimacing with dissatisfaction or nodding her approval.

She'd downplayed her talent earlier, referring to herself as an illustrator rather than an artist, but the difference was insignificant in his eyes. If Judith wasn't an artist, then no one was.

He wondered if their children would inherit her talent, then smiled widely at the thought of children. He was blond, she dark-haired. His hair was straight, hers a mass of beautiful curls. She could draw whatever she saw, he could barely sketch a legible map. Their children would probably be a mixture of looks and talents.

He pictured Judith holding a baby, himself at her side, while they stood in front of the congregation to christen their child.

Maybe it was time to buy that ring he'd promised. Last night she'd lowered whatever roadblocks she had around her heart. She'd been receptive and playful, full of love and good humor. Yes, she would marry him, live in Piney Meadow, and they'd have beautiful, healthy children. Children who would be raised in love and security.

16

On Saturday morning, Jacob frowned over the pile of boxes and bags that overflowed with decorations. "You know, you're only decorating my parents' back yard. Seems to me you've got enough here for three parties."

"I may have gotten a little carried away, but Chloe's worth it."

"I think you're a bit sweet on my niece."

"I think you're right." Judith turned towards the cabin and called over her shoulder. "I just have to get Chloe's gift and I'll be ready to go."

Jacob watched her bound onto the porch and grinned. The past week had been like a chaste honeymoon. Breakfast and morning kisses, followed by good-bye kisses as he left for work. Then a welcome home kiss in the evening and dinner together every night. It was a routine he could gladly become accustomed to.

With a bang of the screen door, Judith jumped off the front porch and joined Jacob at his truck. Holding up the present as if making an offering, she smiled up at him. "Think Chloe will like everything?"

"Chloe is crazy about you. She'd like rotten crawfish if it came from you."

Judith scrunched her nose. "I don't believe that's true."

Jacob slid his calloused hands against Judith's

smooth cheeks and lowered his mouth to hers for the briefest of kisses. "I'm glad to go to Chloe's birthday party," he whispered and kissed her again. "And I'm glad you're coming to share it with me." Another soft kiss. "But being out here alone with you has been…"

Judith gave the tiniest of nods. "Me, too."

Jacob wrapped his arms around her and nestled her head against his shoulder. "Being with you feels like finding my way home on a cold night. Do you feel that way, too?"

She rose to her toes and kissed his cheek. "We'd better get going. I've got a lot to do before the party starts."

Another roadblock. Jacob knew Judith was the woman meant for him, but why God had made her so stubborn was a question he'd never be able to answer. "OK, OK. I know a brush-off when I hear one." Jacob freed her from his embrace and opened the passenger door. "But," he continued, bracing his arm against the doorway to block her entry, "don't think this conversation is over."

᠀᠆᠀

Chloe's birthday party was a blur of laughter, hugs, barbecue, screaming children, and dragons. Jacob's mother declared the paper tablecloths "too pretty to ruin" and taped them beside the banners on the wooden fence surrounding the back yard.

More than once, Judith tried to find a quiet spot away from the crowd, but Chloe and Keneisha kept pulling her back into the midst of the celebration, introducing Judith to the other children and showing them Judith's art work. Whenever the crush of people threatened to overwhelm her, Judith would look for Jacob.

Without fail, he'd grin and wink, sending his love and support over the heads of the children who surrounded her.

If Judith married Jacob, as he seemed so determined to do, family gatherings like this one would be common. Their own children would celebrate birthdays in their grandparents' back yard.

Their own children.

Judith took in a deep breath and blew it out, struggling to calm the fluttering in her stomach. No doubt, Jacob would be a wonderful father. Anyone who saw him with his nieces and nephews would award him that distinction.

Joy passed through her body at the thought of uniting her future with Jacob's. This was where the Lord had led her. She'd prayed for the courage to escape the shackles of fear. God had brought her to Piney Meadow. She'd yet to overcome the doubts that plagued her, but if she held true, if she stayed the course God had set for her, surely everything would be all right.

If only she could be sure.

When the party finally wound down, Judith scuttled into the kitchen to help with the cleanup.

Hope was right behind her. "Oh, Judith. How can I ever thank you for helping today?" Hope asked. "Did you see how happy my little girl was?"

Judith ran water into the sink and began to rinse off a large platter. "She's eight years old now. Not so little."

Hope took the platter and placed it in the dishwasher. "You're right. But part of me wants to keep her young. Keep her safe at home."

Jacob came in, carrying the remains of the birthday cake. "Need any help?"

"Not in here," Hope answered. "But if you could get Chloe to calm down, that would be great."

Jacob stepped behind Judith, laid his hands on her shoulders, and kissed the top of her head. "You doing OK?"

Judith flicked water from the sink towards his face. "Sure."

Jacob smiled, squeezed her shoulders, and left the kitchen.

Hope bumped Judith's hip with hers. "I'm so glad you came to Piney Meadow, Judith. And I'm not talking about your ability to make party decorations."

Hope was talking about Jacob, but Judith wasn't ready to share the quiet joy that warmed her heart whenever she thought about a future with him. "Chloe's such a special little girl. Her imagination is limitless."

"True, but I was talking about my baby brother. Ever since he came back from Houston, he's been restless, like he's searching for something he just can't find."

"Jacob told me about what happened."

"He still blames himself for the death of that hostage. I guess he always will."

"Do you think he misses being a police officer?"

"He says no. He wanted to try his wings, to prove to himself and to us that he could make it on his own. He never talks about returning to law enforcement, but I think he misses it." Hope handed Judith another dirty dish. "But now that you're here, he's got his mind on just one thing. You, Miss Judith Robertson. You."

"I'm sure he thinks about other things. Work, for example."

"Oh, work is work. Has he proposed yet?"

Judith dropped the cup she was holding, splashing suds onto her face.

Hope laughed and wiped Judith's cheek. "Now that was an interesting reaction."

Judith used the back of her wrist to push a stray curl away from her face. "Doesn't anybody in this town mind their own business?"

"All right, Judith, I'll stop talking about your love life. But I'm just saying that if you became part of this family, I wouldn't mind one little bit. Now, where did my husband get to?" Hope started the dishwasher and stepped outside.

Judith finished tidying the kitchen. As she worked, Judith wondered what it would be like if she became part of the Fraser family. She'd have to leave her father, but he'd be retiring from the bank in a few years. Perhaps he'd move closer once he no longer worked five days a week.

A family of her own was one of the many things she'd given up when she'd yielded to fear, yet the Frasers were a large, boisterous, and loving clan.

Judith went in search of Jacob. She found him stretched out on the floor of the den watching one of the videos Chloe had received as a present. The birthday girl snuggled next to him, her head resting on his stomach and the stuffed dragon Judith had bought her clutched in her arms. A movie princess sang merrily about finding her one true love.

Stepping closer, Judith realized that both uncle and niece were sound asleep. She hated to wake them, so she curled up on the couch to watch the movie.

Hope entered a few minutes later, smiled at the sleeping pair, and bent to wake her daughter.

The motion woke Jacob instead. "What? I got her. She's OK," he said sleepily.

"Time to take the birthday girl home," Hope answered.

Jacob eased away from Chloe, then stood and stretched. "I'll put her in the car." He effortlessly hoisted the sleeping child. Cradling his niece in his arms, he left the room with Hope tagging along behind him.

Judith's heart tripped and fell at the sight of Jacob's gentle strength. How in the world had she caught the attention of a man such as Jacob? And why couldn't she accept what he offered without misgivings?

ॐॐ

It was twilight by the time Jacob and Judith headed back to the cabin.

Something was on her mind and the uneasy feeling in Jacob's gut told him he wasn't going to like it. But he'd never been one to put off a problem until tomorrow if it could be solved today. No sooner had they arrived at the cabin than Jacob had Judith's hand, leading her to the rocking chairs on the front porch.

Judith eased into the other chair and covered her yawn with her free hand. "It's been so peaceful this week, I'm beginning to think Dwight Thompson has changed his mind."

That would be an answer to many prayers, but Jacob didn't think this awful business was finished. "Thanks again for helping with Chloe's party."

"I enjoyed it."

Jacob raised an eyebrow in disbelief.

"OK, OK," Judith said with a chuckle. "I enjoyed most of it."

Jacob's heart tightened, but he plunged ahead with the question. "Think you'll ever get used to my family?"

Judith withdrew her hand and crossed her arms, but didn't respond. After several long seconds, she rose from the chair and leaned against the porch railing, her back to Jacob. "I want to get used to your family," she said in a small voice. "When I was a girl, my father used to take me downtown to see the Christmas decorations in the store windows. My favorites were the miniature cities. I wanted to shrink myself and live in those wonderlands where everyone was happy and feathery snow fell outside my window. Sometimes I feel that way about your family."

"You want to be part of them?"

"Yes, but, at the same time, it feels as impossible as that old Christmas wish."

"It's not impossible, Judith. All you've got to do is say yes."

Judith raked a hand through her hair, pulling her curls behind her head. "Every time I think about what you're offering, every time I catch myself yearning to return to my sheltered life in Dallas, I hear one phrase repeated over and over. 'Be of good courage'. There are so many places where that phrase appears in the Bible. 'Be of good courage'. I've discovered that having courage doesn't mean the absence of fear. It means doing something even though you're afraid."

"What are you afraid of, Judith?"

Judith turned to face him. "Are you kidding me?

I'm afraid of the violence that's hanging over my head like a pendulum on a thread. I'm afraid of Beverly or Keneisha being hurt because of me. I'm afraid of disappointing you."

"How could you disappoint me?"

"By not living up to what you want from me. I want to believe that I have the kind of courage it takes to be a good wife and mother, but what if I don't? You wouldn't believe how noisy it is inside my head. The voices of doubt keep up a constant chatter. Then I hear, 'Be of good courage.'" Judith let out a noisy sigh. "It's exhausting."

Jacob rose to stand beside her. "I know how to get the voices of doubt to shut up."

"Please tell me."

"Remind them that you've always had courage."

"Well, that's not quite true."

"I think it is. I know the trauma of your mother's death made you doubt your bravery, but a person who's ruled by fear wouldn't risk violence just so a congregation could have a place to worship. A person without courage wouldn't stand up to the jerks that ran you off the road and put you in the hospital. You're still here, Judith. Don't tell me you're not brave."

"I'm not so sure that's courage as much as anger."

"That's righteous anger, Judith. A fearful person runs when threatened. A courageous person gets angry. Hate and injustice should make you angry, should make you stand and fight."

Judith didn't respond.

Was this the stumbling block that kept Judith from embracing the future he offered? Would her doubts ruin his hopes? "Are you still going to Henry's service tomorrow morning?"

"Yeah."

"Then don't tell me you're not courageous. You know how the hate groups will feel about you attending Henry's church, but you're going anyway."

"I'm going to show that running me off the road or burning my barn won't keep me from helping Henry's congregation. Sometimes I feel like I'm in a big kettle and it's getting hotter every day. Sooner or later, it'll boil over."

Jacob almost wished the arsonists would make their next move. Better to catch them and stop the violence than to keep wondering when they would strike. "I'd go with you to Henry's service, but I promised I'd serve as usher tomorrow. I'd hate to leave them short-handed."

"It's OK. If something happens, it'll be at night, not in the middle of the service."

"You're probably right. Still, I'd feel better if I could tie you to my belt loop and carry you with me."

Judith made a face. "That doesn't sound very comfortable for either one of us."

"I'll do whatever it takes to keep you safe. Speaking of which, it's getting dark. I'll walk you over to Beverly's house."

❧❦

If Judith went to Henry's church service, she'd be setting herself up as a target. Those words echoed in her brain as she dressed for church the next day. Part of her wanted to stand her ground, to look into Dwight Thompson's eyes and say, "Bring it on." But she was frightened. As much as she wanted to deny the truth, her stomach quivered at the thought of another act of violence lodged against her new friends or herself.

She swept through the back door and made her way along the well-worn path towards the church. As she drew closer, she could hear the joyful voices of men and women as they greeted each other.

"How are you this morning, sister?"

"Are you feeling better, brother?"

The members of Rev. Washington's church formed a loving family and Sunday mornings were their reunions. No wonder Henry had wanted a place for them to meet.

Just before Judith stepped into the church, she stopped to touch the worn wooden siding. Hundreds of believers had passed this way before her. Her grandparents, her own mother and father, and now her new friends. A surge of happiness rose in her chest when she thought about the lineage of believers who had built, maintained, and shared the humble building.

Now it was her turn. She could almost hear her grandfather's voice urging her on as a vision of her mother's gentle smile came to mind.

"You gonna stand there all day or you gonna go in and hear some music?"

Judith grinned at the sound of Beverly's voice and turned to see Keneisha and her mother. "Are you in a hurry?"

"Heavens yes, I'm in a hurry. I've got some powerful praying to do today."

"Can I sit with you, Judith?" Keneisha asked.

Judith reached for the girl's hand. "Of course. There isn't anybody else I'd rather sit with."

Keneisha beamed her special smile and skipped into the church, pulling Judith with her. As the girl led

Judith towards the front pew, familiar faces greeted her.

Many of the women hugged her, several of the men voiced their regret at the loss of her barn. Their welcome was so warm, their words so sincere, that Judith soon settled into their loving acceptance and forgot she was the outsider.

After several minutes of noisy conversation, the sound of the electric piano signaled the boisterous crowd to find their seats.

A lone woman stood in front of the choir and sang a single line.

The congregation responded with calls of "Sing it, sister" and "Amen."

The woman's stirring voice lifted the slow, heartfelt melody to heaven.

The choir joined the soloist.

The tempo increased and soon the congregation was on its feet, clapping and singing their affirmation of the hymn.

Keneisha danced in the aisle, her joy so contagious that Judith couldn't hold back. She clapped her hands and smiled as the music filled her heart.

One song followed another until the congregation took a communal deep breath and settled in for Henry's sermon.

Rev. Washington stepped into the pulpit. "Brothers and sisters," he began, "this is the day the Lord has made. Let us rejoice and be glad in it."

"Amen!"

"Let us take a moment for silent prayer."

Judith glanced furtively at the worshippers. Some bowed their heads in quiet thought, others lifted their faces to the ceiling, their hands open as if prepared to receive whatever fell into them.

Rev. Washington raised his head, looked at the congregation, and smiled. "Today, I draw my lesson from Philippians. 'Be anxious for nothing, but in everything by prayer and supplication, with thanksgiving, let your requests be made known to God.'"

"Be anxious for nothing," Henry repeated. "There it is in the word of God. Be anxious for nothing. We all know that Miss Judith's barn was burned a few nights ago and we all know about her accident."

Judith looked at Beverly, who sat with the choir behind Henry. Beverly raised her eyebrows and Judith nodded. They both knew it hadn't been an accident.

"And," Henry continued, "we all know that this old church is the next likely target."

A murmur of concern passed through the worshippers, and Henry waited until the congregation had quieted. "But we are supposed to be anxious for nothing. Now, I know that's not an easy thing to do. Worrying about the little things and the big things that trouble us is human nature. But let's don't forget what the rest of this verse says." Henry paused. The light came into his eyes.

Keneisha slid her small hand through Judith's arm and snuggled against her side.

"By prayer and supplication," Henry said, his voice rising in timbre, "let your requests be made known to God. We know the power of prayer. We've felt it many times before. We've seen the results many times before. And I have faith, brothers and sisters, that prayer will work for us again."

"But," Henry went on, "what is it we're praying for? To protect this church? To punish those who try to terrorize us? Or do we pray for the strength to stand firm in the face of hatred and to turn the other cheek?"

The congregation responded.

Henry resumed. "How many of us have prayed for the arsonists who destroyed our church?"

The sound of dissent moved through the congregation.

A stone of uneasiness lodged itself in Judith's stomach and she squirmed in her pew.

Keneisha, as if commiserating with Judith's discomfort, squeezed her arm.

Judith smiled back and covered the girl's hand with hers.

"I know," Henry said. "You don't have to tell me how hard that is. It's easy to pray for ourselves or for those we love, but praying for our enemies is a whole different ball game. So why does our Lord ask us to pray for those who want to harm us?"

Henry paused, as though giving his listeners time to form an answer to his question. When he continued, his voice was gentle. "I believe the reason we're called to pray for our enemies is because doing so makes a change in us. Praying for our enemies takes us out of our self-centered worlds and forces us to think of someone else. So instead of asking the Lord to protect this little church building, maybe you should be asking Him to change the arsonists' hearts."

Henry continued his message, but Judith's mind was stuck on his suggestion. She'd definitely been guilty of self-centered prayers. Every day she asked the Lord for courage and guidance, and not once had she prayed for the arsonists and Dwight Thompson.

Keneisha pulled on Judith's arm. "One more song and then it's over, and not a minute too soon. I'm starving."

Judith stood with the other worshippers and clapped along to one final, rousing hymn.

But as the men and women filed out of the small sanctuary, an unnatural hush fell upon the crowd.

When she finally made her way through the door, Judith saw the reason for the tension.

Dwight Thompson and his two brothers leaned against the fenders of their trucks, their arms crossed in lazy defiance.

Judith strode towards Dwight, hot words forming on her tongue. The church sat on her private property, and he had no right to trespass. But a hand on her shoulder held her back.

Rev. Washington's face was calm, his voice determined. "Let us handle this, Miss Judith."

She saw the men of the congregation walking slowly towards them.

Henry stepped towards Dwight and his brothers as the men of the congregation formed two phalanxes on either side of their preacher.

"Good morning," Henry began.

"Morning," Dwight answered.

"Is there anything I can help you with?"

"No, I don't believe so. I just came out to see how Isaiah's granddaughter is doing."

Judith touched the shoulder of the man next to Henry, and he moved to let her through. "I'm doing quite well," she said, her chin held high. "No thanks to you."

A slow smile slithered across Dwight's mouth. "I heard about your barn."

Judith glared at him, but didn't take the bait.

Dwight's sly smile never faltered. "It would be a

shame if someone burned this old church, too."

Judith closed the distance between herself and Dwight and leaned in. "Go ahead, you bully. Burn it. Nothing will stop these people and nothing will stop me."

Dwight glanced at each of his brothers, and then chuckled. "You sure got a short fuse, little lady. But things would be a lot easier for you if you'd remember what color you are. Blacks and whites weren't meant to mix. Says so in the Bible."

Judith knew there was no such scripture. "Jesus didn't preach hate. Is your fight with me or them?" she asked, gesturing to Henry's congregation with a nod of her head.

"Who said I was here to fight? I just came out to check on you. When I didn't find you at the cabin, I figured you might be here. Sorry to see I was right."

A thousand sharp words sprang to mind, but Judith forced them back. With her hands fisted at her side and her head throbbing from the pent-up anger, she turned and stomped back through the ranks of men to join Beverly and Keneisha.

Beverly laid a quiet hand on Judith's arm. "Easy, friend. There's more of us than there are of them. They'll leave. Just let it pass."

Dwight and his brothers casually got into their trucks and drove away.

Mumbles of concern passed among the members of the congregation as they watched the trucks disappear down the dirt road.

Henry moved to Judith's side. "You might want to remove anything of value from your cabin. No telling how far Dwight's hate will take him."

Judith watched him walk away, the anger still

popping inside her like water in hot oil.

"Don't be mad, Miss Judith." Keneisha wrapped her arms around Judith's waist and looked up at her. "I'll still be your friend."

Judith bit back her anger and considered Henry's parting words. She hadn't suffered anything like what he and the members of his congregation had. Living with hatred as a daily threat was a problem she'd never had to face. Judith laid a palm against Keneisha's cheek. "That's good, Keneisha. I need all the friends I can get."

17

Jacob's skin prickled with anticipation as he sat on the front steps of Isaiah's church later that night. The air vibrated with the restlessness of nocturnal creatures, as if every living thing knew that hatred was on the prowl, looking for its next victim.

After Judith's confrontation with Dwight earlier that day, there was little doubt the arsonists would strike soon.

Jacob was ready. He'd keep vigil throughout the night, ready to serve as guardian, or witness, or whatever else was needed.

Judith had accepted the risk, but if Jacob could rescue the church from a fiery demise, surely she'd be relieved and happy.

He couldn't stop thinking about her. How he longed to hold her close while they slept and wake every morning to her smile. He'd do all he could to banish any doubts Judith had about marrying him.

The shrill ring of his cell phone startled Jacob. He drew it out of his shirt pocket and glanced at the caller I.D. His heart lurched when he saw the call was from the San Augustine County Sheriff Department. He answered after the second ring.

"Jacob Fraser?"

The man's voice was unfamiliar, but the sheriff had recently hired new deputies.

"Yes."

"Sheriff Miller would like you to come to the station. There's some new evidence in the arson case he'd like you to take a look at. Should I tell the sheriff you're on the way?"

Jacob glanced at his watch. It was almost ten o'clock. What kind of evidence had the sheriff found that couldn't wait until morning? But Sheriff Miller wouldn't have called if it wasn't important. "I'll be there in half an hour."

"I'll let the sheriff know."

Jacob ended the call and headed to his truck. Maybe Sheriff Miller or Mark had uncovered a solid lead.

☙❧

Judith lay in bed and listened to the night noises.

Beverly snored softly in the room next to hers, the kitchen clock ticked resolutely, and the crickets hummed. But Judith couldn't sleep. Memories of the day stomped through her mind. Rev. Washington's sermon had been a powerful reminder of how she'd failed. Never once had she thought of praying for her enemies.

Judith turned on her side and plumped her pillow, intent on getting some sleep, when the faint sound of a bell drifted through her open window. It rang unevenly, as though moved by wind rather than human hands. Remembering how the church bell rang during the storm a few weeks earlier, she climbed to the foot of her bed and looked through the window to check the weather.

The quiet that greeted her filled her chest with apprehension. In the waning moonlight, the trees stood like attentive sentinels, their motionless branches attesting to the calm night.

But something, or someone, was ringing the church's bell.

Judith pulled on jeans under her nightshirt and slipped into her shoes. She went out of Beverly's house and rushed through the woods, the branches slapping her face as she ran along the now familiar path to the church.

An unnatural glow rose above the tree line and a fist of dread squeezed her heart. Not the church. Not her grandfather's dear, little church. She ran faster, her chest aching from the exertion, until her foot caught on a root. Pain shot through her left ankle as she fell on the hard-packed dirt. The church bell rang again, louder this time, as if calling for help. Judith pushed to her feet and swiped the dirt from her sweaty face.

She'd known it had been possible, had known the high price she'd pay if she allowed her grandfather's church to act as a lure, but the possible destruction of the church bit the tender places of her heart. As she neared the clearing, the smell of smoke drifted towards her. "No," she moaned as she staggered forward.

Where was Jacob? The cabin was closer to the church than Beverly's house. If he'd stayed at the cabin, surely he would have heard something. Had he called for help? Was he all right?

At last, Judith reached the clearing and saw what she'd feared the most. Her labored breath caught in her throat at the sight of the church engulfed in flames. Part of one wall had fallen and the roof flickered dangerously. Flames climbed the steeple, their heat causing the bell to cry its mournful plea.

The light from the fire silhouetted figures gathered

near three vehicles. Were the firefighters already there? Why weren't they doing something?

Judith ran towards the group. Maybe Jacob was with them and could tell her when help would arrive. But as she neared the people, a man's voice called from behind her.

"Hey! Stop right there."

Judith turned towards the voice. The man tackled her, and her face hit the ground hard. Her eyes watered as she struggled to get up, but the man sprawled his heavy body on top of hers. She lifted her head towards the people who now jogged to where she lay on the ground.

"That's Isaiah Beecham's granddaughter," said a man wearing cowboy boots. "I thought you said the cabin was empty."

"It was," Judith's attacker replied.

Empty? Where was Jacob?

"Now what are we supposed to do?" asked the booted man.

The man on top of her let out a growl of annoyance. "Go get your wife."

The booted man loped away.

Judith struggled under her attacker's weight. How naïve she'd been to not realize that these people were the arsonists. Maybe she could get a look at his face, or memorize the license plates of the vehicles.

"Keep still," the man snarled, "or I'll have to tie you up."

"Get off me!" Judith shouted and pushed against the man.

"Calm down, Judith!"

She froze. The man knew her? It didn't sound like Dwight's voice, but she could be wrong. Maybe it was one of his brothers.

"You're hurting me," she yelled again.

"I am not, but if you don't lie still somebody might be forced to hurt you."

A woman's voice sounded nearby. "I can't believe you screwed this up."

"I'm telling you, the cabin was empty," Judith's attacker said. "I don't know where she came from, but she wasn't in the cabin."

"It doesn't matter now, anyway. Give me your gun."

They were armed?

Judith's blood chilled as fear replaced anger and grief.

"I'm going to get up now," the man said, "but if you know what's good for you, you'll stay where you are until we're gone."

"Leave her to me," the woman said. "I don't have a problem with shooting her."

The memory of her mother's blood pooling on the kitchen floor sprang into Judith's mind. Would someone find her body the same way? *Please don't let it be Jacob*, she prayed silently, *or Keneisha*. No one should be haunted by that image.

Her attacker got up with a groan and air rushed into Judith's lungs. She rolled to her side, but the woman put her foot on Judith's neck.

"Just stay there, Judith. As soon as the others are gone, I'll let you up."

And then what? Shoot her?

Judith heard cars and trucks start up and drive away. The woman slid her foot away. "OK, you can get up now."

Judith pushed to her hands and knees and tried to

catch her breath, certain she was about to be killed. If she died, her father would be alone.

Beverly might blame herself for asking Judith to get involved in this fight.

Keneisha would learn a hard lesson about the evil of hatred and violence.

And Jacob, sweet, darling Jacob, would grieve for her.

The woman nudged Judith with her foot. "I said you can get up now."

Judith rose to her feet, and then stumbled a bit as she fought for her balance. She could run into the surrounding forest, but that wouldn't stop the woman from shooting. Who was this woman who held the power of life and death in her hands?

Judith turned and saw the face of her killer.

"Remember me?" the woman asked with a confident smirk. "You think my name's Lily White. You let me take all the photos I wanted of your church. You don't know my real name and you don't know my sister's real name, either. Did you really think our real names were Lily and Rose?"

Judith looked at the only vehicle left in the clearing. Perhaps she could see the license plate.

Lily followed her gaze. "Recognize that old truck? It's got a dent on the right side. My husband got in a bad accident a few weeks ago. He had to run someone off the road."

There was no license plate on the truck.

Lily could simply drive away and Judith would have no way of identifying her.

"Remember all those photos I took? They helped us locate the surveillance cameras you put all over this place. We disabled them. And your guard? He was as easy to fool as you are. A phone call was all it took to get him away from here."

Jacob was safe.

Judith's breath rushed out of her as that knowledge solidified in her racing mind.

A loud groan sounded from the burning church as the final walls collapsed and the roof caved in. No one had called for help. Nothing would be left of her grandfather's church.

"You were so nice to us that day," the woman said with a sneer, "I almost hate to burst your bubble. But you've got to learn the truth. We burn their churches to keep them scared. The last thing we need is traitors who cross the line and help our enemies."

Judith threaded her fingers through her hair. "Why are you doing this?"

"If we don't keep the blacks in their places, they'll take everything away from us. Every once in a while, they need a reminder that we have the power to destroy them."

Judith fisted her hands at her sides. "Get off my property."

The woman laughed in her face.

Judith's fists itched with the desire to hit the woman. She wanted to push Lily to the ground and restrain her until the sheriff could take her to jail. Anger popped up the length of her spine. How could she keep the woman here?

Judith ran to the pickup that had run her off the road. If the keys were in the ignition, she could drive the truck away. But the keys were gone.

The woman approached, dangling the keys from her finger. "I'm not the stupid one here." She slid behind the steering wheel and closed the truck door.

"Remember what I told you, Judith. Stay with your own kind. Your life will be a lot easier if you do."

Judith watched the truck pull away, memorizing every detail of the vehicle's color and body style. The fire had almost burned itself out. There was no need to hurry to the cabin or back to Beverly's house in order to call for help. All that was left of the church her grandfather had built was glowing shards of wood and cinders. Acrid smoke hung over the ruins like forlorn ghosts.

Judith collapsed and let the tears come. In the last few minutes, the church had been destroyed and her life had been threatened. Without the surveillance cameras, she was the only witness. But what did she have to report?

Three people, maybe more. No license plate numbers. No names.

And she'd let them in.

Anger warred with grief inside of Judith's mind. She'd risked her grandfather's church and lost. Despite the years she'd shied away from strangers and hidden from danger, she'd learned nothing.

༚

Jacob sped down the highway. The truck's headlights cut through the darkness like a butter knife through a log, but Jacob paid no heed. He knew the road well and nothing would stop him from getting back to Judith as quickly as possible.

The call from the sheriff's office had been a ruse. No one there had known anything about it. There was only one reason someone wanted him away from the cabin and he'd fallen for it.

He hadn't hesitated this time. He hadn't asked to speak directly to either Sheriff Miller or Mark. He'd taken the caller at his word and had left the church unguarded. There was little doubt what he'd find once he got back, but he prayed he was wrong.

Jacob's truck bounced down the dirt road as he headed straight for the church. He was going much too fast for the potholed road but he couldn't slow down. He thought of the cameras the FBI had placed around the property. If the arsonists had struck that night, surely something would be on the videos.

A vehicle without its lights on suddenly materialized on the road. Jacob's throat tightened as he swerved to avoid a head-on collision. His truck bucked and smashed into the low-hanging tree limbs that bracketed the narrow road. With an earsplitting crash, a branch pierced the windshield and Jacob banged his head against the driver's side window. Pain burrowed through his head and down his neck while his thoughts spun like a warped disc.

A car racing down a dirt road without its headlights on couldn't be good.

Blood trickled down his forehead and blurred his vision. He wiped it away with the back of his hand and put the truck in reverse. He couldn't afford to wait until his head cleared. He had to get to the church. He rounded the curve that lead to the clearing, and braked hard. A hollow feeling rose in his chest, as if his heart and lungs had retreated to a safer place. The church was a smoky heap of charred ruins. Once again, he was too late. He'd failed again.

He'd promised himself he'd be the witness the FBI needed, but instead he'd allowed himself to be lured away.

How could he have failed again?

He'd hesitated before and it had cost a boy's life. He hadn't hesitated this time, but the arsonists had done their worst, anyway.

Jacob cut the engine and climbed out of his truck on shaky legs. After several steadying breaths, he reached for his cell phone and called Chief Dutton. The firefighters and deputies would be on the scene soon.

He ended the call to the fire chief and hung his head. How would he ever tell Judith he'd failed when she'd needed him? The dying fire popped, sending up a shower of sparks, but other than that, the night was quiet. Then he heard the sobs. Was that a woman? He walked slowly towards the sound. Then he saw a shape hunched on the ground.

He broke into a run. "Judith?"

Her head lifted and she turned her dirt-streaked face towards him.

Jacob's heart squeezed at the sight of her tears.

Judith struggled to her feet and rushed towards him.

Had the arsonists hurt her?

"Judith," he yelled again as he pulled her into his arms. "Are you all right?"

Judith turned her face into his chest. "I heard the bell," she said between sobs. "The fire made the bell ring."

No, no, no, Jacob repeated to himself. If only she'd stayed at Beverly's house.

"I came to see who was ringing the bell, but the church was on fire."

Jacob stroked her hair, willing her to calm down so he could assess her injuries. "Are you hurt?"

Judith shook her head. "No. But Jacob...the

church…"

"I know," he said into her hair. "It's OK, Judith. We'll rebuild it."

"But I knew the lady who burned it."

The lady?

"It was the lady from the historical society. Remember? The one who took all those photos."

"It's OK, sweetheart. The cameras probably recorded everything."

Judith shook her head again. "No. They disabled the cameras. Oh, Jacob. I let them in."

What was she talking about?

"I've got to call the sheriff, Jacob. And Mark. I've got to tell them what happened."

"I've already called Chief Dutton. He'll inform everyone else. As soon as you've been checked out you can tell them everything."

"I'm fine," she insisted. "But you're bleeding. What happened to your head?"

"It's nothing." Jacob swept her up in his arms and carried her towards his truck. He'd believe she was fine when he got her into the light where he could see for himself.

۟ڤ

The morning sunlight slanted through the cabin's uncovered windows. Judith sat on the couch. Sheriff Miller and Agent Grey sat across from her, and Jacob sat nearby, having his head wound tended by an EMT.

A deputy walked through the back door with Special Agent Charles Lawson in tow.

"Did you get anything?" Mark Grey asked his partner.

"Still checking," Lawson answered as he sat at the kitchen table and opened a laptop computer.

"But the cameras," Judith said, "weren't they disabled?"

"Two of them are definitely out of commission," Lawson answered. "But they didn't find the others."

Judith's gaze connected with Jacob's. Perhaps the cameras had recorded something after all. But Jacob's expression remained neutral.

Sheriff Miller handed several sheets of drawing paper to his deputy. "Miss Robertson made sketches of the women who came to visit. Make copies and get it to the other deputies along with this drawing of the truck that ran Miss Robertson off the road and the boots one of the suspects was wearing. We might get lucky and find them." The deputy nodded and left the room.

Mark spoke up. "It may not seem like it now, Judith, but this is a significant break in the case. Not only can you I.D. the truck, you can also identify the woman. Agent Lawson and I reviewed the videos from the day she and her sister came to visit you, but there aren't any clear shots of their faces."

"If you catch them, will the arsons stop?" Judith asked.

Sheriff Miller leaned forward. "There aren't any guarantees in this business, Miss Robertson, but knowing they can't get away with it usually makes a criminal think twice."

Judith rose and moved to Jacob's side. "If you're finished talking to me, I'd like to get Jacob to the hospital."

"There's nothing wrong with me," Jacob said.

"I'm taking you, anyway. That cut on your head is

turning purple."

Sheriff Miller rose to his feet. "That's it for now. We'll be in touch." He offered a hand to Jacob. "I really wish you'd think about my offer."

Jacob shook the sheriff's hand. "I will."

Judith studied the two men. What offer had the sheriff made that Jacob wasn't telling her about?

∂∽⌒

Judith sat on the examination table beside Jacob. "What do you think Rev. Washington will do now?"

"Meet somewhere else. He may even keep meeting at the site of your church. There's lots of shade there."

"Do you think your minister would let Henry's congregation meet at your church?"

"That's a possibility. Henry would have to change the time of his service, but something could be done. I'll talk to our minister about it."

"Dwight Thompson wouldn't burn his own church, would he?"

"Do you think Dwight was there last night?"

Before Judith could answer, there was a short rap on the door and a man wearing a green scrub suit entered the exam room. "Mr. Fraser? I'm Dr. Jansen. We finally got the results from your CT scan. The good news is there's no bleeding into the brain so all you need is a good bandage to close that cut. I'll send in the nurse." The doctor rushed out of the room.

Judith and Jacob exchanged gazes and chuckled. "We waited two hours to see the doctor and our visit lasted all of thirty seconds," Jacob said.

"But at least we know you're OK. How long do you think we'll have to wait for the nurse? An hour?"

"At least." Jacob took Judith's hand. "Since we'll be waiting for a while, this would probably be a good time to tell you how sorry I am for letting you down."

Judith's heart twisted to hear bitter regret in Jacob's voice. "You've never let me down."

Jacob looked at their joined hands, but not at her. "I promised to watch out for you, but I wasn't there when you needed me. I promised I'd keep an eye on the church, and it's destroyed. I tried to help Sheriff Miller and Mark Grey get some information about a local hate group, and I learned absolutely nothing. I don't know how you could call that anything other than failure."

She shouldn't have involved Jacob in her fight. She'd known she was risking the church, but she'd never considered how she was endangering Jacob. What could she say to make him feel better? "You helped Henry's congregation when they needed it. Not only did you arrange for monetary donations, you pitched in and helped them refurbish my grandfather's church. And the only reason you weren't keeping an eye on the church was because you were trying to help solve the crime."

"Didn't do any good, did it?"

Judith was the one who'd let the ladies explore the church. She had no inner compass when it came to trust. A few months ago, she'd trusted no one. But when those ladies had shown up at her front door, she'd ignored the warnings. "We all knew my grandfather's church would probably be burned."

"But maybe I could have prevented it," Jacob continued. "I definitely could have prevented you from getting hurt. Judith, if anything happened to you..."

Visible guilt and regret dimmed his features, and

she'd put it there. Jacob, whose eyes had twinkled with merriment and whose mouth had always been quick to smile, couldn't meet her gaze because she'd over-reached her ability. How could he think he'd let her down when the truth was that she'd failed him?

Judith's cell phone rang. She pulled her hand away from Jacob's grip in order to answer it.

"Miss Robertson? This is Mark Grey. Are you and Jacob still at the emergency room?"

"Yes, but we're almost finished . Do you need us?"

"There's no hurry. I've got some good news for you."

Judith looked at Jacob. He sat patiently on the examination table, intently listening to her side of the conversation. "Hold on, I'm going to put the phone on speaker so Jacob can hear this." Judith returned to Jacob's side and pushed the speaker button. "Go ahead, Mark."

"Special Agent Lawson got the license plate numbers from the video. The cars belong to people who live in the county so Sheriff Miller was able to move fast. He's already made the arrests. He wants to know if you'll come down to his office to identify the woman you saw last night."

"He's caught them? Already?"

"Seems that way."

"Was Dwight Thompson one of them?"

"No. We're also working on locating the man who called Jacob. Since the call came from a land line inside the sheriff's department, and since we know the exact time it was made, we should be able to narrow down who made the call."

A blonde nurse wearing pink scrubs entered carrying a metal tray with bandages.

Judith pressed the speaker button again and brought the phone to her ear. "Do I have time to go home for a shower first?"

The satisfaction in Mark's voice was unmistakable. "Take your time, Judith. I think we should make Miss Lily White sit in the holding cell for as long as possible."

❧❧

Two hours later, Judith parked her car in front of the Sheriff's Department.

Jacob sat in the passenger's seat, his eyes closed and his head resting against the back of the seat.

"Do you still have a headache?"

"Oh, yeah. If I didn't know better, I'd think some of your fairies were mining for ore in there."

"Did you take the pain medication the nurse gave you?"

"Not yet. She said it would make me sleepy. I'll take some when this is over."

Judith looked at the building's glass door. She'd identify the women and the law would take care of the rest. She'd done what she could for Rev. Washington. His congregation could continue to meet on the site of the ruined church or make other arrangements, but she was finished. She had nothing more to offer him.

Jacob got out of the car and walked towards the building.

Judith remembered the day of the church picnic when she'd admired his strength and agility.

Now his shoulders slumped and his jaws clenched. He turned at the entrance and looked at her.

It was time to finish this.

Mark Grey met them near the dispatcher's desk and shook Jacob's hand. "How's that hard head of yours?"

"Just a bump. I'll be fine by tomorrow."

"Glad to hear it. Judith, if you'll come this way, we have the woman we arrested in an interview room."

Judith followed the agent to a short hallway with windowed rooms.

"This is one-way glass," Mark explained. "You can see in, but she can't see out. Take a good look."

Judith stepped to the window and viewed the gray-haired woman who'd threatened her life. Judith's throat squeezed shut as anger rekindled her outrage. What kind of hatred motivated someone to commit such heinous acts?

Mark opened a folder and pulled out a copy of her drawing. "Your artwork was spot on, Judith. We showed this rendering around the county and more than one person pointed us to the woman you see sitting in that room."

"What's her real name?" Judith asked.

"Barbara Sullivan. We also arrested her husband, Alfred Sullivan. He was still wearing those fancy cowboy boots you drew. No word yet on the other man."

Jacob touched Judith's shoulder. "Is that the woman who threatened you?"

Judith's mind flashed back to the way the woman had sneered at her as the church burned. "Yes."

Jacob's hand tightened on her shoulder. "Are you sure?"

"I'm sure."

"Are you willing to testify to that in a court of law?" Mark asked.

Judith thought of Rev. Washington's congregation. They drew so much strength from each other, and this woman wanted to find a way to put an end to that. "Of course."

Mark smiled broadly. "That's all I need now."

"What about the woman's sister?" Jacob asked.

"We haven't been able to locate her. The suspect says she doesn't have a sister, and so far, all the other woman is guilty of is lying about her identity. But don't worry. This investigation is far from over."

Jacob moved closer to the window. "Are you going to question her now?"

"No," Mark answered. "The suspect has already confessed."

"Confessed?" Jacob's surprise was obvious.

"I can't say too much more because you're both potential witnesses. I just needed the I.D. as a safety measure. We're going to take her back to the holding cell now. You two may want to leave before we do."

Jacob laid his palm against the small of Judith's back. "Let's go. This woman has caused you enough harm."

Judith allowed him to guide her back towards the front of the building. A deputy passed them in the hall and Judith heard the interview room door being opened.

Barbara Sullivan's voice carried down the short hallway. "I'll tell you whose fault it is that old church was burned. Judith Robertson. Her own grandfather built that church, but she didn't have any respect for that. We wouldn't have even known about that old place if Judith hadn't let the blacks use it."

Something cold skittered up Judith's spine. If she'd denied Henry's request, the church would still be standing.

"And you can blame Judith for the truck accident, too," Barbara continued. "That black woman and her little girl wouldn't have even been in the truck if Judith hadn't made friends with her."

Judith fought to keep her tears from falling. The suspect may have been lying about other things, but what she'd said about Beverly and Keneisha was true. They would have been better off if Judith had never tried to help them.

Judith squeezed Jacob's upper arm. "I'd like to go home now."

Jacob reached for her.

Judith stepped away. "I need some time alone." Her hand went to her aching throat. "And we both need some sleep." She walked briskly towards the front door.

She was so close to crying, so close to collapsing in the hallway and surrendering to the anger and self-reproach that bit at the edges of her soul. If only she could get back to the privacy of her cabin where no one could witness her loss of self-control.

❧

Home, in her cabin. Safe. In the last twenty-four hours, Judith had been terrified, threatened, angry, and grief-stricken. She'd cried until her swollen eyes burned. Nothing would keep her awake that night.

Pumpkin jumped on the bed and kneaded Judith's stomach. Pumpkin didn't know how badly Judith had messed up, but Jacob did.

He'd driven her home, helped her into the cabin, and driven away. Not even a good-bye kiss. His feelings couldn't have been clearer. The love he'd once felt for her was buried under disappointment and remorse.

She'd put others in danger. Maybe he'd been right that she was too young to know better when she'd allowed her mother to get murdered, but what was her excuse now? She was certainly old enough to know she shouldn't have let Beverly or Keneisha come to harm, but her stubbornness about the church had put them in danger.

No wonder Jacob had been anxious to get away from her.

He'd once told her he'd waited a long time for her. But she was not the woman meant for him. He needed someone who could make a clear decision without risking someone else's life. He deserved a help mate, not someone who would force him to question his very judgment.

How could she stay in Piney Meadow, knowing what she'd done to him, to his friends? She should go back to Dallas, back to the insular life she'd created for herself. It may have been lonely, but she hadn't hurt anyone.

Sheriff Miller had told Judith she wouldn't be needed for several weeks. She could always come back to testify. Otherwise, she'd make her home in Dallas. She'd concentrate on work and eventually the pain of losing Jacob would diminish.

And surely the hollow feeling inside her would eventually fade.

18

Pumpkin emitted an indignant wail as Judith set the pet carrier on the cold tile floor of her condo in Dallas. Everything was just as she'd left it, as uninviting as a morgue.

She knelt beside the crate and opened Pumpkin's door, but despite the cat's constant complaints during the three hour trip from Piney Meadow, the feline cowered in the corner of her crate, distrustful of the new surroundings.

"I know how you feel," Judith coaxed in her gentlest voice. "This place doesn't feel like home, does it?" Already she missed the summer breeze that wafted through her grandfather's cabin and the constant birdsong that accompanied her daily tasks.

Pumpkin eased her nose to the edge of the carrier and sniffed the air. One small paw tested the floor, followed by a blur of orange as the kitten bolted to the nearest hiding place.

Still on her knees, Judith moved to peer under the couch. "Oh, sweet cat. I'm so sorry. You were just getting used to the cabin and I brought you here." Maybe her father had been right to never allow her a pet. She certainly wasn't doing a very good job with Pumpkin.

The ringing phone forced her to leave the cat where it was. She answered, not surprised to hear her father's voice.

"Are you all right, Judith? I got your message."

"I'm fine, Dad. How are you?"

"Fine, but I'm worried. Why did you leave Piney Meadow so quickly?"

"I've already done enough harm there. Thought it was time to come back home."

"What are you talking about? When I saw you a few weeks ago, you were surrounded by people who obviously loved you. What harm could you have possibly done?"

Judith held the receiver at arm's length so she could sniff back her threatening tears.

"Judith?" her father's voice crackled loudly.

"I'm here," she answered, struggling to keep her voice steady.

"Sounds as though we need to talk. Want to have dinner tonight? We can meet anywhere you'd like."

"Why don't you come here?"

"You're going to cook?"

Despite her sorrow, Judith smiled at her father's incredulous tone. "I learned to make a few dishes while I was away. I can run to the grocery store to get stuff for dinner. Do you like fried okra?"

"Sure." Her father paused, obviously considering the invitation. "OK, if that's what you want, I'll see you after work."

Judith ended the call and slumped against the wall, imagining how difficult the evening would be. She'd disappointed so many people since going to Piney Meadow. Tonight she'd have to disappoint her father because she'd come back.

Her father stepped through the doorway, almost tripping on Pumpkin as the kitten darted for cover. "If you brought the cat, you must be planning on staying for a while."

"Things have been crazy in Piney Meadow. I just needed to get away from it all."

Her father draped his suit jacket over the back of the kitchen chair and sat at the table. "Who taught you how to make fried chicken, mashed potatoes, and fried okra?"

Judith slid into the chair next to him. "Beverly Lewis. You met her at the hospital."

"Oh, yes. Your new neighbor. She seemed like a lovely person."

"Good cook, too. Jacob Fraser once said she made a sweet potato pie so good it would make a man propose."

Her dad grinned at the comment. "That must be good pie. But from what Jacob told me, he wouldn't need any bribe to propose to you."

"He never proposed."

"I find that hard to believe."

Judith took a deep breath and let it out slowly. She'd learned from experience that there was no skirting the painful truth when it came to her father. "Jacob talked to me about marriage, but he never out right proposed."

"Uh-huh. What did he say when you told him you were leaving?"

"I didn't tell him."

Her father's eyes widened. "You left without saying goodbye?"

Judith dropped her gaze but didn't answer.

"You just packed your car and left? Did you tell

anyone you were coming to Dallas?"

Judith winced at the rising tone of disbelief in her father's voice.

"Well?" he demanded.

"I had to leave. Saying goodbye to everyone would have only have made it more difficult."

He let out a long sigh that conveyed his frustration. "Let's start this conversation over. Tell me what happened."

Judith described the night the church had burned. Unlike the account she'd related to Sheriff Miller, she left out the part where she'd been thrown to the ground and threatened with a gun. There was no need to add to her father's worries.

When she'd finished, her father leaned back in his chair and blew out a breath. "The sheriff arrested the arsonists?"

"Yes. I identified the woman and the sheriff arrested three other men. Apparently, one of them gave up the other two in an effort to cooperate with the police."

"In order to get a lighter sentence."

"I guess."

Her father leaned back in his chair and crossed his arms. "I still don't understand why you felt you had to leave. Don't get me wrong, I'm glad you're home, but I wonder if this is where you really belong."

How could she make her father understand? She'd dreamed of a life with Jacob, but those hopes had evaporated in the light of reality. "When I told you about praying for the courage to change my life, I never anticipated how being involved with other people could hurt them."

"You think you hurt someone?"

"I almost hurt Beverly Lewis and her daughter. They were in the truck with me when I was run off the road."

"But you didn't cause the accident. That wasn't your fault."

"I also hurt Jacob."

Her father propped one elbow on the table and rested his head in his hand, as if settling in for a long discussion. "Why do you think you hurt Jacob?"

"He thinks he failed, and it's all my fault. He knew how important Granddad's church was to me, so he tried to find the arsonists on his own. He wanted to guard the church, but he believed the call from the sheriff's office was genuine. He wanted to protect me, but he wasn't there when the arsonists attacked. Don't you see, Dad? None of that would have happened if I hadn't loaned out Granddad's church to begin with. He wouldn't even have been involved."

"Judith, he wasn't just involved with you, he loves you."

The words twisted Judith's heart. She'd had Jacob's precious love, but hadn't known how to nurture it.

"And you left without saying a word to him?"

Judith nodded.

"Oh Judith, I hardly know where to begin." Her father stood and thrust his hands in his pockets. He paced the length of the kitchen before returning to his chair. "Let's start with the church. You knew there was a high probability your grandfather's church would be destroyed, so why are you grieving for that old building?"

"I'm not. Not exactly."

"That church is like a casualty of war. It ought to

be awarded a Purple Heart or something. Maybe you could paint a picture of it, sort of a memorial to its heroic sacrifice."

Not a bad idea, Judith thought, and recalled the day she'd first seen the building. It had been expectantly waiting for its worshipers to return. She'd paint it with Henry's congregation in attendance, their faces alive with devotion and praise.

"Second," her dad said, "we have the issue of Jacob Fraser and his hurt feelings. Jacob's a grown man, Judith. He'll work through his emotions. All you have to do is give him time and support. You don't think he's a failure, do you?"

"Of course not."

"That's all he needs to know. Keep showing him your love and esteem and he'll get over it."

Showing him love and esteem would be easy. But she'd have to go back to Piney Meadow in order to do it.

"Next," her father continued, "we have the question of the help you gave to Henry Washington. Do you regret helping him and his congregation?"

"No."

"Even though it led to all these problems?"

"No. I'd do it again."

"That sums it all up, doesn't it? Surely you don't think that doing the right thing is always easy."

This conversation wasn't going the way Judith had envisioned. Her father was using logic, but he didn't realize the emotional price she'd exacted from her new friends. "But the women who visited, the ones who told me they were from some historical society? I let them in." Judith walked to her front door. "See all these locks? There was a time when I did everything I could to keep out people who would hurt me. But then I tried to change." Judith's voice rose with each sentence. "The whole time those ladies were traipsing around Granddad's church, I had a feeling something wasn't right, but I ignored it, thinking it was just fear shouting its old refrain." She placed her hands on the sides of her head. "I can't tell the difference between the voice of fear and the voice of good sense."

"And how do you expect to learn the difference?"

Judith dropped her hands and lowered her voice. "I don't know. Maybe I can't."

"You may be right."

Anger flickered at the base of Judith's spine. Had her father actually said she'd never learn to live without fear? "What did you say?"

"Since you won't settle for anything less than perfection, you'll probably never learn to tell the difference. You've heard of trial-and-error, haven't you?"

"Sure."

"Well, how can you learn if you never make an error?"

He'd tricked her. She might settle for a small, quiet life without love, but it rankled her to have someone else agree with her. "But what if that error hurts other people?"

"Then you deal with the hurt. But, Judith, I still don't see who you hurt. Beverly Lewis knew what could happen. I'm not saying she expected to be involved in a car wreck, but she knew the reason behind the arsonists' actions, knew they might come after you—or anyone who was with you."

Judith recalled the day she'd spoken with Beverly and Henry after the destruction of her barn. They'd said almost the same thing.

"And I'd bet Jacob doesn't believe you've hurt him, either," her father said. "I understand where he's coming from. When your mother died, I blamed myself for the longest time. If I'd been home, I could have protected both of you. But I went to work that day, never suspecting it would be the last time I'd kiss my wife goodbye, never suspecting the life-long burden you'd live with."

Sympathy flooded Judith's heart. "Oh, Dad, I never knew—"

Aaron waved his hand. "It doesn't matter now. It hurt to see you crawl into your protective shell, cowering from the big, bad world and forfeiting your future, and I prayed for you every day. When you told me that you'd felt the Holy Spirit urging you to claim the life the Lord planned for you, I knew my prayers had been answered."

But she'd given up. After conquering so many of her fears, she'd simply conceded defeat and run back to her hiding place.

Her father took both of Judith's hands in his. "You don't really want to relinquish the small victories you've made, do you? I never want to lose you, Judith, but you no longer belong here."

Judith's shoulders slumped. "I have to go back, don't I?"

"I'll drive you there myself if I have to."

Judith smiled at her father for the first time that evening. He didn't want to lose her, but he believed she belonged in Piney Meadow. Wasn't part of loving someone wanting what was best for them, even if it meant they'd leave? "I need a few days to think things over, but I'll go back."

Her father embraced her. "I'm so proud of you. Always have been."

Judith's eyes had been dry during the entire conversation, but her father's last words filled them with tears of gratitude. How blessed she was to have such love.

❧

Would Jacob forgive her for running away? No matter how she rationalized her departure from Piney Meadow, there was no denying the truth. She had run from her mistakes.

Would Jacob still want her?

Judith's heart pounded in her throat as she turned onto the narrow road that led to her grandfather's place. The small cabin seemed to smile at her as she passed it and drove straight to Beverly Lewis's house. She'd no more than shut the car door when Keneisha grabbed her around the waist and squealed.

"Miss Judith! Miss Judith! Where you been?"

Judith turned in Keneisha's embrace and cupped the girl's chin. "I went to Dallas and visited my father. What's new with you?"

"Where's Pumpkin?"

"Staying with my Dad. That cat does not like to ride in the car."

Keneisha's gaze darkened with concern. "You're not going to leave her there, are you? I mean, you're here to stay, aren't you?"

That was the million dollar question. Everything depended on Jacob. If she'd hurt him so deeply that he no longer wanted to be with her, Judith wouldn't be able to abide living in Piney Meadow. Seeing him around town, but no longer being special to him would be agony.

Beverly's voice boomed from the front porch. "It's about time you showed up."

Judith climbed the steps towards Beverly's welcoming smile.

Beverly wrapped her arms around Judith's shoulders and pulled her into a warm hug. "What took you so long?"

"I...had to get away."

Beverly studied Judith's face. "I feel a long talk coming on. Come on inside."

Judith followed Beverly into the kitchen and sat down.

Beverly eased into the chair opposite Judith and rested her arms on the table. "Now, Judith, tell me all about it."

"I hardly know where to start. What's happened since I've been gone?"

"The sheriff made more arrests. You know that phone call Jacob got the night of the fire? The deputy who made that call was identified and arrested. The word is, he's been spouting names left and right in order to keep himself out of jail. And you remember those FBI agents? We've got ourselves a whole slew of them around here now. The last I heard, they'd arrested more than twenty people."

The loss of her grandfather's church had led to so many arrests. Maybe it had been worth the high price she'd paid. "Has Dwight Thompson been arrested?"

"Not that I've heard of."

Judith grimaced. Yet another mistake she'd made—condemning Dwight without evidence of wrongdoing.

"Does Jacob know you're back?" Beverly asked.

"Not yet. To tell you the truth, I don't know what to say to him."

Beverly laughed loudly and clapped her hands in delight. "Oh, honey, you're not going to have to say much of anything. Just show up and smile."

"Actually, I need to ask you a favor."

"Ask away."

"Will you give me another cooking lesson?"

"Of course. Anything special?"

"Something really special."

⤞⤝

As she mounted the steps to Jacob's office, Judith balanced the sweet potato pie as though it was fragile crystal.

"You won't need a pie," Beverly had told her, but Judith had wanted a peace offering.

She knocked timidly on the door.

"Come in," his familiar voice answered.

Judith's chest ached from the tense breath she'd trapped there, and her fingers trembled as she turned the knob.

Jacob's back was turned as he bent over his desk, writing on an unseen sheet of paper.

Judith fought her shaky knees as she stepped into the room and closed the door.

But still he wrote, unmindful of her thundering heart.

She set the foil-covered dish on a nearby table and took several deep breaths. If only she could see Jacob's face she'd be able to judge his reaction. Would he be angry? Hurt?

"Jacob?" she said, her voice just above a whisper.

He spun at the sound of her voice and fixed his gaze on her. With two long strides across the office floor, he pulled her into his arms and held her tightly against his chest. "Thank you, Lord," he whispered into her hair.

Judith relaxed into his strength.

His hands bracketed her face and tipped her gaze up to his. "It's about time you came home. I was about ready to make a trip to Dallas."

"You would've come after me?"

"Of course. I wanted to give you time to think, but I can only stand so much."

"You're not angry?"

"Of course I'm angry. I've been worried sick about you, praying every hour for you to come back to me. Have you come to stay?"

Not answering, Judith nodded towards the table where she'd set the dish. "I brought you something."

Jacob's eyebrows rose in question.

Judith uncovered the pie.

"Is that what I think it is? Did Beverly make me a sweet potato pie?"

"It's Beverly's recipe, but I made it for you."

The smile of comprehension lit Jacob's face. "Now why would you make me a sweet potato pie?"

"You said once that Beverly's pie was so good it would make a man—"

"Propose. I remember."

Judith reached into the back pocket of her jeans and withdrew a fork. "Would you like to taste it?"

Jacob kissed one side of her mouth. "You didn't need a pie." He kissed the other side of her mouth. "You've always had everything I've ever wanted."

19

Autumn sunlight streamed through the stained glass window and reflected off the gold band Judith wore on her left hand. She silently lifted her thanks to God. Whenever she realized how close she'd come to giving away her happiness, a shudder passed through her body.

Jacob's hand covered hers. "Everything OK?" he asked in a low voice.

The ring on his left hand caught the same beam of sunshine. "Couldn't be better," she assured him.

Chloe and Keneisha, dressed in identical blue dresses, appeared at the end of the pew. "It's almost time to start," Keneisha said. "Momma said I should sit with you."

Jacob moved away from Judith to make space for the girls, and the two youngsters squeezed between them. Judith felt a hand on her shoulder and turned to see her father's smile.

"You made it!"

"Sure did," he said after hugging his daughter. "I didn't want to miss this." He reached across Judith and the children to shake Jacob's hand. "How's the new job, deputy?"

"Going well. Between scouting for the mill and working for the sheriff, I keep busy." Jacob moved farther down the pew so that Judith's father could sit next to her.

From behind them, a man's powerful voice sang out.

The choir repeated each line, the singers increasing in volume and joyfulness with each repetition.

Henry Washington, the choir, and the congregation got to their feet, singing and clapping along with the music.

The singing finally ended and the congregation sat with a collective sigh.

Henry stepped up to the pulpit and beamed at the congregation.

"Here we are, brothers and sisters. We finally made it. Our new church, bigger and better than the last one." Henry's resonant voice boomed over the crowd. "We have much to celebrate today. Once again, we have proven that love conquers hate. When evil tried to defeat the love we have for each other and for our God, we held steadfast in our faith. And today we sit in this fine church. Man may harm us, but God will always rescue us."

Shouts of "amen" and "hallelujah" echoed through the church.

"As the Lord says in Jeremiah," Henry continued, "I know the plans I have for you. They are plans for good and not for disaster, to give you a future and a hope."

Henry turned to the choir and they launched into another song.

Chloe and Keneisha jumped to their feet to clap and move with the music.

Judith looked at the happy faces around her and breathed in the jubilation that filled the new church.

The boisterous church service lasted well over an hour, and when Judith stepped out into the fresh autumn air, she was met with Beverly's smothering embrace.

"Here she is!" Beverly called to the crowd. "Here's our Judith!"

Cheers and applause resounded through the gathering.

Judith covered her face with her hands and looked for Jacob.

He stepped away from a group of men and went to stand by her side.

"You have to get used to this," he said, gently lowering Judith's hands from her face. "There are a lot of people in this town who love you."

"But you did just as much as I," she protested. "You made sure there was enough money and building supplies. You even helped to build this new church."

"But you helped them in a way no one else could. Plus, those paintings of Henry and Mr. Isaiah's old church hanging near the front door couldn't have been done by anyone but you."

Before Judith could argue, Beverly spoke up. "We'll be eating in just a few more minutes. Jacob, there's places for you and your new wife next to Brother Henry."

Judith would never get tired of hearing those words. She was Jacob's wife.

Her father was already seated at the colorfully covered table when she and Jacob found their seats. "Thanks for inviting me to today's service," he said. "I've never attended a church service where people were so happy."

"You're always welcome to visit us," Jacob replied. "Don't need an invitation."

Judith's father took a long drink of iced tea. "How's the new house coming along?"

"Slowly but surely," Jacob answered. "We should be able to move in just after New Year's Day."

"We're doing OK in the cabin for now," Judith added. "But the new house will have a room for you."

Her father smiled and patted her arm. "Once you move, what are you going to do with the cabin?"

"Turn it into a studio for Judith," Jacob answered. "She's been working there for almost five months."

"Still working on the illustrations for that book about mermaids?" her father asked.

"Yeah, and then I start on a new project about angels."

"I'd rather be surrounded by angels than mermaids," Jacob said. "I'm beginning to see mermaids in my coffee."

Judith's father chuckled and turned to look at Henry Washington's new church. "This building is much nicer than Isaiah's old place. Everything turned out for the best."

"After we get settled in the new house," Jacob said, "I'm planning on building a chapel in the spot where Isaiah's church was."

Judith gazed at Jacob. "I didn't know that."

A small grin played at the corner of Jacob's mouth. "I thought it would be a nice place for our family."

Her husband would build a place of worship just like her grandfather had done. The circle was complete.

Judith's heart warmed at the thought of creating a family with Jacob. Married life was so much more than she'd ever imagined, and she would be forever grateful that she'd saved herself for him.

A soft breeze fanned the tablecloth around Judith's legs as Henry and Beverly joined them.

Henry raised his hands and the crowd quieted. "Lord," he called out in his deep baritone, "we ask You to bless this food that nourishes our body, to bless Your children who love and serve You, and to bless our lovely new church. Amen."

"Amen!" the people shouted.

Judith sat back in her chair and watched the people around her.

Chloe and Keneisha were already at the dessert table, eyeing a triple-layer chocolate cake.

Henry Washington and his wife smiled broadly at Beverly as she served them food.

Her father was in deep conversation with the man beside him.

Three cars drove into the parking lot.

"Isn't that—?" Judith asked Jacob.

"Hey, it's my family," he answered. "I thought they might come."

The children tumbled out of the vans first, followed by ten adults carrying foil-covered plates of food. Jacob walked out to meet them, taking his niece from her father's arms and perching the baby on his hip.

Judith stood to embrace her mother-in-law. "How nice of you to come."

"Wouldn't miss it. Aaron, nice to see you again," Emma said as she hugged Judith's father.

Hope was right behind her and greeted Judith with a warm embrace. "You didn't think we'd let you and Jacob enjoy all this good food by yourselves, did you? Now where do I put this potato salad?"

Beverly took Hope's elbow.

Judith greeted the remaining members of the Fraser family. To think that she'd once been afraid of these people. She'd come to love each of them.

Especially Emma. Jacob's mother would never replace her own mother, but the empty spot in Judith's heart was slowly being filled by Emma's unfailing love.

Judith walked away from the table to stand in the shade of an oak a few feet away and survey the scene. She'd prayed for courage and she'd been given adversity.

Wasn't that the Lord's way? He'd had blessings planned for her, but she'd had to find the courage to receive them.